ONE

ON THE MORNING of June 16, 2022, at precisely 10:34, a well-dressed man carrying a leather shoulder satchel walked into the Chase Bank located at 301 Grant Street in Pittsburgh and deposited a check for the value of nine hundred and forty-two thousand dollars into the account of William Carlson. Nobody batted an eyelid as the transaction took place, the man thanking the teller with a pleasant good morning before calmly walking out of the branch, where he hailed a nearby cab and directed the driver to take him to the airport.

That might have been the end of the story were it not for a murder that had taken place several hours earlier, and the suspected killer identified by a passerby who called police. Officers put out an APB for the suspect, and when the man tried to check in for his flight to Switzerland, his very short stint as a wanted fugitive came to an end.

The reason I know all of these details is that the man in question became my client just a few hours after being taken into custody and transported to the Zone 1 Police Station. What he didn't know is that I tried my absolute hardest not to take the case for one very good reason. Brian Watson happened to be the father of my deceased wife, a man with whom I hadn't spoken in more than five years. Were it not for a very persuasive boss, who knows who would have ended up with the case, but after a long and bitter argument, I gave in and agreed, thus becoming the man's lawyer.

I'd very nearly spoken to him just the previous day, even before the events I described above. In fact, I had every intention of doing so at the time, but things quickly changed when I saw two specific men walk into his place of business while my investigator and I sat parked in front of his building. Those two men opened my eyes to a reality that immediately shook me to the core, a reality I still struggle to comprehend fully. In short, they shouldn't have been there, and yet seeing them confirmed my suspicions in ways I could have never predicted.

When Riccardo Costa first sent me a card containing a cryptic message pertaining to my late wife, I was so sure of finally uncovering some dark secret that I willingly risked another case to find it. Despite the advice from my friends and colleagues, I couldn't believe that Costa would use me for his own amusement, and yet that's exactly how the subsequent meeting with him went.

Costa played me like a fiddle, more so face to face, when he smirked his way through a meeting that ended with me being dragged from the room and later having to eat humble pie for ignoring the advice of my friends. And yet everything I had believed before that confrontation came flooding back the second I saw those two men walk into Brian Watson's building.

The thing is, Linda and I had been in good spirits up until that moment. The previous twenty-four hours had been quite eventful, given the final confrontation with Corinne Lucas and her hired hitman. Linda even managed to find some information on Morris, who turned out to be a less-than-exemplary

FINAL
DEFENSE

ISBN-13: 978-1-63696-454-6

ISBN-10: 1-63696-454-0

Cover design by: Damonza

Printed in the United States of America

www.righthouse.com

www.instagram.com/righthousebooks

www.facebook.com/righthousebooks

twitter.com/righthousebooks

David
ARCHER

Oliver
BLACK

A framed man.

FINAL

A broken lawyer.

DEFENSE

And a secret that ties them to a deadly conspiracy.

A **Ben Carter** LEGAL THRILLER

RIGHTHOUSE

hitman after all. His real name was Angus Shaw, and if I had to use a single word to describe him, bumbling might come to mind.

Don't get me wrong; The hitman managed to slice Dale Rich up like a Christmas ham, but let's face it. He'd surprised the guy from behind, rendered him helpless within a couple of seconds, and finished his victim off while he lay bleeding on the ground. What he didn't know was that his employer had set up a video camera to film the attack and then blackmailed him into doing her bidding.

In a way, the recording she had orchestrated to blackmail the hitman out of his payment turned out to be a blessing. I don't think she ever expected to get arrested for the crime herself, and she used Morris to hire me, something he covered up well during our meetings. While Lucas played Morris, Morris played me, and I was the clueless schmuck at the end of the line lapping it all up.

Getting back to Linda and me sitting out front of Watson's business, seeing those two men walk in felt like a sledgehammer to the gut for me. All the volatile emotions I experienced during those brief days after finding Costa's card returned in an instant, the realization that it might not have all been complete bullshit after all. One look at Linda after that initial shock, and I could see the same thoughts running through her head, no doubt wondering whether her advice to me at the time had missed the mark.

Let me tell you what emotions like that feel like. In a weird kind of way, reality takes a sudden sidestep as a new existence takes its place. The temperature in the car immediately skyrocketed as raging heat seemed to rise up out from my collar. Beads of sweat formed on my brow in an instant, while the former slow and steady beating in my chest changed gears. Even my eyes reacted, the vision no longer clear and precise but somehow tinged red from the blood rushing to my face. My fingers shook from what I thought was fear, but I think they trembled from the body trying to use up an overload of energy caused by the sudden adrenaline dump.

"Ben, wait," Linda snapped when she saw me grab the door handle.

"Why the hell are they going to see him?" I could barely articulate the words, thanks to the adrenaline also numbing my lips. "I have to find out what—"

"No, not yet," she said, cutting me off with a tone surprisingly calm. I think she knew that if I heard or felt any sort of excitement or panic from her, it would have triggered my own. "There'll be plenty of time."

"Lin, I have to go *in* there," I said, but she only shook her head.

"I gave you bad advice the last time you came to me for help, and I am not going to fail you a second time, Ben Carter."

I think her second-naming me somehow conveyed the seriousness behind her words. She reached over and touched my arm as if needing a connection to convince me.

"What if Costa did know something about Naomi's accident? What if..." I paused to look through the windshield toward the car the two men had arrived in. "What if he had something to do with it?"

"Then we are going to find the connection and deal with it accordingly," Linda said.

All I could do was sit there and stare at the entrance to the building. My brain barely functioned, too stunned to think about anything but the numerous possibilities it now played out, each scene laid out end to end with the next. I barely noticed the silence in the car or Linda looking at me cautiously while no doubt wondering just how quickly I'd lose control if I did climb out.

We stayed long enough to watch the two men walk out again, just twenty minutes later. I noticed one of them rubbing the knuckles of his right hand incessantly during the walk from the entrance to their car and had a strange suspicion as to why. Linda also noticed, but the look exchanged between us didn't need words. The SUV remained sitting curbside with its engine idling for another few minutes before it finally drove off. I got a good look at the occupants when they passed us by and thought I recognized one as being the driver from the day Costa first met me in the parking lot of the prison, but I couldn't be sure.

When Linda started the car for us to also leave, I asked her to hold off and considered going in to see Brian anyway. He wouldn't have known about me seeing his most recent visitors, and I could have ascertained his condition at the same time. If the knuckle-rubbing had been due to dishing out a beating, then I could make sure he wasn't severely injured. I did, after all, still need answers.

This time, Linda didn't intervene the way I expected her to. Instead, she sat there silently gripping the steering wheel with one hand while resting the other on the gear shifter. I just sat there staring through the windshield, unsure of which decision would be the right one. If we left and Watson really was severely injured, then whatever happened next would be on me. If, however, he wasn't, and my highly emotional state persisted, then I could possibly blow my one chance to get the answers I so desperately needed.

"Catch 22," I whispered, more to myself, but Linda answered anyway.

"Better to have a choice than none at all" was what she said.

"Let's get out of here," I said once I knew I wouldn't be able to trust myself.

I had to face the harsh truth of knowing how unpredictable

my own emotions would become if the situation didn't go as planned. Given my wrathful sense of urgency, I couldn't even imagine my reaction if Watson had greeted me with disrespect and refused to talk, especially with me now aware of his connections to a man who claimed to have knowledge about Naomi's accident.

Linda drove in silence, and for the next twenty minutes or so, it felt like each of us sat in our own bubble. She dropped me off in front of my building, where I thanked her for the ride before quietly making my way up to the apartment. Sleep didn't come easily, and when the alarm I'd set for early the next morning began jingling near my ear, I almost launched the cellphone across the room in disgust.

It took me quite a long time to manage keeping my eyes open, thanks to the fatigue refusing to let go, but it wasn't entirely wasted. Memories of Naomi and me resurfaced, mainly conversations I'd had with her, recalling how a lot of the animosity she'd had for her father came about. It's funny how life sometimes plays out. I never in my wildest dreams thought that I'd ever need to recall those conversations for something as important as investigating her death, and yet there I lay with that exact thought running through my head.

The fatigue only truly faded away completely when I greeted both Grace and Linda in my office at around nine that morning. The latter had brought in a bag of donuts, and I think the sugar helped wake me up properly, it and the double-shot espresso I'd sipped on the way in.

"I can't believe I'm sitting here talking to you guys about investigating Naomi's father," I said once I put away the last of the chocolate iced donut I'd been manhandling.

"I've already done a bit of poking around," Linda said, "and I might have found something interesting." She pointed to my laptop, and when I waved her forward, she spun it around and began typing. After a few seconds, she turned it far enough for both me and Grace to see what she'd brought up. I immediately recognized the website.

"Derby's?"

The transportation company operated dozens of trucks across the Eastern Seaboard, including both long- and short-distance routes. It offered varying distribution networks to all manner of clients, from small corner stores needing their wares transported from the local markets to huge factories needing raw materials. It wasn't exactly a secret that criminal gangs used transportation hubs to move drugs, money, stolen goods, and whatever else they needed shipped discreetly between locations. Derby's Transport would not have been my first guess at what Linda was about to share.

A man named Peter Derby owned the business with his brother, Jaxon, the pair inheriting the company from their father, who had passed away almost a decade earlier. Being the older brother, Peter not only made all the business decisions but was also the face of the company, quite literally. It was his grin that made up the company logo and stared out at the nation's traffic from practically all sides of each vehicle.

"Watson has been handling the accounts of Derby's for years, but what isn't so well known is that Derby's has also been under constant investigation by the IRS. They've audited the company twice in the last four years. Your old father-in-law has two full-time employees working just on this account, one of whom only started a few months ago because the previous guy got arrested for money laundering." Linda opened her cell phone screen and checked her information. "Lance Baker, sentenced to four years for laundering close to a quarter of a million dollars over six months."

"Laundering Derby's cash?"

"That we don't know," Linda said. "Baker owned a Go-

Kart joint in Lawrenceville, which he'd purchased nine months before his arrest. He worked for Watson during the day and ran his own business at night with his wife. They somehow got themselves caught cooking the books and laundering a lot of cash through the business."

"I don't understand what this has to do with Derby's," I said.

"Authorities charged Jaxon Derby with possession of counterfeit notes last year," Linda said. "He was eventually acquitted of all charges, but some of those same notes just happened to be found at the Go-Kart track of Lance Baker."

"It was Jaxon Derby's money that Baker could have been laundering?"

Linda shrugged her shoulders. "Money had to come from somewhere, right? But that's not all. The lawyer representing Jaxon Derby?" She paused, waiting for me to answer, and when I didn't, she finally revealed the connection. "Winthrop Curtis."

Hearing the name immediately stirred something inside me, having seen the man on several prior occasions. I'd never met him personally or professionally, but I'd come close on one occasion. Originally from somewhere inside the United Kingdom, he spoke with this obnoxiously arrogant British accent that I called English snobbery. I should also probably mention that Winthrop Curtis only had a single client...the Costa crime family.

"Curtis represented Jaxon Derby?" I couldn't quite believe my ears. I might not have met the man myself, but I knew him by reputation alone, and that was enough to understand the significance of such a revelation.

"I thought that might prick your ears," Linda said. "Tell me there isn't a connection between the Derbys and the Costas."

"And given that we already know the Derbys to be a client of Brian, it's a link between him and the Costas," I finished. I pondered the idea for a few seconds, the vision of the two men walking into his building coming back to me. "But just how deep does that connection run?"

"That's what we have to find out," Grace said. "Let me get everything I can on this Jaxon Derby case for you. Must be something in there we can use."

"Am I interrupting?" We all turned to see Dwight peering around the corner.

"Not at all," I said as the rest of Dwight's body appeared. "Just going through our plan for investigating Brian Watson."

"Perfect," he said, walked into the room, and effectively changed the course of my day.

TWO

"SORRY TO SPOIL THE MOMENT, but I gotta run," Linda said as she got up and gestured for Dwight to take her place, and then to me said, "But I'll deep-dive into Derby a little more to see just what they have going on behind closed doors."

"Thanks, Linda," I said.

Nobody spoke again until Linda disappeared through the door, and for some reason, I felt the air in the room suddenly grow uncomfortable with tension. Grace sat quietly watching, also unaware of what Dwight had in store. I think he was ready for a fight when he eventually broke the silence.

"Listen, Ben, I know you've got your blinkers on with Brian Watson and getting answers to some pretty traumatic questions. Plus, you've only just finished with this whole Corinne Lucas fiasco, but I need you to jump back into the saddle."

"Jump into the saddle with a new client?"

"I know it's not exactly an easy time, and normally I wouldn't even bother you with this. God knows I understand what you're going through, but this one requested you specifically."

I hated people beating around the bush, and Dwight normally wasn't one to do it, which is why it surprised me. The second I heard him say that the client had asked for me, an uneasiness washed over me, evoking a feeling of déjà vu, reminiscent of Walter Morris.

"Who?" I asked. Dwight exchanged a look with Grace, but not being clued in either, she stared back at him questioningly.

"Brian Watson."

The name hung between us for what felt like an eternity. I'd heard it clear as a bell but wasn't sure my brain had deciphered it properly. A part of me wondered whether my subconscious had somehow inserted it by mistake.

"Who?" I repeated.

"It's true, Ben. Brian Watson has been charged with murder and is currently sitting down at Zone 1 waiting for you."

"Murder?"

I honestly felt like English was no longer my first language, the words tangling themselves around invisible roadblocks between my ears and brain. Even Grace shook her head in disbelief and asked her husband to confirm it.

"Are you sure it's the same Brian Watson?"

"Yes, my love, it's him," Dwight said as he turned his attention back to me.

"I'm...I..."

Stuttering didn't help me confirm the reality any more by slowing the words, but it did give me enough time to understand the gravity of the situation.

"No," I finally managed, the word short, sharp, and fully intentional. Dwight didn't understand its meaning at first.

"Yes, Ben, it's true. He's down there. I confirmed it myself."

"No, I won't represent him," I said, clarifying it for him, for the first time since Naomi's death feeling like I owed it to her to avoid her father. Dwight, however, wasn't taking no for an answer. He looked at Grace and subtly nodded his head toward the door.

"Would you give us a minute, dear?"

Not one to argue or get in the middle of anything between her husband and me, she did as asked. She quietly closed the door behind herself, and once we were alone, Dwight tried to make his case.

"He insisted on you, and only you," he began. "Said he would refuse anybody else we sent down there to represent him."

"I don't care," I said. "Not only would it be a direct conflict of interest with what I'm already doing, but the emotions alone would impair my judgment." I shook my head as if needing a visual aid to amplify my answer. "No."

Dwight had never been one to force a client on to one of his lawyers, even ones with specific requests, which is why he surprised me. I could tell from his body language alone that he wasn't going to accept my answer.

"This is actually what you need, Ben."

"Oh yeah? How so?" I felt my temper rising, the heat intensifying with each passing second.

"You're already planning to investigate him. This is the perfect opportunity for you to get inside his head, his business, his entire life." Dwight leaned forward enough to drop his arms on top of the desk. "Think about it. You can ask any questions you have directly of the man himself. There is no need to waste valuable time and manpower, and you can send Linda to investigate other matters."

"No," I said, barely able to register his words. Looking back now, he made a valid argument. I just wish I had seen it earlier.

"Damn it, kid, see the logic in this."

"Stop calling me kid like I'm some junior around here," I snapped, my temper getting the upper hand. "This is about family, and I have the right to refuse."

I expected Dwight to fire back, his own temper ready to retaliate, but unlike me, he managed to control whatever emotion the argument stirred inside him.

"Brian Watson is a suspect in a murder investigation and needs representation. He's also somehow involved with a person who claimed to have knowledge about your wife's accident."

He spoke with an unbelievably empathic tone, the words holding just enough volume for me to hear them.

"Take away the fact he just happens to be Naomi's father, and you would jump at this case."

"That's a pretty big aspect to ignore," I said, still refusing to admit that he was right. All I could see was Watson's expression the last time he and I had stood face to face. "Get someone else to represent him and let me run this investigation from the sidelines."

"He's not accepting anybody else," Dwight said. "You don't go down there, and he'll end up represented by another firm. He did mention that Winthrop Curtis had already tried to represent him, but for some reason, Watson refused."

Hearing the lawyer's name for a second time inside an hour pricked my ears the way it had the first time.

"He said Curtis wanted to represent him?"

"He did," Dwight said. "And we both know who that man already represents."

While I tried to picture the pompous snob walking into Zone 1, Dwight leaned back in his chair and just stared at me. I think he could sense my defensive walls begin to crumble just a bit and tried to figure out a way of smashing them completely.

"You know, I had a similar dilemma myself a few years ago." He chuckled. "Actually, a *lot* of years ago. I had to defend my father after he knocked a cyclist off his bike and almost killed him."

"You defended your father?"

"Look, it was nothing like this situation, of course, but I think the emotions feel somewhat similar. I didn't want to defend him, no, sir."

"Why not?"

"My father wasn't known for being the most sober man around. He enjoyed his drink a little too much and often wouldn't make it much past eleven in the morning before cracking a bottle."

Dwight shook his head and looked up at the ceiling as I felt myself ease back into the chair.

"I hated hugging him, the stink of alcohol on his breath a permanent reminder of what I saw as his illness. Most days, he'd either remain home and drink himself into oblivion, or he'd walk down to the bar on the corner and then stumble home whenever the money ran out. But not that day."

"What happened?"

"That day, he hit the golf course with a couple of friends and then drove home around eight that night. He apparently didn't take losing too well and drank a lot more than usual. He also almost never ate, which meant he had nothing but alcohol in his gut. Well, he rounded the bend a little too wide, hit the cyclist, and pushed the unfortunate rider into the path of an oncoming car. Dad swerved about a second too late, smashed into the back of a cab, and ended up in the hospital for a few hours."

"Was he hurt?"

"Who, my dad?" Dwight sighed. "Only his pride. Concussion and a broken pinky finger. The rider, however, ended up in a wheelchair thanks to a broken spine." He shook his head and snapped his fingers as he must have imagined the scene. "Just like that, life changed in an instant."

"What happened?"

"What happened is that I got the call. Dad ended up with several charges and needed a lawyer to defend him."

"And I'm guessing you didn't put your hand up?"

"Not at first, no. I was disgusted. The man had nearly killed an innocent road user, a new father. The poor guy had only become a dad for the first time like a week earlier, and my father had robbed him of his legs."

"Did you end up defending him, though?"

Dwight didn't answer at first. Instead, he pushed himself out of the chair and walked to the window, where he stood with his back to me.

"I remember seeing the man's photo in the newspaper and feeling so much shame." He turned back to face me. "My father had become the type of man people would openly crucify for being so reckless, and here I was being told that it was my duty to defend him."

"Can't have been an easy decision."

"It wasn't," Dwight said as he slowly walked back to the chair, stood behind it, and leaned down enough to grab the backrest. "But sometimes, it's not really our decision to make. Sometimes, fate has a plan all of its own, and we just end up grabbing hold and seeing where it takes us. I ended up defending him, and because of that case, I opened up this business. I wanted to be the one to decide which cases I worked."

"Did you win?"

Dwight looked at me and grinned. "I think you're missing

the point. See, it wasn't about winning but about the case taking me somewhere I never predicted."

"I understand that part, but did you win?"

"No, I didn't," Dwight said with a shake of the head. "It wasn't a case for me to win. My father pleaded guilty, and I negotiated with the prosecutor."

"What did he end up getting?"

"My father had an unblemished record up until that moment. He ended up picking litter off the side of the road for a couple of hundred hours and paid a fine." Dwight retook his seat and again leaned over the desk to get his point across. "But this isn't some drunken mistake. This is about so much more than that, Ben. You could really get some answers out of this if you play your cards right. Imagine getting up close and personal with a man possibly linked to someone who already stated knowing something about Naomi's accident. How often does this kind of opportunity come up, huh?"

I finally heard his words in a vastly different light from the one I'd had at the beginning of the conversation. They made so much more sense to me, and it was at that moment when I finally realized what my decision should be. With his eyes locked on me for my answer, I leaned forward and gave him the only one he wanted to hear.

"Fine, I'll do it," I said and effectively took on a fresh murder suspect just two days after my previous.

———

THREE

I CAN COUNT on one hand the specific trips in my life that felt like defining moments set to shape my existence in some way. The most obvious to you, of course, would be the drive to the hospital after Naomi's accident. Those precious minutes spent in the car on my way to the ER felt like hours...*endless* hours, each passing second an individual moment in itself.

I can still recall the individual thoughts that ran through my head during that drive, a drive I insisted on taking myself, despite offers from others to drive me. I remember thinking that I couldn't trust anybody else to get me there, with me being the only one capable of reaching the hospital. The fear of not reaching Naomi in her time of need kept common sense out of reach, and I stubbornly drove myself.

Another drive I vividly remember is the one in the backseat of a car while sitting next to my aunt while driving to the church for my parents' funeral. I can still feel the smooth fabric of the black dress against my fingers as Aunt Shirley held my hand in her lap while dabbing at her eyes. While a five-year-old may not fully comprehend the finality of a plane crash, there's something to be said about seeing a grown-up crying in such close proximity.

There are two other drives I could explain to you, but they don't matter much to this story, and I doubt you'd find them interesting anyway, not the way you might find the latest addition to the list. When I walked out of the office shortly after finishing my talk with Dwight, I swear a boat anchor had somehow found its way into the pit of my stomach and made itself right at home.

The drive to Zone 1, where the police were currently holding my latest client, felt all too familiar, the dread of a meeting I'd put off for half a decade about to come full circle. Brian Watson never had much time for me to begin with, a trait that didn't really surprise me at the time of our first meeting. What father welcomes his daughter's husband with open arms the first time anyway? Perhaps someone who had organized an arranged marriage and been involved in choosing the proposed partner, but certainly not someone like my eventual father-in-law.

Given the strained relationship between father and daughter, I didn't hold out much hope for ours to fare any better, and so I had simply opted for a backseat when it came to deciding family events. Naomi took charge of that side of our life, and in a way, each of us understood our role. With no mother around to add some maternal influence, it was left to Naomi to shape those connections.

What might surprise you to know is that during all the years since Naomi's death, and all the countless times I had gone to visit her grave, I never crossed paths with her father. Not once. There was one time when I did see his vehicle parked in the cemetery parking lot, but I simply drove past the entrance and continued on down the street as if nothing had happened. I don't know whether he had actually gone to his daughter's grave or remained sitting in his car; I never found out. I didn't really care.

When I say I cut the man from my life, that is exactly what I mean. Our paths never crossed, his face never entered my mind, and each of us simply got on with our lives. I did my mourning on my side of the world, and he mourned on his side. I continued to visit Naomi's grave on the anniversaries of both her birthday and our wedding day and on random days when I just needed to be close to her. And in all the years, not once did Brian Watson and I cross paths.

The boat anchor shifted position when I turned the Mustang into the Zone 1 Police Station parking lot, the drive finally coming to the pivotal conclusion. I didn't climb out immediately. It felt surreal to be sitting there knowing that the man I'd avoided for all those years was literally sitting a few dozen yards from my position and awaiting my arrival. I mean, he was actually *waiting* for me to walk into whatever interview room they were holding him in and start defending him. The speed with which the direction of one's life can change truly is mesmerizing.

When the anticipation became too much for me, I shut off the engine, grabbed my briefcase, and climbed out. A heavy scent of diesel exhaust hung in the air courtesy of a recently departed bus pulling away from the stop in front of the station. I could still hear its engine but shut it out almost immediately as I turned for the precinct's front door. The time for me to put on my game face had arrived.

The turmoil in the building's foyer was exactly how you might expect to find the entrance to a popular police station. A number of people lined the main counter, the group standing three deep as a single officer tried to deal with them. I could see the frustration on his face, especially when one of the women, asking about her boyfriend or husband, called him completely useless.

"That is what they told me, ma'am," he said with forced calmness, "and if you don't wish to wait until then, you're more than welcome to return after three."

She didn't bother responding and was muttering something under her breath when she passed me on her way to the door. Thankfully, the cop recognized me from my multiple previous visits to the place.

"Straight up the stairs," he called to me. "Detective Perkins is the second door on the left."

"Thanks, Merv," I called back with an accompanying wave. A couple of the others waiting in line glared at me for jumping ahead of them, without me ever intending to, but I didn't stick around long enough to apologize for it.

I found Perkins sitting in his office, just as Mervin had told me. Introductions weren't needed, of course, due to my previous interactions with the detective. Normally, he was a friendly kind of guy, so it did take me back some when Perkins ignored my greeting completely.

"I'm surprised you agreed to take this one on, Carter," he instead said.

"Why is that?" The question caught me off guard, considering our relationship up until that moment had always been purely professional. In fact, the question annoyed me.

"You haven't heard what this son of a bitch did?"

"Whatever he did, he still deserves representation, does he not?"

Perkins shook his head in disgust and didn't bother trying to hide his contempt. "You lawyers are all the same," he said with overcompensated arrogance as he walked past me and out into the hallway. I wanted to respond but decided to bite my tongue instead.

When Perkins opened the door to the interview room where Watson was being held, he made some remark about it appearing as if his lawyer had finally arrived to save him. He did give me another up-and-down glance on his way back out of the room and closed the door. That was when the silence amplified the already tense emotion hanging in the air.

At first, I avoided looking at the man sitting at the table. I walked around to the other side, set my briefcase beside my chair, and took a seat. I could feel his eyes boring into the top of my head as I sat, still unable to look at him. Aside from the intense thumping in my chest, it was the smell hanging in the air that stirred memories for me. The cologne was something of a signature smell for him, Creed Aventus, the fragrance first bought for him by Naomi for a birthday. She told me that he became almost obsessed by it and bought several bottles shortly after that day in case they stopped making it.

That's the thing about Brian Watson. If he had been born several decades later, he might have found himself diagnosed with various conditions often described by a bunch of letters, namely ADHD and OCD. Throw in arrogance, pride, and a guy who laughs at his own jokes, and you might have an idea of the man I was dealing with.

"Wasn't sure you'd answer my call for help," Watson finally said when the silence became too much for him to sit through. His words were enough to draw my attention to him, and I finally laid eyes on the man I had sworn to cut from my life.

"I'm not here because I want to be," I said. "So don't think I've come answering the call for help."

"But you are here, and that means you are going to give me legal representation, are you not?"

I wish I could have said no, every fiber in my body telling me to get up and walk from the room, but I knew I couldn't.

"Yes, I'm here to provide you with legal representation," I said, the words feeling like woodchips in my mouth.

Watson grinned, his lips stretching wide enough to show teeth. He leaned back in his chair, and I half-expected him to fold his arms across his chest, but he didn't. I also expected him to start gloating about me folding first on whatever differences we had between us, but he again surprised me by changing course.

"Look, Ben, I know this isn't easy for you." He sighed and almost...*almost* sounded sincere. "It isn't for me either, but here we are, so maybe we can set aside our differences for the time being and focus on proving my innocence."

"So you're saying you didn't murder your neighbor?"

"I certainly did not," he snapped before lowering his defensive walls again. "I happened to like Libby. She always had a kind word to say."

"How long had you known her?"

"About a year. She moved into Donna Herrod's place after the old stick finally dropped off her perch."

"Mrs. Herrod died?"

It actually hurt me to hear of the old woman's passing. It was Naomi who introduced me to her during the first few months of our relationship, and while she did have a stern exterior that took some getting used to, she also baked the most delicious macarons in existence. The only person she couldn't tolerate also happened to be her neighbor, Brian Watson.

"She did, yes. I heard that it was a peaceful transition." He tried to sound sincere, but it came across as more arrogance.

"Well, let's hope she doesn't come back to haunt you," I said.

"Highly unlikely," Watson said. "Anyway, Libby and her husband moved in about three months after Donna's passing."

"And now you've been identified by a passer-by as leaving

your neighbor's home just minutes before she was found dead inside."

"Libby was fine when I left her."

"What were you doing inside?"

He didn't answer immediately. Instead, I watched him shift in his seat, and it took me a second to realize the uncomfortable way he looked down at his hands. A blind man would have felt the guilt emanating from him, and so I went directly to the next most obvious question.

"Did the husband know?" It seemed like the least intrusive of the numerous questions I had.

"I suspected that he knew to a certain extent, but I couldn't be sure. In any case, I guess he really knows now," Watson said.

"How long have you been sleeping with his wife?"

"Look, it wasn't like that." When he saw that I wasn't buying his story, he tried to change tactics. "Her husband cheated on her himself. They had a kind of understanding. I wasn't Libby's first either."

"They had an open relationship?"

"I don't know if it was official or anything, but yes, that's how Libby described it."

"So tell me what happened?"

"We had our usual get-together on Wednesday night, which should have ended with us parting company at around nine with a kiss and a hug."

"Where would you meet?"

"Mostly my place, although there was a time or two when she wanted to spice things up and asked me over to her house. Sometimes, we even visited a hotel. That night we met at her house against my better judgment, although it wasn't as intimate as it normally would have been."

"The parting with a kiss and a hug didn't happen?"

"No, it did not," Watson said. "She had seemed distracted

more than usual for the entire evening, and it was only when we finished our...our..."

"I get it," I said when he couldn't bring himself to say the actual word. "Special cuddles?"

"When we finished our intimacy," Watson corrected, trying to keep his ego in check. "It was only then that she brought up the matter about her husband, said she was tired of all the cheating and needed to concentrate on her marriage."

"So she was calling it quits on her extra-marital affair, namely the relationship with you," I said, still feeling a need to come down on him as much as possible. I just couldn't make it easy on the guy, not when he had made Naomi's life such a misery and still appeared to spread the same type of torment to the present day.

"That's what she told me."

"And how did you take the news?"

"We got into an argument."

"You didn't agree with her decision?"

"It wasn't that I didn't agree with it," Watson said. "It's just that I know how much of an ass her husband is, and given the fact that we'd been discussing the possibility of her leaving him and moving in with me, her sudden change of heart just caught me by surprise."

"The police report states that a neighbor heard the two of you arguing," I said, holding the report in one hand while taking quick glances at it. "A Mrs. Herrington."

"Hillary Herrington is what you might call the neighborhood gossip. The woman constantly sticks her nose in where it doesn't belong."

"I see she also reported you leaving the Young house the next morning."

"Yes, I went back over to see whether Libby had cooled off during the night."

"And yet you had already booked your ticket out of the country and were just a few hours from boarding your flight," I said, skipping to the part of the story that really intrigued me.

That was when Watson looked down again, his expression losing all emotion as he turned on his poker face. I waited a few seconds for him to gather his thoughts before continuing with my questions.

"Tell me about the bank deposit."

"The deposit," Watson said, not asking but rather stating a fact. He closed his eyes and rubbed his forehead as if truly contemplating life.

"Nine hundred grand isn't exactly small potatoes," I said to bring him back into the room. "The thing is, the police aren't exactly sure why, considering the account is held by a man currently living in a Philly medical facility." When Watson still didn't answer me, I continued probing. "How long is it going to take them to find out who this money was really intended for?"

"They'll never find out," Watson said from under his hand before he lowered it to the table again and gazed over at me. "They'll never find out," he repeated with a more direct tone.

"Then tell me who," I said. When he slowly shook his head, I pushed harder. "Look, Brian, I am your attorney, bought and paid for. That gives you lawyer-client privilege. Anything you say to me is held in the—"

"Yeah, yeah, I know all that, but it won't be enough to protect you from...from them."

"From who?"

He didn't answer for a long time, but his eyes continued staring at me just the same. I could feel him weighing up the consequences of sharing whatever secret he felt he needed to hang on to.

"Brian, tell me who."

"You still don't get it, do you?" he snapped when his frustration became too much. "They won't stop with just me. They never do. If they find out that you know, then they'll kill you just as surely as they will me."

"Nobody is listening to us right now."

"No, but they will already be watching us. I guarantee it."

He was scared, not just for me or himself but scared of something more. I could feel the fear more than see it, radiating off him while he tried to cover it as best he could with little effect.

"Me being your lawyer isn't much of a secret, so if they know I'm in here talking to you, they're going to assume you told me anyway," I said. "So you might as well tell me now and save me needing to ask the same question multiple times."

"If they kill you, don't come back blaming me," he said with a hint of humor that didn't quite hit its mark. "Have you ever heard of a man named Alex Kent?" I scanned my memory banks for the name, but nothing came to mind. "I doubt you would have. Costa made sure to keep his kid separated as far as possible from himself."

"Costa? As in Riccardo Costa?" I felt myself sit a little taller hearing the name.

"The one and only. Only a few people knew of his existence, including me, for obvious reasons. Can't work the books without knowing all the payees."

"Wait, Costa has a son named Alex Kent?"

"That's him, yes, although Costa changed his surname after the kid's mother died. Used to be Gonzales. Anyway, that check went into his account, and it will be the kid who spends it."

"But it's in the name of William Carlson," I said, needing to clarify the information my brain continued to try to file.

"And so it will remain until whoever takes over from me decides to move it elsewhere."

"I don't understand," I said, and I really didn't.

"Carlson still owns a viable business, a construction company he set up forty years ago. It still operates just as it has for years, with one minor detail changed."

"What detail?"

"While the company is officially Carlson's, it's actually controlled by a conglomerate working for Costa, which the kid is now the head of."

"Money laundering?"

"It's amazing how much money can be moved through a business like that," Watson confirmed. "Carlson's daughter runs the office and works the phones, but she's well looked after by the silent partner." He leaned a little closer. "And this isn't even the only one. There are at least half a dozen other such setups operating right now. All with the same scenario. The owner is no longer able to look after the business; they take it over and run it as needed."

"This Alex Kent. How old is he? He can't be much—"

"Turned twenty-one earlier this year. Costa got his girl pregnant when he was sixteen. The family initially tried to hide it for the sake of their reputation, but that ended up becoming more permanent when Riccardo became more involved in the dark side of his business."

"OK, so they run an extensive money laundering operation," I said once I understood the basics. "But surely there are more sophisticated ways of transferring money between accounts. Why the check?"

"Because that money didn't come from any of their businesses." He sighed, looked at his fingers, and made a couple of fists. "That was *my* money."

"Yours?"

"I owed them for a personal debt," he said with barely enough volume for the words to reach me. "Let's just say I screwed up and needed to pay my way out of it. I promised to drop a check into the account, after which I planned to leave the country."

"Did they know you were planning to leave?"

He shook his head. "I wanted to buy myself some time with the check. They initially wanted cash, but I convinced them to funnel the money through the Carlson account."

"You could have transferred the money directly from your account into theirs," I said. "Why the theatrics?"

"Like I said, I needed time to make sure I could escape. I did the check so I could get to the bank and see if anybody was following me. I expected them to."

"I'm guessing when you saw nobody following, you high-tailed it to the airport?" He nodded. "And as it turned out, your plan failed to take into account the murder of your neighbor."

"Not something I could have foreseen," he said and looked over at me. "So I'm guessing bond is out?" I expected him to laugh at his own joke, but it appeared to be the day for continued change. Watson didn't even crack a smile.

"Yes, bond is out," I said. "I'll try and get you a bail hearing at the very earliest possibility, but I wouldn't be holding my breath on that one either." I leaned closer and lowered my voice. "These guys know about your connections, and I highly doubt they're going to risk letting you out and using them to facilitate your escape." That's when he did laugh, albeit a shallow one.

"I ain't jumping ship, Ben," he said. "Only a guilty man would be that stupid."

FOUR

I DIDN'T KNOW what to think while walking out of the police station, nor what to focus on. To be honest, I couldn't work out which part of the story shocked me the most: the part about him working for a criminal gang, sleeping with his married neighbor, or being charged with her murder. It all felt so surreal, and given the sheer shock factor, my first instinct was to drive to Naomi's grave and tell her everything. I considered questioning him on the whole Derby's connection as well but then figured it might be just a touch too much informational overload. Better to stick to the main part of the case first and gradually work my way around to everything else.

At one point, I had to stop walking so I could take a deep breath and refocus my attention. There were certain things that needed to be done, and if I was going to work my way down the list, then I would need to get my head in the game and concentrate. I only began walking again once I pulled the cell phone from my pocket to call Grace, but I barely managed to unlock the screen before a strong hand suddenly grabbed the back of my collar.

"Is that son of a bitch in there?" He pulled me in close enough where I felt his breath on the back of my neck. "Did you talk to him?"

While the hand grabbing the back of my shirt wasn't exactly overwhelming, the man's voice rose well above the rest of the foyer's standard noise, so much so that a lot of the people nearby stopped and turned to watch what was going on. Already on edge thanks to my client's recent revelation, I spun around fast enough to pull my clothing free from the man's grip, but that only served to bring him in even closer as he got right into my face.

"Answer me, is Watson in there? Did you speak to him? You're his lawyer, right?" One question rolled over the next, my brain barely able to comprehend the first before the next had already filled the air.

"Sir," the cop standing behind the reception desk called out, "I already told you to settle down or you'll be placed in a cell until you do."

The guy completely ignored the cop and remained fixed on me, muttering something about killing Watson. Blazing eyes stared back from mere inches away, close enough for me to smell the tobacco on his breath. He wasn't huge by any means, much shorter than me. I could sense his fists ready to strike and saw him flinch with the intention of doing so, but before he had a chance to use them, a couple of pairs of hands much stronger than his own grabbed his arms. The man's defenses immediately kicked into overdrive. He began fighting against the human restraints, and when he realized there was little chance of breaking free, he launched into a tirade of abuse that only served to speed up his removal from the room. I could hear him for another brief moment after he disappeared through a side door before the voice faded out completely.

A person didn't have to be a genius to know that the

potential attacker was none other than the husband of the woman my client had been charged with murdering. Colin Young didn't appear to be a man who might stray from the wife he loved, not after the way he passionately came to defend her honor, yet that is precisely what crossed my mind. Grief alone wasn't the driving force behind his coming to the police station; that much was obvious. No, there was definitely something much stronger behind that grief. The raw anger of confirming her infidelities, perhaps?

I exchanged a look with the cop on reception duty, a single nod between us enough to acknowledge the potential attacker and the thanks for stopping him. With the phone still in my hand, I headed for the door and hit the Call button, glad to finally be on the other end of the interview.

If it hadn't been for Grace not answering her phone, who knew if I would have noticed the two men in the car watching me, but why question fate's objective? My assistant not answering gave me reason to pause when I reached my car, and it was then, after shutting down the attempted call, that I happened to look across the street to see the same SUV I had seen parked near Brian Watson's business. I couldn't make out the guy in the passenger seat, but the driver? Riccardo Costa's bodyguard.

We made eye contact, and despite an overwhelming urge to look away gripping me, I ignored it and held the man's gaze. He muttered something, although I wasn't close enough to know whether it was under his breath or to his partner. If it was the latter, the second man didn't appear to react, not that it made the slightest difference to me. If it really was me they had come to check out, then Watson's fears for both his and my safety had just been confirmed. One thing was for sure: They now knew who was representing their accountant.

It was Henry Altera, the bodyguard, who broke first when

he looked back at his partner and said something. I saw a faint puff of exhaust smoke escape from the tailpipe, and a second later, the SUV took off down the street. Altera didn't bother looking in my direction again. I remained standing next to my car until theirs disappeared from view.

Before pulling out of the parking lot myself, I first sent Linda a message asking her to meet me back at the office, after which I sent Grace one informing her of my prospective arrival time. I needed both of them to be ready so we could begin working the case in earnest. It felt like I had a lot of information to work through, the least of which remained a murder investigation that still felt somewhat alien to me. Had I really agreed to such an intensive job after what I'd learned about Costa?

The drive back to the office flew by, mostly due to my thinking about the meeting with my former father-in-law. Or was he still classed as my current? I remember the words *till death do you part* as being among my vows, but how much did they really mean when you get right down to it? It wasn't a debate I ever thought I'd have with myself, but that afternoon, I did just that, trying to decide whether Brian Watson was still my father-in-law or a former one. Legally, death doesn't end the in-law relationship as such, but that's not what I tried to determine. For me, it had never been a question of legality.

Somewhere between the police station parking lot and the office, I came to the conclusion that it remained a personal choice. It wasn't as if I addressed him as such, but rather how I described him to others. I guess when it came to the case, I would continue to call him my client, just as I would for any person I defended in court. Funnily enough, it came up the second I walked into the office and was met with Grace's opening question.

"How was the meeting with your ex-father-in-law?"

"My *client* appeared quite calm and controlled given his current situation," I said while setting my briefcase on the desk. I barely got it open before Linda walked in ahead of her new accomplice, Brody. "Good timing," I said to her. "Just walked in myself."

"Well, let me bring you up to speed on what *I* have while you get yourself ready," Linda said, taking her seat. Brody remained standing, just as he always did.

Brody Atkins was what you might call a business partner with a difference. While he did work for Linda per se, he also ran his own investigation business to a certain extent, but he'd elected to take a break to help his friend. With limited work coming in, Brody needed a cash injection to keep his mortgage in check, and Linda just happened to need help. Call it a win-win situation all around.

"You already have information?" I said after spotting the look on her face.

She grinned at me. "I don't sit around on my laurels, boss," she said with an air of smugness. "I prefer to earn my dollars."

"And that's why I insist on keeping you around," I joked and dropped into my chair. "Let's have it."

"Jaxon Derby left the US three months ago, caught a flight to Bangkok, Thailand, stayed there for a week, then caught another flight to Vietnam and disappeared." She greeted Grace as my assistant took her seat and then continued. "Word on the street is he not only has unfinished business with the IRS, but he also has some unpaid bills with the Costas, and they're looking to bring in the debt collectors."

"Vietnam doesn't have an extradition treaty with the US, do they?"

"No, they do not," Linda said. "But," she added, pointing one finger toward the ceiling to make a point. "There's also a rumor he won't be needing extradition from there anyway, or a flight to anywhere else for that matter." I looked at her curiously. "He's apparently already buried somewhere in the Vietnamese jungle. His brother recently launched a second team to try and locate Jaxon, but they've turned up nothing to date."

"What about the connection with the Costas?" Grace asked. "There has to be a reason why they would send Winthrop Curtis to defend him."

"To protect their interests is my guess," I said, and Linda nodded in agreement.

"That's what I was thinking too, especially when I found out about the half a million dollars he owed Riccardo."

"Sounds like they've been calling in a few of their debts," I said and began to explain what my new client had told me about the money he had deposited for Costa's son. The revelation took Linda by surprise.

"Costa had a kid who now runs the outfit?"

"According to Watson, he does. Or at least as much as the rest of them are willing for him to run."

I walked over to the small bar fridge and pulled out a bottle of water. Linda motioned for one, and I tossed her a bottle before returning to my chair.

"The way I'm thinking we run this case is to keep maybe the two sides separate," I said after cracking the bottle and taking a sip. "Grace, you and I will work on Watson's murder defense directly. Let's start by finding out what we can about his neighbors...*all* of his neighbors." I took another sip of water before putting the bottle down and continuing. "Focus on Hillary Harrington at Number 4246, directly across the street. Let's see if we can determine how involved she is with her community." I turned to Linda. "If I can get you to work backwards for me, start with Costa and find me everything you can on his connection to Brian Watson. There's gotta be a reason for them trying to bring Winthrop Curtis into this."

"All right, you got it," Linda said. "Did Watson mention them at all during your chat?"

"No," I said. "I held off asking him about it. Figured there would be plenty of time to stray into enemy territory once we get the foundational information about the murder."

"Makes sense," Linda said, looking at her partner. "Shouldn't be hard finding a connection given that we have a pretty decent starting point." Brody nodded.

"Just keep me updated. I'd rather stay ahead of the curve on this one."

"I will. Got any plans for dinner?"

"I hadn't actually thought that far ahead," I said, suddenly aware of the rumbling in my middle. "You can hear that?"

Both Linda and Grace erupted at the same time, their laughter echoing back at me from the corners of the room.

"I wasn't sure whether *you* could," Linda said when the giggling finally eased.

"Neither did I," Grace added. "Was starting to think you'd lost your hearing."

"How long has that been going on?" I asked. "I didn't even realize it until now."

"Since you sat down," Linda said and promptly pushed herself out of the chair. "And I'll take that as our cue to go," she said to no one in particular, but then pointed at me. "I'm doing burgers tomorrow night, if you want to come around. Just be there by six as I'll be hungry and won't wait for you."

"I'll be there," I called after her when she didn't wait for my response and subsequently disappeared through the door without replying. Brody gave me a final wave and followed Linda out.

"Think I'll get on to this neighbor of Watson and see what I can find," Grace said and went to rise from the chair, but I motioned for her not to.

"Do you think I did the right thing taking on Watson as a client?" She looked at me curiously, her head tilting just enough to remind me of a puppy hearing a new sound.

"You think you made a mistake? You know, if you think that Dwight overstepped his—"

"No, no, nothing like that. I respect Dwight too much to ever think him capable of such a thing."

"But he convinced you to take the case, and you're not sure about Watson."

"True about Watson, yes," I said. "But while Dwight might have pushed hard, it was always my decision to take the man on as a client. And, in a way, I'm glad your husband had that talk with me."

"But you're still not sure?"

I didn't answer immediately, my brain flipping back and forth between the husband confronting me in the foyer of the police station and the two men watching me from their car across the street from the parking lot.

"I just don't want to find myself too distracted, if that makes sense," I finally said.

"You think because of what Costa said about Naomi, your focus is going to be constantly looking for new clues to help answer the multitude of questions you have."

"Exactly," I said. "I'm just not sure whether I'm the right person to be defending this case."

"I think that is *precisely* why you're the perfect person for this case," Grace said without hesitation and stood. "And Brian Watson is a lucky man to have someone as experienced as you fighting for him."

Like Linda, Grace turned without waiting for me to respond. Just before she reached the door, I called out to her.

"Hey, could you please organize a meeting with William

Carlson for me? Oh, and I'm also going to head off an hour early today. I have some things I need to take care of."

"Yes, I'll get on to it right away," Grace said of my request. "Will you be coming in tomorrow?"

"Yes, I will," I said. "And thank you."

There was a reason I had to leave early from work, a reason that I wasn't ready to share with the rest of the world, regardless of how close they were to me. What nobody knew was that I had quietly been searching for a specific venue for the better part of three months. This venue, if you will, would hopefully start to help me heal from the past, a past I just couldn't find myself able to escape.

FIVE

WHEN I EVENTUALLY WALKED OUT of the office, I felt like every eyeball in the place watched me from the instant I walked through the doorway to the moment I exited the building. Was it a guilty conscience? Perhaps. It was no secret that I struggled with my past, more so now that I was also defending my father-in-law. For me, however, the situation had taken a turn some time earlier in the year. What nobody knew was that, for the first time since leaving my previous counselor some years before, I had been actively looking for a way to vent, to share, and to open up without needing to rely on my friends or family for support. In a way, I felt like I had already leaned on them enough and wanted to find a way of helping myself.

I'd spent my evenings going through various forums looking for the right kind of group. You know the kind I'm talking about, the kind of group offering support to those dealing with the loss of a loved one, usually coming together in some church back room or hall where the coffee just isn't hitting the spot but the donuts do. I also wanted a place close enough for me to reach comfortably within a reasonable amount of time, but also far enough from my place in the world so as not to risk running into anybody associated with anybody else in my life.

"Have a great night, Carol," I told the receptionist on my way past her desk, and she gave me a wave before turning her attention back to the computer screen.

The sensation of being watched didn't end when I reached my car. It felt like they continued staring at me through the wall of windows facing the parking lot, hidden faces shielded by the reflective glass from dozens of offices. Only when I finally pulled the Mustang out onto the street and joined the late afternoon traffic did I finally believe myself free.

The bereavement group I found myself heading to wasn't one I'd found easily. I'd spent weeks, perhaps even months, trolling through websites, trying to find one with the right feel and location that suited my needs. While I did find a similar group up in Cleveland, the distance felt a little too far, and I opted for one just a few miles closer. My destination? Canton, Ohio, population seventy thousand, give or take a few hundred, home of the final resting place of our 25th president and a bereavement group holding its meetings at 7 p.m. every other Thursday night.

I drove in silence with nothing but the sound of the V8 engine making short work of the miles. The scenery didn't change much between states, not that I really noticed. Most of my focus remained firmly inside my head, where multiple scenarios of the upcoming meeting played out. How would the people react to hosting a stranger from out of town, even from out of state? And more importantly, how much would I really benefit from unloading my deepest pain to complete strangers?

Grief is such a pain in the ass, and yet ask anybody who's lost a loved one, and I bet if given the option, they'd prefer to keep it. For me, it has the power to keep the connection alive, to keep my loved one within easy reach of my soul. I was still trying to figure out whether I had made the right decision driving to the place when I pulled into the parking lot of St. Mark's, and as per instructions on the website, maneuvered my way to the far end, where I pulled alongside a couple of pickups.

The sky had already lost most of its color when I climbed out of the car with just a bare hint of dusk hanging near the far western horizon. I paused to take it in for a few seconds before turning to where a couple of other people were heading toward the same small building where I needed to go. One of the women had some of the longest blond hair I'd ever seen, the ponytail dangling past the back of her knees. They did give me a passing stare when they saw me turn and walk in the same direction, but it appeared more empathic than anything else. Perhaps the woman with the long blond hair sensed a familiarity about me, the grief somehow recognizing itself among us.

There were already about a dozen people sitting in a circle set up in the middle of the room when I walked in behind the two women.

"Help yourselves to a hot drink before taking a seat," someone called from the gathered people, and I saw the source of the voice waving at us from a doorway at the other side of the room. "There are also tags and a marker for you to put your name on."

I followed each of the instructions in turn, although I wasn't quite sure whether to write my real name on the white label. I wasn't exactly thinking *Mission Impossible* type of secret agent stuff, just more so a protective instinct telling me to guard my personal life. Something about feeling vulnerable and opening up to complete strangers felt way too uncomfortable to me.

"Hi, I'm Ronnie," the woman who had called out the initial instructions said to me as I neared the circle of chairs with my hot drink in hand. "First time here?"

"Yes, I'm Ben."

"Welcome to the group," she said and motioned for me to choose a chair. "Anywhere will do. Don't feel pressured into talking. We're all friends here and know how it feels to open yourself up to complete strangers," she added, almost as if she'd stolen a sneak peek inside my head.

"Thank you," I said and took a seat away from most of the others. A guy four seats down smiled at me but didn't throw in any additional words, and so I returned the gesture with a matched response.

Approximately twenty chairs stood in a neat circle with two opposing gaps allowing people to enter the ring and take their places. Judging by the multitude of hushed conversations, most of the participants seemed to know each other, although I did spot several who looked just as vulnerable as I did. I assumed them also to be fairly new, but of course, I couldn't be sure. Taking the occasional sip from my drink, I sat in silence and watched more people arrive, follow the same routine I did, and then take their seats. Soon, I had people sitting on either side of me.

Ronnie waited until only a couple of empty chairs remained, and after checking her watch a final time, opened the meeting with a warm welcome.

"I see a few new faces among the group," she said with an empathic smile after greeting everybody at once. "Don't feel pressured into speaking on your first night, or even subsequent nights. There's no rule for participation. All we ask is that you be mindful of others and remain respectful at all times."

"And no jokes about orphaned seals," someone three chairs

up from me said out loud and immediately caused a low laughter to roll across the group.

"Yes, Jerry, no more jokes about orphaned seals," Ronnie said while looking at another man sitting opposite me. He gave the group a thumbs up, but I could see color rising in his cheeks.

Ronnie was about to continue with something else, but the main door suddenly opened behind her, and she was interrupted as another participant walked into the room.

"Sorry I'm late," the woman called out with a wave, and after closing the door again, she rushed to one of the few remaining seats.

My heart just about jumped out of my chest as I watched the familiar face give the group's leader a smile after taking her seat, a smile I had seen multiple times before. I didn't quite recognize the voice when I heard it, but I did feel a hint of familiarity about it. It wasn't until she sat down in full view of me that I finally confirmed what my brain had tangled itself up over in panicked confusion.

It took Elsa Schwarz almost two whole minutes to spot me sitting on the other side of the group, and I think her shock at seeing me matched my own. It was one of the few times when I saw the smile disappear entirely from her face, the surprised look almost chiseled into place. Her brain must have also questioned the validity of what her eyes were showing her because I swear it felt like looking into a mirror, this one reflecting emotions instead of vision.

What are you doing here? she finally managed to mouth silently after letting go of the initial shock. Unsure of how to answer the question in silence, I simply nodded and smiled in return as Ronnie continued the meeting without our attention.

It took almost an hour before Ronnie called for the first

break, and we finally had a chance to chat in person. The meeting felt genuinely great, but the truth is, I couldn't relax as much as I wanted to because of Elsa being there. I had built the whole thing up with the expectation of not knowing a single person and being able to unload some of my deepest pain, and yet there she was, not that I held it against her.

"Ben, what are you doing here?" Elsa whispered to me when she came to where I stood alone with a fresh cup of coffee. Others were also congregating into little groups during the break with just a few remaining sitting in the circle, talking with our host.

"To be honest, I'm not really sure," I said, still confused at being discovered. "Wasn't expecting to run into anybody I knew, that's for sure."

"That's why you chose this place, isn't it? Because you didn't want to risk running into anybody you knew." She drank from her own cup, her eyes studying me. "That's why I came here, too, although I've been frequenting this place for the better part of four years."

"I didn't know you had a..." I began but then stopped, unsure of which work to continue with.

"A husband? Yes, married for ten years before Marc passed from brain cancer."

"Brain cancer? Oh geez, I'm so sorry."

"It's OK, I've had plenty of time and good support over the years. Marc and I had been dating since way back in high school. Actually knew each other since kindergarten." She looked around the room while taking another sip, the cup cradled between her hands in front of her lower face.

"You know, I could always leave and let you—"

"No, don't you dare," she snapped almost immediately. "Knowing how these people helped me, it would be a crime for me to deny you the same help. Please stay." She sounded genuine, and I couldn't help but feel empathy coming from her. "Promise."

"I promise," I said. "Although to be honest, I'm still trying to figure out how all this works."

"It's funny how it helps you. At first, you feel uncomfortable and blend into the background while others share their stories, and then one day, you just feel this need to share your own."

At first, running into Elsa felt like a shock to the system, but she was right. After that first break, we went right back to our seats and continued with the meeting. Halfway through the session, I introduced myself and ended up taking almost ten whole minutes of their time, sharing little bits about Naomi and how she died. By the time I eventually jumped back into my car around ten that night, my head felt a lot clearer than it had going into the place. And Elsa and I? We agreed to catch up for coffee sometime the following week. Now that we had found some commonality outside of our respective workplaces, who knew where it might lead?

SIX

SURPRISINGLY, the meeting did wonders for me. When I woke up the next morning, the focus for the case returned with a vengeance, along with the kind of drive I hadn't felt in a very long time. I felt almost possessed from the moment my eyes opened, my brain already activated into work mode. All throughout my morning routine, I kept thinking about my meeting with Watson and the information he'd willingly shared with me. I couldn't get over how easily he'd transitioned from stand-offish father-in-law to needy client looking for a viable lawyer to save his ass.

Grace messaged me just before I walked out of my door to not only remind me of the bail hearing I had for that morning but also to inform me that a meeting with William Carlson would be impossible since the old man had passed away during his afternoon nap the previous day. I thanked Grace with a quick reply and continued preparing for the day ahead.

I wondered how the death of Carlson would affect the business that the Costa gang used to launder their money.

Given the extensive planning the crew put into their operation, it wouldn't have surprised me to know that they would have foreshadowed such an event, given the age of their accomplice. It was while slipping on my tie that I imagined the distinguished Winthrop Curtis arranging wills and whatnot for when such a day rolled along. Watson told me that they worked more than just Carlson's business, and I wondered just how many. How many businesses would an outfit like theirs need to launder all of their money?

I was still rolling the numbers through my head during the drive to the courthouse when Linda phoned me to say that she had found out Alex Kent hadn't quite taken over the business as we had assumed.

"It appears as if some of the older heads want him to shadow his father's former Number 2 for a while," she told me while I sat stuck at some lights behind a cab.

"Henry Altera is running the show?"

"It appears that way. And from what I hear, he's a definite step up from Costa when it comes to dealing with people." I thought back to the first time I'd laid eyes on the man while standing outside the prison and talking with his boss, the late Riccardo Costa.

"Sounds like the kid's got a role model to follow."

"That he does. Kent isn't exactly an angel himself. Already done time for assault and battery, car theft, and enough of a list of other crimes worthy of his father's name. Anyway, I'll keep digging around."

"Thanks, Linda."

I ended the call just as the lights changed and continued on to the courthouse. Once inside, I immediately headed to the back and arranged for a quick meeting with my client. To say that Watson appeared to be having it rough would be an understatement. Despite the snappy suit, he looked like someone who'd roughed it for the better part of a month, his hair almost as unkempt as his unshaven face. To finish the look, he also harbored a purplish bruise the size of a quarter underneath his right eye.

"What the hell happened to you?" I asked once we were alone. "You look like you climbed into some ghetto dumpster looking for shelter."

"I don't think I'm quite cut out for life behind bars," he said as he took a seat.

The thing is, I didn't have a very positive vibe about him getting out anytime soon, not with the murder and the attempt to leave the country hanging over him.

"We'll get it sorted out," I said. "Just be sure to try to look remorseful."

"Remorseful? But I didn't do anything," he snapped defensively.

"Yes, but there's a dead woman's family needing answers, and right now, all eyes are on you."

"I understand. Just get me the hell out of here." He looked around the room and shuddered. "Just the idea of prison gives me the willies."

I took Watson through the process, and despite feeling less than confident of winning him his immediate freedom, I did maintain a positive vibe for him. It felt strange to be representing someone I'd once considered family, especially when defending him from such extreme charges. I'd never had a family member as a client before. Naomi's father was definitely the last person in the world I ever expected to defend in court.

Just before leaving the room again, Watson called out to me. I immediately saw something heavy weighing on his mind, and after a few seconds of silence, he spoke the words I never expected him to say.

"Thank you for doing this, Ben," he said, the words just

above a whisper. "I know we've had our differences, so this means a lot to me."

There were a million different ways for me to respond, and yes, I could have returned the civility with which he intended his gratitude to be received, but I just couldn't do it. The knife that he'd effectively embedded into my soul during Naomi's funeral remained intact, and it would take a lot more than simple words to remove it.

"Don't worry, Brian," I said. "I have every intention of charging you accordingly."

I didn't wait for his response and continued to the courtroom, where the prosecutor Cliff Hoffman was already sitting at his table. He gave me a cursory head nod as I walked by but stopped short of verbalizing his greeting. I returned the gesture and took my seat. Less than ten minutes later, all the pieces had taken their places, including Judge Crispin Jenkinson on the bench.

We argued back and forth from the start, our sides presenting their points over the course of several minutes. Hoffman wasted little time raising his objection to my client getting bail, namely for the fact that he'd already been caught trying to leave the country.

"Your Honor, Mr. Watson's very apprehension took place at the boarding gates. It was only through sheer luck that police were able to arrest him before he could execute his plan to escape the country."

"Your Honor, if I may," I said, more than happy to interrupt the prosecutor after it looked like we weren't going anywhere fast. "My client had no knowledge about the murder at the time of checking in for his flight, and I'd like to highlight the fact that he not only purchased a return ticket, but he also bought the ticket almost a week earlier, and not on the morning of supposedly committing this murder." I turned to look at Hoffman. "The prosecutor is also well aware of my client's exemplary record as a citizen of this city and his endless devotion to volunteering both his time and money to a number of charities."

"I hardly think that donations are a fair distraction from first-degree murder, Your Honor," Hoffman continued. "This is a most heinous crime, taking the life of a much-loved mother and wife, a pillar of her community, and people deserve answers from a man who tried to evade authorities and deny them those answers."

"All right, gentlemen, I've heard enough," Jenkinson cut in.

At first, I thought the judge just wanted us to pause long enough for him to reorient himself. We had been going at it for at least five straight minutes without interruption, and I guess our arguing might have caused something of a brain block of sorts. Imagine my surprise when he indicated otherwise.

"Mr. Hoffman, I've looked into the specifics of this case, and while you do raise some very valid points, I also have to consider the wider details surrounding the case." Jenkinson turned to look directly at the defendant. "I'm setting bail at half a million dollars on the provision that your client willingly agree to the fitting of a tracking device to your person, Mr. Carter."

Dumbstruck is perhaps the best word I can think of to describe my initial reaction. Looking at Watson, I saw a similar expression on his face. I doubt either one of us considered the possibility of winning bail, and yet here we were.

"Thank you, Your Honor," I said, but Hoffman wasn't about to roll over.

"Your Honor, I strongly insist you reconsider your decision. This man—"

"I've made my ruling, Mr. Hoffman."

"But, sir, this isn't how—"

"MR. HOFFMAN," Jenkinson snapped, his voice echoing from the corners. The silence rolled across the rest of the room in an instant as everybody hushed to see just how far the prosecutor would push his point. Only when the final hint of echoes disappeared did the judge continue. "I am not in the habit of repeating myself. You came here for my decision, I gave it, now move on."

I could see Hoffman consider the notion of arguing again, but the look Jenkinson gave him was enough of a deterrent, and he slowly closed his lips. Instead of responding, the prosecutor simply dropped the notes he held in one hand into his briefcase, shut the lid, and left the courtroom. He did give me a cursory glance before turning toward the door, but aside from pursing his lips, he held in whatever other reactions he continued to fight. The only person who *did* react was the one standing beside me.

"What the hell just happened?" Watson asked under his breath.

"What happened is you got bail."

"Seriously?"

Watson's disbelief mirrored my own, although his lacked the insight I possessed. Bail should never have been granted, and yet there we were, minor victors in what could be considered a pre-war skirmish. The prosecutor was right, of course. Not only was my client a significant flight risk, but he also wasn't the poster boy for man of the year. I wasn't even sure how he'd managed to avoid prison for so long, given the information I was finding out about him and his associates.

"Yes, seriously," I said and led him back out to be processed.

While Watson organized his bail money, I walked off to the

side to phone Linda. The thing is, I hadn't contemplated actually winning, and now that I had, I faced another significant problem: what to do with my client now that he was effectively free to walk out of the courthouse. Given the circumstances surrounding the check deposit and his urgent plans to leave the country, it didn't take any kind of genius intuition to know what kind of danger the man now faced out on the street.

"Ben, hey, what's up?" Linda asked after answering on the second ring.

"Linda, could you meet me..." Where? Too preoccupied with losing, I hadn't fully considered the consequences of winning the argument and so hadn't thought far enough ahead. I had to think fast. "Can you meet me at the office in, say, an hour?" I watched Watson signing paperwork at the counter as I talked.

"Yeah, sure. Anything I need to prepare for?"

"I might need you to watch Brian Watson until I can arrange for some protection."

"He got bail?" She sounded just as surprised as the rest of the world.

"Apparently so," I said. "Just finishing up at the courthouse. Should be back at the office in around forty minutes or so."

"No problem," Linda said. "I'll see you there."

Speaking with my investigator kind of put things into perspective for me. Maybe saying things out loud brought the previous minutes into reality for me, and I began to list the things I needed to move forward mentally. Linda would be OK to watch my client for a day or two, but after that?

While Watson disappeared through a side door to get fitted with his ankle monitor, I tried to call a man I hadn't physically seen in close to four years, a man whom I'd once helped move across the country after a heartbreaking divorce. When Rhett Hardy didn't answer after my second attempt, I sent him a message instead, asking if he was still in the game. Having grown up with the guy, I knew he was someone I could trust. When I still didn't get an answer by the time Watson emerged again, I turned my attention to getting the hell out of there.

SEVEN

WE TOOK a side exit out of the courthouse to avoid the waiting media pack and managed to make it back to my car without getting spotted. Watson walked in silence a little behind me, and his demeanor didn't change once we got underway. I wasn't sure whether he fully understood the situation his release had put us in, but before I had a chance to ask, he seemed to give me the answer on his own.

"This is what I meant by them always finding a way," Watson said as he sat in the passenger seat, staring out into traffic. We'd gone about three blocks by then and were currently stopped at a set of lights. Pedestrians filled both sides of the street, the bustling sidewalks almost resembling a parade, and I could see him watching the people passing back and forth.

"You think they had something to do with you getting out?"

He didn't answer, just a slight head nod being the only confirmation that he heard my question. I detected a sense of heaviness in his tone that didn't come from fatigue or weariness. He knew something he still wasn't sharing, which is why I dropped a suggestion at that moment.

"I don't think you should be home alone right now." He looked across at me just as the lights changed. "I actually don't think you should be home at all."

"What do you suggest?"

"I'll have my investigator stay with you for today."

"And tomorrow?" He didn't sound overly impressed by the idea, but his lack of protest told me he agreed with my point.

"I'm working on finding someone to watch your back. Just going to take me some time. I think I have just the man, but I'm waiting for him to get back to me."

Watson again fell into silent contemplation as I took care of the traffic. We got to within about four blocks of the office when he suddenly turned to me.

"You know, just for the record, I never felt any animosity toward you for what happened at Naomi's funeral."

Now it was my turn not to answer, hearing my wife's name enough to clamp my mouth shut. I didn't want to blurt out some reflex response that would just inflame the conversation with unnecessary malice. He didn't seem to mind, happy to continue the conversation on his own.

"If anything, I actually felt kind of glad, in a way, glad that my daughter had someone as devoted to her as you. She knew how much she meant to you, and I could see how protective you were of her." He paused to take a breath, briefly looking out through the windshield before continuing. "I wasn't the best father, not by a long way, and that is one regret I get to live with for the rest of my life. I'm grateful that you gave her the kind of happiness she deserved."

Brian Watson had never shown emotions before, at least not to me. As far as I knew, the man epitomized the term hard-ass; his heart was nothing more than a brick. So you can imagine my surprise when I saw him turn his head to wipe away a tear.

"Linda should be here in a few minutes" was all I thought to say, subtly changing the topic as I pulled into my usual parking spot. I think Watson appreciated the move as he didn't respond and simply climbed out of the car once I shut the engine off.

Linda happened to pull up just a few seconds after we began walking toward the office building. I slowed and introduced her to my client when she eventually caught up with us. The pair of them shook hands and greeted each other with standard hellos before we continued on. Once inside, I introduced him to Grace, who joined us in my office, and the four of us sat down for a debrief. Just as I was about to begin the meeting, my cell phone began to vibrate on the desk, and one look at the screen was all I needed to know that I had to answer.

"Give me a sec, guys," I said and excused myself as I headed for the door. "Rhett, so good of you to return my message," I said when I reached the foyer and continued on to the sidewalk running along the front of the building.

"Ben, my man. Geez, how long has it been?"

"Too long," I said with a smile. "I'm guessing life just swallowed you up, huh?"

"If you're asking for an apology for me ignoring your calls, then I'm sorry, but yes, life did sink its claws into me."

"I forgive you," I said.

The thing is, I didn't actually think Hardy had avoided me on purpose. If anything, the fault of our somewhat separation lay at my feet, since I was the one too busy struggling with my grief at the time. I think Hardy tried to do the polite thing by subtly stepping back and giving me the time and space I needed.

"And to answer your question, yes, I'm still doing the occasional protection job. Why do you ask?"

"I have a job for you, if you want it."

"Seriously? I could do with one, for sure. Things have been a bit tight around here lately."

"You still in LA?"

"I am, but I'm happy to come to you. Still in Pittsburgh?"

"I am. I've got a client who needs a bit of watching." I shifted my gaze out to the street, where a Challenger's engine suddenly roared to life, smoke rising from its rear tires as the driver opened the throttle to full capacity.

"You at a racetrack?"

"Nah, just outside my workplace," I said. "Rhett, listen, this isn't a straightforward protection job. I'm holding some serious fears for my client." I paused to consider whether to share the truth about who the job actually was. "It's Naomi's father."

"Naomi? As in your wife, Naomi?"

"Yes," I said. "Brian's been charged with murder and managed to get bail earlier today. I don't think anybody will come for him, but there's always a chance." Never one to sugarcoat anything, Hardy immediately set me straight.

"Bullshit, my friend. You wouldn't be calling me if you didn't think he was in real danger. So who's the threat?"

"Riccardo Costa's crew," I said, the name familiar to a former Pittsburgh resident.

"I heard he bought it recently."

"Riccardo, yes, his crew no. They're still very much active, and from what I just heard, toying with the idea of a new leader to run them."

We spoke for a few extra minutes, and once Hardy had all the details he needed, he promised to jump on the very first flight the following morning. I thanked my friend, ended the call, and headed back inside, where I found the trio still sitting in my office awaiting my return.

"Sorry, folks. I had to take that."

"Brian was just telling us his theory on getting bail," Linda said as I took my seat.

"Oh, really?" I said, not sure whether I was ready for the assumption, one that I'd silently already predicted.

"They did this," Watson said.

"They?"

"The Costas. They made it possible for me to be out on the street so they can kill me." He sounded remarkably calm about the prospect of facing death at the hands of his former associates.

"You really think they paid off a judge?" I asked it as purely rhetorical question but didn't let on the idea to anybody else. At that point in time, my suspicions remained my own.

"I wouldn't put it past them," Watson said with a shake of the head. "It's rare for those bastards to lose."

If Watson was right, and something in my gut agreed with him, then we faced a much bigger challenge in the courtroom when it came time for the actual trial. I made a mental note to test the waters when it came time for the arraignment which had been scheduled for the following Wednesday.

"As much as I want to put a corrupt judge at the forefront of our case," I began, "right now I think I want to focus on keeping you out of harm's way." I turned to Linda. "I'm thinking nearby hotel for tonight, and I'll let Rhett decide the rest once he gets here." Linda's ears immediately pricked.

"Rhett Hardy?"

"Yes," I said, the tone in her voice catching me off guard. "I wanted someone from outside the city. The Costas' reach just seems to stretch a little further than I like. The judge being one such example." I looked at Linda curiously. "Is there a problem with bringing him onboard?"

"You could have just used Brody," she said.

"I could have, but like I said, right now, I need people from out of the city."

"You mean people you trust," Linda snapped, and that was when I felt the very air in the room fill with tension.

"Yes, if that's how you want to put it. I need someone whom I can trust, just like I do you." I wished I could have asked the others to leave the room, but I knew it wouldn't help the issue. "It's not a question of getting personal, Lin. I need every hand on deck, including Brody, who I intend to use where he will be the most valuable."

"I'm sorry, boss," Linda said, and I could see she meant it. "Just a bit under the weather."

"Let it go," I told her and turned to Grace. "How are we going with Mrs. Harrington?"

"Actually, it isn't missus," Grace said. "The woman's never been married."

"That explains a lot," Watson said under his breath and immediately held a hand up. "Sorry, she just rubs me the wrong way."

I ignored him. "OK, how are we going with the Harrington woman?"

"From what I've been able to gather, she's made no less than fifty-four individual reports to police since 2017, most about her neighbors. She is also responsible for dozens of phone calls to 9-1-1 about suspicious vehicles and people near her home."

"So a busy lady, then," I said. "She'll certainly be near the top of the page when it comes to the prosecutor's witness list."

"I told you she was a pain," Watson added, and this time, I tended to agree with him.

"Pain or not, she's going to be testifying against you," I said. "So I need to know every little piece of dirt she's going to be dishing on you to the prosecutor."

"There's nothing other than what you already know about Libby and me."

"Just how open were you two about your relationship?" I asked.

"We weren't exactly hiding in the shadows," Watson said, again composed like a man relaxing with a cold beer on a Sunday afternoon. "Libby told me her husband had his suspicions about us, but since he had his own affair running parallel to hers, they never really clashed about it."

"Yeah, you're right," I said. "I wouldn't call sleeping with his wife in his own bed hiding in the shadows either." Linda and Grace both looked at him. Watson met their gaze and held his hands up in a so-what gesture.

"That's how she liked to play, and I wasn't going to argue with her."

That was when I realized I needed to delve deeper...much deeper if I was going to get the answers I so desperately needed, and the timing just seemed to feel right. What I didn't want was for my client to use other people as a shield.

"Grace, Linda, would you guys give us a minute?"

"Yes, of course," Grace said and was the first to get up. Linda continued looking at Watson as if trying to get inside his mind but eventually followed Grace from the room before closing the door.

"This sounds serious," Watson said, no doubt trying to break the mood. I was beginning to remember how he dealt with conflict and tension.

"I'm going to cut to the chase, Brian," I said as I pushed myself back from the desk and leaned into my chair. "If I'm going to help save your life, I'm going to need to know just what it is we're up against." I looked at the ceiling to get my mind into position before looking back over at him. "Tell me why the Costas are after you so badly. Tell me about the deposit you made and why you had to pay nearly a million bucks to them."

At first, he didn't answer, instead trying to hang on to his relaxed composure. He appeared to study me with eyes that continued to hide their secrets. When he did speak, he kept his voice low, as if suspecting someone standing outside the door with their ear pressed against it.

"Defending me is one thing, Ben, but stop short of trying to take on the Costas."

"I don't see the separation between the two right now," I said. "If you didn't kill this woman, who do you think did?" The thought had already floated through my brain, and I was beginning to see a direct connection between Watson's release and the murder.

"Do you really want to know?"

"Yes, I really want to know, Brian."

"I think they did. Most likely Altera, but I wouldn't be surprised if he sent one of his men."

"Henry Altera?" It was a name that continued to show up, and I wasn't about to overlook the possibility that Watson was right. "Why?"

"To squeeze me," Watson said. "They knew I was sleeping with her. These guys love nothing more than to hold something over a person. Altera's right-hand man saw me leaving her house one night when he came to deliver a personal message."

"What sort of personal message?"

"The kind that leaves bruises," he said, again trying to use humor and sarcasm to deflect his own fears. "He certainly wasn't coming around to share tea."

"What was the message?" I asked. Watson sighed, still

unsure of whether to answer the questions once and for all. I was beginning to think that he was hiding something specific.

"That my time to pay the money was fast running out."

"You skimmed from them, didn't you?" It was the only conclusion I could come up with.

"Not so difficult to do when you're already cooking their books. With the sheer number of operations they have going on at any one time, it didn't take long to build myself a nice juicy nest egg."

"Why not just kill you on the spot the second they find out? Isn't that their usual plan?"

"Yes, most of the time," Watson said and shifted his weight from one side of the chair to the other. "But I held all the cards at that point in time. Killing me would have killed their business, quite literally. They needed me, and I knew it."

"So you managed to buy yourself some time and eventually concocted a plan to escape the country. Why bother paying them at all if you knew you were going to disappear?"

"I guess because it was their money to begin with," he said with little hesitation. "Figured if I gave it back, then they might just grow tired of chasing me and shift their attention elsewhere." Given what he had already told me, just a single question remained for me to ask, one I didn't think he'd respond to.

"Still think that's true?" His silence was answer enough.

EIGHT

LINDA ENDED up taking Watson to a nearby hotel for the night while Grace and I continued with our case building. She ended up heading home around six, and I wasn't far behind her. The day had been a long one, and it felt like it didn't actually end, not when so many questions remained hanging in the air. Did I believe that Costa's men murdered Watson's neighbor with the hopes of pinning it on him? Maybe, but I wasn't completely convinced. The last thing I wanted was to be blindsided down the wrong track and find the blinkers blocking the actual truth from me.

Linda messaged me just as I walked through the door of my apartment to tell me they had made it to the hotel and Watson was at that very moment settling in with a beer and a movie in the room right next to hers.

"He did ask whether I wanted to share a drink with him, but I politely declined the offer," she said without bothering to lower her voice. "His eyes firmly staring at my chest probably swayed my decision somewhat." I grinned, picturing the exchange between them.

"Just be sure to keep an eye on him," I said. "Something tells me he might get visitors if somebody manages to bribe an official at the monitoring company. Do you have Brody with you?"

"He's just grabbing us some food and then coming over. I didn't want to order in."

"Probably a wise decision," I said. "Keep me posted."

"I will," Linda said and ended the call.

The final text of the night came from Hardy, who messaged to say that he had secured his flight and was landing in Pittsburgh around nine the following morning. I offered to pick him up, but he declined, stating that he was picking himself up a rental. I replied with nothing but a thumbs-up emoji, plugged the charger into my cell phone, and lay down on the bed.

That night, I must have fallen asleep almost the instant my head touched the pillow because I cannot remember a single moment of time lying awake before my alarm woke me the next morning. My head felt like it had been dipped in brain fog, the thought process frustratingly slow to kick in. At first, I couldn't remember actually going to sleep, which made me question the time displayed on the phone. I had to look at the sunrays pushing past the edges of the curtains to confirm daylight.

My investigator had sent me a text message at one that morning to say there had been no disturbances worth reporting. She mentioned that Watson had crashed into bed around eight and snored his way through the first half of the night. She and Brody had taken shifts watching him. I shot back a quick reply and jumped in the shower, anxious to get the new day underway. I had plans, including meeting with Hardy and then Linda once Watson had his new protection in place.

When one of my oldest friends walked into my office just

before eleven that morning, it took me a moment to recognize the face hiding under a thick bush of growth. Hardy looked as if his features had somehow switched places, the usual thick locks on his head now residing across his jawline, while the freshly-shaven dome of his head shone under the fluorescents. Not only that, but I swear he must have added a good hundred pounds of lean muscle to his frame, the T-shirt sleeves struggling to contain the ripped biceps of his upper arms.

"Surely that can't be you," I said with a huge grin stretching my lips apart. "Rhett?"

"It's me, old buddy, in the flesh."

"What the hell happened? Where's the clean-cut lad I remember?"

"Image is everything in this business," he said, "and if you don't look the part, then it's tough finding work."

We came together and hugged each other, throwing in a couple of decent back slaps for good measure. When we pulled ourselves apart again, Hardy seized me by the shoulders and stared at me.

"Speaking of appearance."

"Oh, stop it. I look just the same as ever." I gestured to myself and walked around to my side of the desk before dropping back into the chair. "Thanks for coming up, man. I really appreciate it."

"No sweat. How is Brian doing?"

"As well as expected. I've had Linda watching him. They're on their way in now. I don't want to know where you take him, just as long as it's out of the way. I'll let you know when and where we need to catch up. I've got the arraignment in a few days. I'll need him present in the courtroom."

"Sounds fair. Is he happy to be watched? I'd hate for him to bail on me."

"Nah," I said. "Brian is OK. Pretty easygoing, in fact. He won't cause you any grief."

"Excuse me, Ben?" I looked over to see Grace standing by the door. "The district attorney would like to see you this afternoon, if possible. Around two."

"Thanks, Grace," I said and made the mental adjustments to fit the visit in.

Linda dropped in with Watson just a few minutes later, and after some brief introductions, Hardy led my client back out of the office and disappeared into the day. Linda took his seat and gave me a quick rundown of how the rest of the night had gone. Once she finished, I turned the conversation to current needs, as I saw them.

"Listen, I know I've got you working all over the place right now, but I want you to focus your efforts on Henry Altera for now. I need to know everything you can find on him. Who he hangs around with, his closest associates, anything you can find. Watson seems to think that it was Altera who murdered his neighbor."

"I'll get in touch with some of my connections," Linda said. "Want me to get Brody to start tailing him?"

"Maybe not just yet," I said. "I don't want to risk him spotting our eyes on him."

"All right, I'll get on it," Linda said.

I opened my laptop once I was alone again and continued my research into Riccardo Costa's background. I had already looked into the man plenty of times before, but there was still a lot I didn't know, especially the part about him having a son. Now that I knew the kid's actual name, it made finding information a lot easier, especially with the advancement of social media.

While I did see the physical resemblance between father and son, nothing could be further from the truth when it came to their character. I've always believed that you can tell a lot about a person just by looking at them, and the two Costas were the perfect examples. There was a darkness in the father's eyes, a kind of evil essence living behind the dark pupils. Not so with Alex. A warmth seemed to radiate off the kid, his smile showing genuine emotions that would draw people in. The emotional distance between father and son could have stretched across chasms.

I traced Alex's social media profile across three different platforms, taking note of the kinds of posts he shared, those he interacted with, and what sort of comments he left. Not once did I find anything nefarious coming from him. It appeared as if he didn't have the slightest hint of meanness about him. If it wasn't for the shape of his nose and the distinctive Kirk Douglas chin dimple he shared with his father, I would have questioned him being the son at all.

By the time I eventually left the office to go and visit the DA, I was still trying to get my head around the father-son relationship and how it just didn't seem to make sense that the kid was now slated to follow in his father's footsteps. The other question I still didn't have an answer for was the one pertaining to Watson's substantial deposit. Too many details just didn't seem to fit, and yet I struggled to find the key to unlock the mystery.

Pulling up in front of the DA's office building on Grant Street, I found a parking spot close by and immediately jumped out, only to see a familiar face coming the other way.

"Bartell, what are you doing here?" I asked as I spotted the prosecutor coming from the building's front entrance in the company of a guy almost as big as Hardy. "I hope you're not considering coming back to work."

"Carter, hey," Xavier Bartell said with a smile. "No, just

wanted to pick up some files." He pointed to the pile of folders held by his caregiver as if to prove his answer.

"How are you feeling?" Just seeing him walking around, albeit with a slight limp, proved a surprise.

"I'm OK. The stroke wasn't as severe as they initially thought. The weeks of physiotherapy they said I would need turned into just a couple of days. Think I'm just too stubborn to stay put anyway." He pointed at the building. "You going in to see Clements?"

"I am, yes. Hopefully, he's in a good mood."

"Hmm, I hate to be the bearer of bad news," Bartell said. "Today is probably not one of his better days." I leaned in a little closer and whispered to him.

"They usually aren't," I said. "A man gets used to it."

"That they do." Bartell gave my shoulder a playful slap and continued on his way. I watched him for a few seconds, still shocked at seeing him at all, before I turned and headed inside.

Bartell hadn't been exaggerating about Clements. I could hear the man barking orders from where I stood in the reception area and watched people come and go from his office like dogs called to heel. After around ten minutes of standing around, his secretary finally gave me the go-ahead to walk in. Clements didn't even give me time to sit before starting on me.

"Ah, Carter. Thanks for coming," he said, his words lacking any hint of gratitude. Hoffman stood a little off to the side, pretending to be reading something on a sheet of paper. "I'm still trying to figure out how you managed to convince the judge to grant bail in this matter." He pulled a pack of breath mints from his shirt pocket, shook one into his hand, and popped it into his mouth before returning the pack without offering me one. "Needs to be an inquiry into the man," he continued to nobody in particular. "An inquiry."

"I'm sure Judge Jenkinson took everything into consideration when he made his decision," I said, but Clements barely heard me, continuing to mumble about his inquiry. "In any case, I understand you wanted to see me?"

This time, Hoffman took a step forward as Clements leaned back in his chair, seemingly happy for his prosecutor to take over.

"I think everybody knows the non-spoken details of this case, specifically about who your client works for."

"Who does my client work for?" I asked, playing dumb. "And what bearing does his employment have on a murder charge? Last I heard, Mrs. Young was killed in her home." Clements wasn't about to take my act quietly.

"Oh, cut the horse shit, Carter. We all know Brian Watson is in bed with the Costa crime family." He looked up at his prosecutor. "Just give him the damn deal so we can all move on." Hoffman looked almost embarrassed at being spoken to like a college trainee.

"We're going to give your client a chance to walk out of prison again in his lifetime, provided he gives us information leading to the arrest of specific members of the Costa crime family." He looked up from the sheet of paper. "Watson could be out and enjoying freedom again in twenty years, maybe earlier with good behavior."

"Brian Watson runs an accountancy firm, the last time I checked," I said, "and I have no interest in finding out who his clients are. This is about a murder charge you currently have against my client, and that is what I'm here to negotiate."

"I knew he wasn't going to listen," Clements said to Hoffman while looking directly at me. "Go and deliver the offer to your client."

"I certainly will," I said, rising to my feet. "But I think we both know what the answer is going to be. We'll see you in court."

NINE

WHILE I DID phone Watson with the offer from the district attorney, he knocked it back just as quickly. I did mention the part about him offering up information about some of his clients, but he didn't even bother acknowledging the request. Instead, he asked whether he needed to be at the arraignment set to be heard in just a couple of days, and I said he did.

The thing about arraignments is that they really don't bring anything new to the table, other than formalize the charge or charges against a defendant. With just a single charge of murder against him and Watson pleading not guilty, the whole thing was over in under an hour. I know the prosecutor did try to expand the charges to include something about the substantial sum of money my client deposited into a certain bank account, but due to its legitimacy, their hands were tied.

Where things really took a turn for me was after the arraignment had concluded and the judge set a date for the trial. Jenkinson announced Monday, September 16, as the day, and I made a note in my diary. I was just finishing up when Watson made an off-the-cuff comment.

"That's a long time for us to be trying to stay alive" was what he said.

"Speak for yourself," I replied, not really paying attention as I packed my things back into the briefcase. That was when he said something that immediately drew my attention.

"They won't stop with just me," he muttered under his breath. "They never do."

My ears immediately pricked, a sense of déjà vu washing over me. I'd heard him speak the same words before, and yet this time, they didn't pass between us quite as unnoticed as the first time.

"What exactly do you mean by that?" I asked, turning to him as the courtroom continued to empty out behind us. He looked at me but somehow *through* me. I felt his eyes looking further beyond as he focused on something inside himself. "Brian?"

"Never mind," he finally said. "I just don't want anyone else hurt because of me."

He pushed himself off the chair and took a few steps toward the exit before pausing to wait for me. I snapped the locks of my briefcase closed and followed him out into the foyer. There was something about the words I couldn't shake. No, not the words, but the way he spoke them. Pain, *real* pain, seemed to drive the words out as he said them, as if encapsulating each inside a bubble of emotion. Most men didn't speak that way, not unless...

Hardy remained where we left him, standing near the foyer doors. He gave us a wave when we approached.

"That was quick," he said, but I skipped past his words.

"Can you take Brian back to the hotel? I need to rush back to the office."

"Sure thing," he said. "Anything you need help with?"

"No," I said with a forced grin and a sideways glance at my client. "Just something urgent Grace needs me to do."

"All right then," Hardy said. Brian shot me a wink of gratitude and followed his bodyguard out the door.

While I remained standing in the foyer for a few extra seconds, pretending to be doing something on my cell phone, my attention remained firmly on the man walking slightly ahead of his bodyguard. Something had awakened inside me, a suspicion that felt too frightening to consider. At one point, I walked out of the courthouse but just enough to continue watching the two men continue trekking down the street until they eventually disappeared completely from view. Only then did I send a text to my investigator asking if she could meet me at the office.

I barely remember taking that drive at all, my brain caught in an endless loop of visions and thoughts. At one point, I completely missed a red light changing to green and had to be prodded by an incessant horn from the lady sitting behind me. She did drive around the obstacle in her way and flipped me off on her way past, but I ignored the finger, still too caught up in my own head.

When Linda walked into my office an hour later, she immediately noticed that something was bothering me. It must have been written across my forehead because she didn't even reach the chair before mentioning it.

"Something has really got you thinking," she said, skipping a greeting altogether.

"Close the door and grab a seat," I said, causing her to raise an eyebrow.

"What's going on?"

I waited until she sat down before sharing just a brief

snippet of what had been plaguing my head since the courthouse.

"I need you to double down on looking into Altera," I said. "I want to know everything there is to know about him, and I mean *everything*."

"Did something happen down at the courthouse?"

"I wish it were that simple," I said. "I need to know exactly how Watson is connected to them. I know he's cooking books, but there's more to it than that. I need to know the secrets."

"If you could tell me what specifically it is you need me to find, then perhaps I can focus on a specific thing."

"I wish I knew," I said.

"I did find something interesting this morning about him. Just haven't had a chance to tell you about it yet," Linda said. "He's got a brother in jail."

"A brother?" My ears pricked.

"Bobby Markle," Linda said as she pulled out her cellphone and unlocked the screen. "Nine years younger. Different fathers, but yup, his brother."

"He's not part of the Costa gang, though, is he?" I tried to run the name through my internal database, but nothing came up.

"He's been serving a life sentence in Cumberland County Jail for murder since 2011," Linda said. "I've tried looking deeper, but there's no mention about him by anybody connected to the Costa gang. He used to run a low-level car theft ring back before his arrest. Chop-shop, of sorts. His crew stole whatever they could get their hands on, broke the vehicles down, and then distributed the stolen parts all over the state."

"Who is he accused of killing?"

Linda did some scrolling on her phone before stopping. I watched her eyes dart across the screen several times before she answered. "According to reports, a hitchhiker named

Rodriguez Salazar. But that's not the part that caught my attention. I found something a little more interesting. The judge who sentenced Bobby Markle? Judge Crispin Jenkinson."

"Jenkinson also tried Altera's brother?" I tried to connect imaginary dots. "Could be just a coincidence," I said, but I wasn't convinced. Coincidences like that don't just happen, especially not when there are a few of them. I know from experience that when a lot of coincidences begin to pile up, there's usually a reason for it. "I'll see if I can arrange a meeting with Bobby Markle. Maybe he'll have something to share with us."

"Really think he'll talk to you, though? I mean, if he's anything like his brother..."

"Who knows? It will be worth just trying to find out the relationship between the two brothers. And this one's been in jail for several years. Who knows how his incarceration has affected him?"

We continued spit-balling a few scenarios between each other before Linda had to take her leave. Alone again, I first asked Grace to contact Cumberland County Jail and try to arrange a meeting with the long-lost brother before I turned my attention to some more research. Finding out about the brother certainly intrigued me, and I immediately brought up everything I could about the Bobby Markle murder case.

The details I found immediately raised my suspicions, and that was after just a couple of paragraphs from one news article. Markle was suspected of picking up a hitchhiker halfway between Lewistown and Harrisburg. A patrol car stopped the vehicle around two that morning, and when the officer grew suspicious of the passenger, further investigation revealed the man was deceased from a suspected drug overdose.

From what I could gather, twenty-four-year-old Salazar had a significant criminal record, most notably vehicle theft and carjackings. The officer who arrested Markle said that the driver also appeared under the influence of drugs, although initial testing for illicit substances proved negative. When law enforcement looked into the dead passenger's background, they found that he was more than two thousand miles from his home in Las Vegas, where his girlfriend hadn't heard from him in days.

Salazar had no logical reason for being in Pennsylvania, much less dying there. He had a good job, a supportive partner, a baby on the way, and the kind of life most people would have dreamed of. Apparently, he'd turned his life around when he found out he was going to be a father, quitting all illegal activities and drug taking.

According to his girlfriend, who was eight months pregnant at the time of his disappearance, Salazar left for work that Tuesday morning just as he usually did, only this time, he never showed up. His boss phoned the girlfriend two days later, informing her that he was ready to fire her man if he didn't show up the next day. Her boyfriend turned up dead on the other side of the country just a day later.

The strange thing is that there had supposedly been no interaction between the two men prior to that night, and yet a text message from an unknown sender containing Markle's details was found on Salazar's cell phone, which ultimately led the prosecution to charge Markle with second-degree murder. He pleaded not guilty but ultimately lost and ended up with a life sentence.

The moment I knew something more suspicious lay beyond the articles was when I found a photo of Markle in the company of a man that caused the hairs on the back of my neck to stand up. It was a man who shouldn't have had anything to do with the defendant, given his price tag, and yet there he was, Winthrop Curtis smiling graciously at the cameras while accompanying his client into the courthouse.

Seeing the lawyer standing next to Bobby Markle raised yet more questions for me, considering the man had always represented just a single family's interests. What business did he have representing a two-bit hood running a poorly organized stolen car racket? It didn't make sense to me, not in the least. Leaving the image on the screen of the laptop, I leaned back in my chair and just stared at the scene, the man's smile starkly contrasting with the frown of his client.

"I've got you a visit with Bobby Markle for 12 p.m. tomorrow," Grace suddenly said, pulling me from my thoughts.

"Thanks," I said and turned the laptop around enough for her to see the screen. "Why do you think this guy would represent someone like Markle?"

It was almost a rhetorical question, since Grace knew just as well as I did that Markle was far from the kind of client Winthrop Curtis would take on, and I mean *way* beyond the possibility.

"My guess is that maybe Markle is a lot more important than people give him credit for," Grace said as she took a seat.

"Hmm, that's my thinking too. I'm guessing he knows something these guys want to keep secret."

That was when an idea struck me. No, not an idea, maybe just a random thought that was supposed to just roll through but instead stood out quite by accident.

"I don't understand why he lost," I said, verbalizing the thought. "Any lawyer with an honest education should have won that case, so why wouldn't a man like Winthrop Curtis win?"

"Do you think he lost on purpose?" Grace asked, and hearing the question only served to solidify the idea even more in my head.

Looking at the photo again, the lawyer's smile came across differently, the slight curl of the upper lip on the right-hand side giving the expression a kind of twist. It reminded me of another expression I'd seen recently, that face harboring a similar kind of deceit, the kind you could only see if you really looked hard. That face belonged to a particular judge, and after knowing what I knew now about Jenkinson, I'm surprised I didn't see it a lot sooner.

TEN

I DECIDED to wake up early the following morning and get on the road before the traffic had a chance to build. Grace decided to come for the drive with me, and we met in the office parking lot around seven that morning. Due to thick clouds blanketing the city, plus the slow and steady drizzle that was already going when I stepped out of my apartment, Grace remained sitting in her car until I pulled up beside her.

As if the universe sensed the moment, the heavens finally unleashed the moment I rolled to a stop, the scene through my windshield immediately turning into the rear side of a raging waterfall.

"Oh dear," Grace muttered as she slid into the passenger seat and slammed the door shut again. Drops of rain flew across the cabin, a couple hitting me in the face.

"I think somebody upstairs was watching," I said with a grin.

"Just a bit of water," Grace said as she pulled a tissue from her purse and dabbed at her face.

It felt good to get out of the city, and once I turned the

Mustang onto I-76 heading east, we settled into a relaxing mix of conversation and low-volume music to mask the endless drone of tires on asphalt. Grace shared plans she had organized for her and Dwight's upcoming twenty-fifth wedding anniversary, a surprise to fly the two of them to Thailand for a week.

"He's always wanted to visit there, and I have to admit, I'm kind of excited after researching the place."

"Lots of sun," I said with a hint of sarcasm.

"And beaches," Grace added.

We should have reached the prison by ten that morning but ended up with an unplanned hitchhiker joining us, a four-inch screw invading the thick rubber of one of my brand new front tires. I felt the steering wheel begin to vibrate after a metallic flapping began to emanate from under the car and immediately flicked on the turn signal to pull over. When I eventually stopped the car and climbed out to investigate, I found the tire damaged beyond repair and kicked it in frustration.

It took almost twenty minutes for me to fit the spare, and thankfully, the delay didn't threaten to impede on the appointment. We reached the prison with plenty of time to spare, and I walked into the foyer with about twenty minutes still up my sleeve. Grace remained in the car, of course, having come purely for the drive itself. This kind of meeting needed subtlety, and I've always found one-on-ones far better when trying to extract information from a complete stranger.

Unlike the big city jails, this one didn't have too many people waiting to be processed inside, and I made it through to the other side in just a few minutes. A female escort walked me through to an interview room, and I patiently sat down to await the arrival of someone whom I was beginning to think of as a wild card. You know what I mean, right? A wild card in a case is someone who has the potential to bust things wide open, their potential far outweighing what you might think they have. I had no clue when it came to Markle. All I could do was guess at what he might know and, more importantly, what he was prepared to share.

I heard the inmate approaching long before I laid eyes on him, his footfalls echoing down the hallways right alongside the guard walking beside him. He called out to someone just before they reached the door, his opening shout sounding like a gunshot through water.

"Yo...Reb," the shrill voice barked, followed by a hyena-like laugh.

"Quit it," a much more authoritative voice said, effectively silencing the laugh just as the door opened.

The man who walked in ahead of his escort looked to be a distant relative of a young *Die Hard*-type Bruce Willis. He walked with a kind of smugness about him and locked eyes with me the second he saw me sitting at the table. The second the guard turned to leave, he threw his first question at me.

"You're the guy defending Brian Watson?"

"I am," I said. "I didn't realize it was front-page news, though. How did you know that?"

"Any news is big news in here," he said. "That's probably the only reason I agreed to talk to you in the first place. Heard you had some questions for me."

"I do, and thanks for agreeing to answer them."

There was something about the way he grinned at that, a twinkle in his eye that just rubbed me the wrong way. I'd seen the same kind of look the previous day when searching the Internet for information on the man and found a website containing a photo of him and his lawyer. It was the same look I spotted ever so briefly on the face of a judge, and I was beginning to think that perhaps most people caught within the web of the Costa crime family shared it.

"Tell me why Winthrop Curtis represented you in court. How did you meet him?"

"My lawyer?" He stared at me with surprise, and I couldn't work out whether his reaction was genuine or not. "You drove all the way from Pittsburgh to ask me about my lawyer?" He slapped the table playfully and shook his head. "I don't know whether you noticed, Mr. Carter, but he didn't exactly win the day for me, if you dig my words."

"Yes, he lost, I understand that, but how did you happen to have him represent you in the first place?"

"Bobby arranged it," Markle said. "Told me to let the man do his thing and accept whatever happened."

"Your brother arranged your lawyer?"

Markle nodded. "He did. He damn near turned up almost the same time I reached the station that night. I was damn surprised by how quickly he showed up. Didn't even need to use my phone call."

"Wait," I said. "Your brother arranged your lawyer without you ever calling him and saying you needed one?"

Again, Markle nodded. "Told me he was scanning the police bands and heard my name mentioned."

"And yet, the lawyer lost. Wasn't exactly a win for you."

He pursed his lips and tilted his head slightly. "Not much he could have done with an open-and-shut case like mine. That's what he called it. An open-and-shut case."

"But you were innocent, were you not? You don't strike me as much of a killer, but I could be wrong."

That was a lie, of course, but I needed to keep him onside if I was going to build enough trust for the real questions I had traveled three hours to ask.

"I *was* innocent, yes, but Bobby told me to just accept the verdict and he would fix things when the time was right."

"Your brother told you to accept a life sentence?"

"When my brother tells you to do something, you learn fast to shut up and do it."

"But a life sentence?" I couldn't believe my ears.

"Even a life sentence."

"And how much longer will you need to serve before your brother steps in to fix things?" I asked. That was when he shifted uncomfortably in his seat, the exact reaction I was hoping for. It appeared as if the younger sibling was growing restless, waiting for his brother to act. It appeared as if the fear was the only thing holding him back.

"We'll see."

"And what if you acted alone? Try to get a new lawyer to start working on winning you a retrial? You know, I looked at the details of the case, and there's a lot of information that could be brought up."

"You don't understand, Mr. Carter. You don't cross my brother and expect to come out untouched on the other side."

"I doubt he'd be able to intimidate you. You're just as ruthless as he is, aren't you?"

"Just because the same blood runs through our veins doesn't mean we're alike. My brother is a born killer, hence why he surrounds himself with a gang. Me? Not so much." He looked genuinely scared, so much so that I couldn't let it go.

"But you're still brothers," I said. "Surely you don't think he would actually hurt you, do you?"

He grinned, a low chuckle rising into the air. "You don't get it. My brother is loyal to nobody. Not even his boss. You know he once called *Riccardo* his brother, and look how that turned out."

That was when I stopped, his words catching me off guard as I replayed them in my head a couple of times.

"What are you saying? Your brother had Costa killed?"

"You didn't know that?" The chuckle evolved into a laugh.

"He couldn't run the business with his boss still giving orders from jail, and so he had a couple of his boys do the deed. If he could do that to someone he loved, he certainly isn't going to think twice about ending me the same way."

"Why do you think he's keeping you in here, Bobby? Surely you know that your brother had the lawyer lose the case on purpose?"

That was when something in the inmate's demeanor changed, so much so that a faint scowl began to emerge, eclipsing any hint of the grin that had once lit up his face. When he spoke next, he did so with a tone of someone fully intent on making himself heard.

"I didn't agree to this meeting to talk about my brother," he said, lowering his voice for what I assumed to be dramatic effect.

"But I need to understand him if I'm going to have a chance of saving—"

"And I'm not here to talk about fucking Brian Watson. That piece of shit deserves everything he's got coming to him." His words actually stunned me, and I wondered just how well planned out the meeting really was.

"He's still my client, though."

"And I'm going to be yours."

"Wait, what? Why would I take on your case? I already have a case I'm working on."

"And now you'll have another."

Markle suddenly fell into this weird kind of silence. He closed his mouth and just stared at me, the silence between us heavy and thick with mystery. I could have broken it, but the truth is, I became intrigued by his intentions. I suddenly felt that the meeting was serving a different purpose than the one I had arranged it for.

"Why did you agree to this meeting?"

"Because I heard the name Ben Carter and knew you would be my one shot to get out of here alive."

"Because of Brian Watson?" He slowly shook his head, the eyes remaining fixed on mine.

"Forget about Watson," he said, lowering his voice even further as if to draw me closer. "This is about you."

Chills ran down my spine like I hadn't felt in a long time. Something about the way he spoke those final four words gripped me with intrigue.

"About me? What do you know about me?"

"I've got answers, Mr. Carter."

"Answers? What kind of answers?"

"The kind that brings closure to a man like you."

Visions of me sitting in my office with Grace suddenly flooded into my head, the conversation we'd had pertaining to Riccardo Costa knowing something about Naomi's death. She tried to warn me about falling for an inmate's ruse, and I didn't listen. Was I about to make the same mistake?

"What the hell are you talking about?"

At that moment, I felt like I was about to lose grip on the conversation, Markle on the cusp of winning control and running with it. As much as I wanted to avoid such a scenario, I felt powerless to avoid it, feeling myself drawn in by the power of a single statement.

"I'm talking about the answers you've been searching for for a long time, Ben Carter."

"You know something about my wife," I said, the words falling out in a whisper before I had a chance to vet them properly. I must have looked like a reeled-in trout dangling on the end of a line. Markle grinned with glee, but he wasn't about to reveal the only cards he held.

"All in good time, Mr. Carter. You get me a retrial, and then we'll sit down and talk."

The power of déjà vu felt almost too real as Markle's face was replaced by that of Riccardo Costa. I could hear the man seated before me, but the words were spoken with the mouth of a murdered gang leader.

"Tell me now and we'll discuss the possibility of me working for you."

He knew he had me. With a grin wide enough to show teeth, Markle leaned back in his chair and slowly shook his head.

"I'm calling the shots here, counselor. Get me a retrial. Then we'll talk." As if needing to show me that he now held the power, he solidified his position by effectively ending the meeting. "GUARD."

I watched in silence as the door opened and the previous guard walked in. Markle stood and turned to face me while he was cuffed again. He never spoke, submitting himself to the cuffs in silence as their metallic clinking filled the air. When the ratcheting clicks announced their closure, Markle shot me a final wink and said, "The sooner you make it happen, the sooner you get your answers."

ELEVEN

THE FRUSTRATION inside me just about boiled over by the time I got back to the Mustang, but that wasn't what drove me to walk completely past the car and continue toward the outer edge of the parking lot. Somewhere behind me, I heard the car door swing open before Grace called out to me.

"Did you forget what your ride looks like?" When I didn't respond, Grace closed the door and tried again. "Ben?"

I couldn't stop nor slow down enough to answer her. What drove me to the very edge of implosion was knowing that I had opened myself up a second time to be played in the exact same manner as Riccardo Costa had played me...by using my dead wife as bait.

Grace didn't speak when she neared me but instead stopped and just watched me as I paced back and forth, shaking my head. It took all of my self-control to finally stop long enough to share what had happened.

"He knows something about Naomi," I said with my hands held out wide as if challenging her to charge at me like a raging bull. "You don't have to speak because I already know what you're going to say," I continued. "I couldn't believe it either, at first, but it's true this time. It really is."

"How could Markle possibly know anything about Naomi?" Grace asked, and it was a fair question.

"That's what I'd like to know, too, which is why I'm going to get Linda to find the answer for me." That's when I knew what I had to do and pulled out my cell phone. Linda answered on the second ring, and I didn't bother with greetings. Instead, I gave her a brief rundown of the twenty minutes I'd spent with Altera's brother, including the part about him telling me his proposal, and then finished by asking her to work her magic to find me something.

"I'm not sure how long it will take me, but I do have one interesting bit of information that you might find intriguing."

"Go on," I said.

"One of my contacts told me that Alex Kent has gone missing, and what's even more notable is the fact that Henry Altera has put out a contract on him."

"Altera wants the kid dead?"

"According to my sources, yes," Linda said.

"Well, that *is* interesting, especially after finding out that he also was the one responsible for the hit on Riccardo Costa." I closed my eyes as I ran the information through my already-overworked brain.

"Like father, like son," Linda said, and that's when it hit me.

"Listen, I have to go," I said, pointing to the car for Grace to follow me. "Let me know if you find anything else."

"I will," Linda said and ended the call.

I wasn't kidding when I said I knew exactly what I needed to do next, and it had nothing to do with finding more answers. It actually had to do with confronting someone with the truth that I believed I had managed to figure out all on my own. All I needed was for the right information to fall into place, and the rest would quickly follow.

We drove most of the way back to Pittsburgh in total silence. Grace didn't seem to mind. At one point, she slipped her earbuds in and began listening to an audiobook, something she had begun doing a few weeks earlier. She said that she never expected much from the experience when she first gave it a try, but had since listened to more than a dozen books, thanks to the freedom of being able to do it most of the day.

While Grace listened to whatever the narrator was whispering into her ear, I continued running bits and pieces through my head and trying to find more pieces to fall into place. One thing was clear to me, and that was the fact that Henry Altera was responsible for a lot more than just his former boss's death. What I wanted to know was just how much the rest of the Costa crew knew about the man's actions. I wondered how open he was with the men and women who had such loyalty to their former boss.

I must have spent the entire three hours of the drive caught up inside the deepest recesses of my mind because I barely remember anything happening outside the car during that journey. I think I only came back out once we reached the office building parking lot, and instead of pulling in, I stopped at the front doors.

"I've got to head out and run an errand. I'll be back in about an hour," I told Grace, and while she did look at me funny, she didn't complain.

"All right, then. I'll see you soon" was all she said before climbing out.

What followed can only be described as an awakening, a moment of enlightenment, if you will. I pulled out my cell phone and called Hardy, waited for him to answer, and then asked a single three-word question.

"Where are you?"

"Super 8, by the airport, Room 12," he told me.

"I'll see you in ten." I ended the call, tossed the phone onto the passenger seat, and took off again.

I drove as if on autopilot, my fingers gripping the steering wheel tighter with each passing mile. My insides churned with anger, the muscles in my jaw constantly flexing and relaxing. Naomi used to call it my gills working overtime, and while it had made me smile at the time, no such humor came to me at that moment. I was pissed and for very good reason.

The penny dropped when Linda told me about the contract Altera had put out on the kid. His disappearance was one thing, but the contract? That put the rest of the mystery into context for me, and now I needed the final confirmation from someone who knew more than he was letting on.

I pulled into the parking lot of the hotel at speed, the tires of the Mustang protesting with squeals as I whipped the steering wheel toward the entrance. The car struggled to make the turn, but my faith in it remained. Besides, I was too angry to care about losing a bit of tread. I shut off the engine, removed my seatbelt, and opened the door in a single motion. My feet hitting the ground felt something akin to finally reaching the destination of my intuition, the place where I would unlock the mystery once and for all.

OK, so that's a little dramatic, but I did feel a lot closer to getting answers than ever before. I did feel my fingers cramping a bit and realized I'd turned them into tightly clenched fists. I used one to bang on the door while relaxing the other, and the second the door opened, I pushed my way inside, bypassing Hardy and making a beeline to where Watson stood with a bottle of water in hand.

"Ben, we weren't expecting to—" was all he got out before I reached him and grabbed the front of his shirt. His eyes widened in shock as I propelled him back into the wall behind him. "What the hell are you—"

"You lied to me about the kid," I said, pushing the words through my gritted teeth with a little too much venom. "You weren't paying back some debt. You put that money in the account for him to use for his escape."

"I don't know what—" he tried to get out, but I wasn't in the mood for more lies.

"Quit it," I snarled. "The kid has disappeared, and Altera's put a contract out on him."

That was when realization flooded over him. His hands let go of my arms as he understood that the lies had failed him. Just seeing his walls crumbling was confirmation enough for me.

"Damn it, Brian, you *lied* to me."

"To protect the kid," Watson said, finally sounding legitimate for the first time.

"All this time, I've been struggling to understand why you'd pay that money into the account before disappearing," I said while looking at a bewildered bodyguard. "But now it makes perfect sense. You wanted to protect Costa's son."

"Alex is a good kid," Watson said with his hands held defensively out in front of him. "He hates his father and wants nothing to do with him or his crew." He looked from Hardy to me and back again as if hoping for someone to come to his defense. "He was never going to become the head of the organization, and with Henry anxious to take the reins, there was little chance he was going to let the kid live."

"You also knew Altera had Costa killed in jail," I said. He nodded, confirming his knowledge on the matter. "And you kept this from your lawyer for what reason exactly?"

"I'm trying to save you here, Ben," he said. "This kind of knowledge gets people killed."

"And it also helps people survive," I said, shaking my head in disgust. "How many more secrets must I discover before you tell me the whole story?"

"Look, Ben, I'm not trying to win any awards for keeping secrets here. I'm genuinely concerned—"

"Save it," I snapped. "How the hell am I supposed to build a case to prove your innocence when you're effectively hindering me at every turn?" I took a few steps back to put distance between us. "How close is Altera with his brother?" He looked surprised at me mentioning Markle. "Yes, I know about him. Spent the morning speaking with him, in fact."

That was when Watson's face lost all color, all the strength seeming to drain out of him at once. I thought he was going to fall over and prepared to catch him if he did.

"Look, take a seat on the couch," I said, pointing at it as if he needed a visual cue as to the direction to walk. Watson did as I asked and dropped down onto the seat without breathing, his eyes seemingly avoiding mine.

"You spoke with Bobby Markle?"

"I did, yes."

"What did he say? What did he tell you?"

"Told me enough about his brother to know that he has the capability to kill."

"What else?" Watson sounded scared, genuinely scared, like everyone else I'd spoken to about Henry Altera.

"He told me about the circumstances surrounding his arrest."

I decided to leave out the part about him wanting a retrial and the promise to share details about some other secret. I didn't really know what to say about it anyway, and I didn't want to give Watson anything else to hide behind. I needed him to open up, and I figured throwing in more questions wasn't going to help.

"This is getting out of hand," Watson whispered under his breath, and if I hadn't been standing so close to him, I probably wouldn't have heard it.

"Then help me get this guy. If you genuinely believe him to be the one who murdered your friend, help me prove it."

That was when he did look up at me, his expression almost pleading for me to work some kind of magic to make everything disappear with the flick of my fingers.

"These are dangerous people, Ben," he mumbled. "*Very* dangerous people."

"Which is why we need to put them away," I said. When he still didn't look like he was ready to spill something, I lost my cool for the second time. "DAMN IT, GIVE ME SOMETHING," I just about screamed loud enough for him to flinch himself almost off the couch. He looked at me wide-eyed, shocked by my outburst.

"The gaming hall," he blurted out, throwing the words at me like a defensive shield.

"Gaming hall? What gaming hall?"

"That's...that's what they call it. It's not a hall, as such, just some house behind a golf course in Wildwood."

"OK, but what is it?" I asked as I sat next to him.

"It's a gambling house, their own private casino, if you will. An illegal gaming place where a lot of people go to try their luck. Bottom floor looks like any regular casino with your usual assortment of gaming tables. Craps, roulette, you name it. The second floor is where the high rollers go, the card tables divided into half a dozen rooms. That's where the big money is won and lost."

"That's where you got yourself into debt with them?"

He nodded, lowering his eyes in shame. "That's where I lost a lot of money."

"That's where they turned you into an asset," I said with a

shake of the head. "Entice you with the lure of winning big and end up owning you through your own stupidity."

"Something like that, yes," Watson said, for the first time accepting his fate.

"How often does this game hall operate?"

"Twenty-four-seven," Watson said. "They bring in enough clientele to run it nonstop. Sometimes, they fly people in; most of the time it's just locals."

"And how often does Altera visit?"

"Nothing regular, but he does have a taste for the ladies. Likes to hang out with one in particular. Calls herself Tilly, but her real name is Dana Erickson." I mentally filed the name for later use.

"So you knew Altera was going to kill the kid and decided to just front him a million bucks, is that it?"

"I used the debt I owed as a cover," Watson said. "Alex told me about how Altera was beginning to treat him differently, and he felt in danger. I changed the access and cards linked to the account at the last minute and then went to the bank with the check. That way, nobody but Alex could get access to it. I'm sure that if we check, those funds would have already been withdrawn."

"Do you know where the kid is now?" I wondered if questioning Costa's son would open yet more doors for me.

"No, but I have an idea. I didn't want him to tell me, just in case I got caught and questioned." I opened my phone and handed it to him.

"The address," I said, pointing to the screen.

At first, Watson hesitated, continuing to look at me with those same questioning eyes, but when he saw that I wasn't going to back off, he lowered his eyes and began typing. When he finished, he held the phone up to me.

"Your guess is as good as mine if you'll actually find him

there, but it's about the best place I can think of. It's a farm between Sarver and Freeport, a place his uncle used to take him before getting killed by Riccardo."

I read the details he had typed for me, some nondescript address on a random rural road a couple of hours outside Pittsburgh. I forwarded the details to Linda and asked if she could take her colleague for a drive to check it out and see if they could grab the kid. She responded a minute or so later, confirming my request, and I turned my attention back to Watson.

"If there is anything else you want to tell me, Brian, now is your chance," I said as I sat down beside him. "I promise you. The next time I find out you've been holding out on me, I'll pull my guys and dump your ass."

"There's nothing else. I swear to you," he said, and while he appeared to be telling the truth, I wasn't so sure. Something about him still didn't add up.

TWELVE

IT TOOK Linda and Brody a couple of hours before they managed to reach the address given to us by Watson, and after spending almost another hour looking around the deserted property, they found nothing of interest aside from an abandoned cabin. Linda said it didn't look like anybody had been there in years, the only sign of recent life being a few cigarette butts left at the foot of the stairs to the secondary cabin at the very back of the place.

I thanked her for the update, ended the call, and continued fighting my way through peak-hour traffic back to my apartment. What I really wanted to do was get home, kick my shoes off, and dump myself on the couch with a beer and whatever I could find on the first streaming service my fingers happened to fall on. I actually didn't think my eyes would stay open long enough to last much past the opening credits, but I wasn't going to let that stop me. One single text message changed the course of my evening.

Elsa Schwarz – *Feel like a catch-up?*

The second I saw the name, a phantom hand reached into the pit of my stomach and squeezed, a hand I hadn't felt in a very long time. It wasn't a bad kind of sensation, like fear or dread, but rather something more akin to waiting in line for a rollercoaster ride. I'm fairly certain the previous time I had felt the same sensation was while preparing to ask Naomi out for our first official date.

Sure, I replied after a few seconds of hesitation. The thing is, I had wanted to ask her out long before that moment but always found myself pulling back out of guilt. I couldn't betray the connection I still had with Naomi, and it just didn't feel right for me to even consider the possibility.

Continuing to fight my way through the traffic, I kept stealing glances at the cell phone screen sitting just a few inches in front of my face in the screen-mounted holder. It took a few more minutes for Elsa to reply, and when she did, her suggestion caught me completely off guard. Rather than propose a neutral place like a café or restaurant, Elsa simply sent another four-word question. *Your place or mine?*

My mind raced as I considered the options. I'd feel more secure in my own home, of course, and could control the situation better. This was, without a doubt, one of those precarious questions holding way too much weight than it should have. My answer should have been simple, easy, and immediate, and yet I hesitated to commit to any one response. But that was when I remembered the place where we found each other at our most vulnerable.

Elsa faced exactly the same issues as I—perhaps even more so, being a female. She, too, had been grief-stricken, and who knows whether she'd dated anyone since the loss of her husband. While I might have thought of myself as taking a chance, it occurred to me that she might have been taking an even bigger one.

Yours, if that's OK, was what I sent back after deleting the words twice to try and make them sound a lot more sincere. I then followed it up with, *My place is a bit of a mess right now,* suddenly feeling a need to explain my decision.

My place at 7, she sent back almost immediately, followed by her address, and I replied with a simple *OK.*

With the appointment set, my heart should have slowed again, now that the exchange had finished, but it did the complete opposite. By the time I pulled into my usual parking spot, a light sweat had descended over me, small beads breaking out across my brow. A few broke free when I stood in the elevator watching the floor numbers slowly ascend, and the first thing I did when I reached my apartment was jump in the shower.

Never in my wildest dreams did I ever think I'd be that nervous meeting a woman for a date, and there I was, feeling like a sixteen-year-old about to go on his very first. When I once asked my counselor how I'd know when I would be ready to date again, he told me that I would just know in my heart, and I think he was right. Anytime I'd even approached the idea during the previous few years, I felt the same kind of sinking feeling of betrayal, like I was somehow cheating on my dead wife. Not so tonight.

Elsa felt different, or at least she had since I'd seen her in that grief support group. Despite the hesitation, I felt like I had finally met someone who wouldn't look at me with pity for my past trauma. I saw her as an equal, someone I might be able to share my experiences with, to grow beyond that endless cycle of grief and guilt that had already plagued me for so long.

The next couple of hours did indeed feel a little confronting, passing by as if dragging its heels, but all of my apprehension faded away the second Elsa opened the door to answer my knock. The smile I had so often seen from a distance appeared to intensify when our eyes met, and she pulled the door open wider to welcome me in.

"Hey, it's good to see you," she said, gesturing for me to walk in. Seeing the shoe rack by the front door, I removed mine. "You don't have to. Just a habit I picked up during my many trips to Thailand."

"That's where my assistant is heading with her husband for their anniversary," I said as I followed Elsa into her living room.

"Oh yeah? Ever been yourself?"

I shook my head. "No, not yet, but definitely open to the idea."

"The place is amazing," Elsa said as we dropped onto opposite ends of the couch. "They call it the land of smiles, and it truly is." She pointed up to where several photos of her standing next to Asian couples on different beaches hung on the wall above the television.

"How many times have you been?"

"I try to get there at least once a year, sometimes twice, but you know how it is with work and stuff."

"Yeah, I get it," I said before Elsa changed the subject.

"I can't tell you how surprised I was to see you at the group." She turned herself slightly toward me and pulled one of her legs underneath the other one. "It really did catch me off guard."

"Me too," I said with a grin. "To tell you the truth, I spent so long trying to find somewhere close enough to reach with a modest drive, and yet far enough from home to ensure I wouldn't know anybody."

She laughed at that, the sound almost enough to melt the last of my apprehension away completely. I felt my shoulders physically relax and leaned a little farther back into the couch's backrest.

"That sounds way too familiar," she said when the laughter

died down again. "I don't know how many meetings I went through before I finally felt comfortable enough to open up, and even then only because the place was filled with nothing but strangers."

She paused to reflect, her eyes almost glistening as she looked past me toward the table lamp and its soft glow, which she used to illuminate the room. I wanted to break the silence, but in a way, I found it somewhat comforting hanging between us.

"Oh, sorry," Elsa suddenly blurted out. "I didn't even offer you a drink. What would you like? I've got beer, sodas, wine..."

"I could go for a beer," I said as she stood.

"Do you need a glass?"

"No, ma'am," I called after her, and when she reemerged a few moments later, she did so with a couple of cans of Bud in her hands. Seeing them made me smile, which Elsa noticed when she handed me one of the drinks.

"Why are you smiling?" she asked.

"Thanks," I said, taking the can. "Just took you for more of a wine girl, or something classier, like an import."

She chuckled at that. "There are just some things a girl can never walk away from," she said as she popped the beer and took a large swallow. "My grandpa used to sit me on his knees after a hard day at the steel mill while drinking beers with Daddy and his work buddies in our garage. I was only little, but I can still remember the smell of the cigarettes, the sounds of the beers cracking open. Just a small taste of one of these instantly takes me back."

I could see the warmth of the memory in her eyes as she took another swallow, and I have to admit that the beer did taste a lot better after hearing the story. We sat in silence for a minute or so, each of us caught inside our own memories, before I turned the conversation in a new direction.

"So how would your boss feel about you fraternizing with the enemy?" I asked.

"Who, Arthur?" She sounded quite surprised by the question.

"Clements isn't exactly a fan of mine," I said, but that was when I saw her smile change to something much more sinister, as if she'd been harboring a secret of sorts. "What?"

"He's not my boss anymore," Elsa said, and at first, I didn't think I heard her correctly.

"Say that again?"

"Arthur Clements isn't my boss anymore," she repeated.

"Why the hell not? Did he fire you? Did he find out about us?" Elsa almost giggled as she held a hand up for me to slow down.

"Ease up, soldier," she said. "Firstly, as far as I know, there isn't an us...yet. And secondly, he didn't fire me. I quit."

"Wait, what?" My brain felt like it had somehow stalled like a big old diesel engine, the words I heard not computing in the right way. "What do you mean you quit?"

"Exactly that," she said. "I quit."

"You quit your job at the DA's office?"

She nodded. "I did, yes."

"Why would you do such a thing?"

The revelation caught me completely off guard, considering how driven the prosecutor had always appeared. To me, Elsa seemed to flourish in her position, a position she would have worked hard to achieve. I couldn't for the life of me understand why she would throw it away so easily.

"It's complicated to explain," she said.

"Try me...if you want to, of course."

We sat in silence for a few seconds as she considered my request. She had this habit of chewing the inside of her cheek whenever deep in thought, and I could see the jaw muscles flexing ever so slightly as she tried to engage the trait.

"I want to do what you do," she finally said.

"Huh?"

"OK, maybe not *exactly* what you do, but I want to go back to help people. I've already arranged to do some work for the public defender's office next week." She sighed long and hard. "I haven't felt a passion for work in so long, and the second I thought about doing some pro bono work again, it just felt so right. I want to get back to the core reason why I became a lawyer, and quite frankly, working for the DA's office just wasn't cutting it for me anymore."

"They can certainly use some real talent down there," I said. "I've seen some of the lawyers trying to cut their teeth down at the courthouse, and I swear I actually saw a couple of the defendants visibly shudder when meeting their legal counsel."

She giggled at that but suddenly changed her expression. After setting her beer down on the coffee table, Elsa slowly set her raised foot back to the ground and slid a little closer. I felt something stir inside me.

"There's another reason why I quit my job," she said in a low whisper while continuing to push herself closer. I swallowed hard, suddenly aware of the distance between us closing.

"Oh, yeah? What's that?" I asked when she got close enough for her knee to touch the side of my thigh. She didn't stop there, and when her upper body continued moving toward me, I suddenly found myself staring into her eyes from just inches away.

"Conflict of interest," Elsa whispered, and when her lips touched mine, the rest of my skin broke out into goosebumps, effectively robbing me of any will to pull back.

THIRTEEN

WHEN I WALKED into the office the following morning, it didn't surprise me that Grace noticed the smile on my face almost immediately. I, too, had felt its unabating presence since the moment I woke up.

"Someone's a happy boy," Grace said when I walked into the foyer and saw her standing by the reception desk.

"Looks like someone might have had company," Carol whispered to Grace without any attempt to hide her words.

"Good morning, ladies, and no, definitely no company," I said. "Maybe it's just because of the beautiful morning we're having."

"Yeah, right," Carol mused and subtly elbowed Grace in the ribs, who giggled.

The thing is, I wasn't lying. While Elsa and I did reach a point in the night where we could have taken our intense smooching into the bedroom, we decided that it would probably be better to stick to second base for the time being. It wasn't that we didn't want to, nor that we weren't comfortable with one another. Call it taking it slow, if you will.

The smile remained, however, feeling as if it had remained on my face for the entire night. I think I walked back into my apartment around midnight, and when I woke up at seven and walked into the bathroom, there it was. The couple from the apartment next to mine noticed it in the elevator but didn't mention it. Neither did Nick, the building's overnight security guard. Grace and Carol, however? They don't miss a thing, especially when it concerns a worthy gossip topic.

I could still hear the women whispering to each other when I reached my office, and so I closed the door before heading to my desk. My cell phone vibrated in my pocket just as I sat down, and when I checked, I found a message from Linda telling me that she and Brody Atkins were going to head back out to the farm to see if they could find any trace of Alex Kent. I acknowledged her text and told her *Good luck*.

No matter how hard I tried to focus on my work, I couldn't get Elsa out of my head. The previous night had surprised me, given how easily we seemed to fall into each other's arms. We had a connection, sure, and so many similar interests, but the one aspect that proved our bond beyond the rest was the similar grief we shared. We weren't physical with each other the entire evening. In between our cuddles and kisses, Elsa shared her story with me, and I reciprocated with my own. And by the time I eventually walked out of her home, it felt as if we'd known each other a lot longer.

I eventually managed to push through the distraction enough to get some work done, but the universe had other ideas. Less than an hour after I opened my laptop and began a deep dive into the victim, Libby Young, my phone began to vibrate several times in quick succession. When it vibrated a fourth time to indicate yet another incoming message, I picked it up to find Hardy sending me rapid texts, each just a couple of words in length.

Got company read the first. *Two men* read the second. The third was the name of the place where he'd taken Watson, while the final one consisted of just a single word...*Help.*

I jumped out of my seat without hesitation, grabbing my car keys and wallet in one smooth motion as I rounded the desk. Grace, sitting in front of her computer, called something out to me as I startled her on the way past, but my feet barely touched the ground as I fumbled through my phone to message Linda. When I still hadn't managed to send a message by the time I reached my car, I waited until the phone connected to my phone's Bluetooth and called her instead.

Three failed attempts to contact my investigator were all I managed before I gave up and focused on getting to the hotel. The morning traffic still hadn't totally dissipated, which slowed me somewhat but not enough to keep me from getting to the hotel in record time. I took a couple of shortcuts along the way, avoided one breakdown by veering onto the wrong side of the road and another by sneaking the wrong way down a one-way street.

Gilbert's Motor Inn sat on Route 65 near Avalon on the northern side of Pittsburgh. A large gravel parking lot fronted the building that ran parallel to the road with twenty-something rooms sitting in a neat line. The police cruiser, already parked near the far side with its lights flashing, gave away the mystery of where I would find my client and his protector, and when an ambulance pulled up immediately after I rolled to a stop, I feared the worst.

I barely managed to climb out of my car before I saw Hardy sitting on the ground beside the open door to his room. With no sign of Watson, I rushed toward the scene with my mouth hanging open and would have run into the room were it not for the cop who saw me approach.

"Hold it," he called while I was still several steps away from crossing his path.

"It's OK, he's with me," Hardy told him and sent me a half-hearted wave.

"What the hell happened?" I asked through struggling breaths when I saw the cop take up a position in the doorway to block me.

"He saved my life, that's what happened," another voice said from behind me, and I turned to find Watson sitting on the ground with his back against the police cruiser. Blood ran down the side of his face from a cut somewhere above his right eye.

Looking from client to bodyguard and back again, I couldn't see any significant damage other than the blood on Watson's face, which immediately eased my mind but did little to quell the confusion.

"Was it an attack? Did Altera send someone to hit you guys?"

"Was an attempted robbery," the cop still standing in the doorway said. "Your pal here managed to get one of them. My partner's got the other one in custody down the street."

"A robbery?" I wasn't sure I'd heard correctly, despite my brain telling me I had.

"I'd just come back from grabbing us breakfast," Hardy said. "They rushed me the second I opened the door to get inside. Pulled a gun on us and tried to get our things." He pointed to the doorway. "Managed to shoot one when he hit Brian over the head with his gun."

"So one is dead?"

He nodded.

"As a doornail," the cop said before his radio began to emit static mixed in with voices, and he turned his back to us.

"Jesus Christ," I whispered to myself while still struggling to pull enough air into my lungs. Expecting the worst during the drive had dumped a bucketload of adrenaline into my system, and it wasn't thanking me for it. Turning to my client, I knelt down to get a better look at him. "You sure you're OK?"

"I'll be fine," Watson said. "Just a damn headache."

"A headache that's going to need a couple of stitches," I said, noting the open wound I saw on top of his head after closer inspection.

Watson ended up with four stitches and a night in the hospital. The paramedics finally transported him to the nearest hospital, where a doctor examined him in more detail. While he didn't say so, I could tell that the attack had rattled him, so much so that he almost thanked me profusely for asking Hardy to remain by his side.

Watson wasn't the only one rattled by the attack. While it had only been a couple of junkies looking for a quick score and not the attack we had been expecting to come from Altera and whoever he had paid off, it could have been so much worse. Hardy had been caught off guard, and the two of them were put in mortal danger because of it. I couldn't risk another such mistake, not when the stakes appeared to have been substantially raised.

The second I left the hospital later that afternoon, I messaged Linda and asked whether she would be OK with assigning Brody to help with guarding Watson. She agreed without hesitation, and I thanked her before continuing on my way. Once back at the office, I closed the door, shut the blinds, and grabbed a seat just to give myself a moment of solitude.

The days had begun to feel like some random roller-coaster ride, the track completely unscripted and materializing in a random pattern I struggled to track ahead of time. I was actually beginning to regret having been awarded bail, but then I remembered that it was never up to me in the first place. Thanks to what I still believed to be a corrupt judge, Watson's fate had been sealed long before I ever walked into the courtroom to fight for his freedom, paid for by someone I still hadn't fully gotten to know.

It was beginning to feel like Henry Altera was the one driving the train, building the track, and deciding which direction things should go. He was the shadow master, the new head of a gang known for ruthless tactics and some of the city's worst crimes. I had been reading about them for a long time, like most people in the state, but never thought I'd be the one to go up against them.

What frustrated me most was not knowing whether Altera had a genuine issue with Watson or whether he was just toying with him, maybe scratching an itch to torment some poor schmuck. If it was the latter, then I figured he might grow tired of pursuing someone who would eventually be out of reach and maybe move on to someone else. If, as I suspected, it was because of an actual issue between them, like helping the son of his former boss escape, then our problems were only just beginning. While the most recent attack didn't come from Altera, who was to say the next one wouldn't?

The question for me was how far Altera would go to make Watson pay for helping Alex Kent escape. Was it worth killing him for? I didn't think a man like Altera really cared about murder. To him, the line in the sand was non-existent, murder just another tool to be used by people who shunned the laws of common people. I imagined him to be someone who didn't care about repercussions, someone who simply looked for an alternative option when the chosen one didn't work out. If he couldn't get Watson put away, then he'd take care of him in a more direct manner.

It was that very thought that suddenly made me sit up and open my eyes. What if the junkies had been sent by Altera after all? Who was to say that they *weren't* working for him? The man had a habit of paying people to do his bidding, like the guys who'd killed Riccardo Costa in prison. It wasn't as if they wore a recognizable uniform or displayed some tattooed symbol of allegiance. Men like Henry Altera used their strongest tool for getting others to do their dirty work...cold, hard cash.

I grabbed my cell phone, thumbed the screen to life, and waited for the Face ID to do its thing. One unlocked, I opened the message app and sent Hardy a question, asking whether he was sure the duo had been trying to rob them. He responded a minute or so later, saying that they demanded their wallets and watches, and one of them went looking through their bags. I thanked him, but I still wasn't satisfied, and so I sent an additional message to Jack Barnes asking if he could check something out for me. I needed to know if anybody had any idea how much money the junkies had in their pockets.

Jack got back to me about twenty minutes later with an answer that both surprised me and opened my eyes to a danger that had only been assumed up until that point.

They found two folded-up hundred-dollar bills in each man's pockets was the reply that came through. *Two hundred-dollar bills,* I thought to myself. I leaned back in the chair a second time, eyes open and staring at the opposing wall. How odd is it to find the exact same amount of money in the pockets of two men living rough on the streets?

"Not odd at all when that money has been handed to them by someone paying them for a job," I whispered into the darkened room.

There wasn't a shred of doubt in my mind as to how the men ended up with the money in their possession nor who had facilitated the payment. Now that the threat had all but been confirmed for me, I had to ensure my client's safety moving forward. With the trial still a couple of weeks in the future, I knew we would have our work cut out for us to make sure that Brian Watson would make it to the courthouse alive.

FOURTEEN

THE DAYS PASSED by a lot slower after that initial attack, but they eventually turned into weeks, and before I knew it, the first day of the trial finally arrived. The good news was that Watson managed to survive to the start of his trial, although having said that, it's also fair to say that we didn't hear so much as a peep from any potential attacker. The truth is, I had begun to wonder whether I hadn't misjudged the idea that the two robbers had been sent by Altera in the first place.

Hardy and Brody watched Watson around the clock, and maybe Altera grew tired of waiting for the right opportunity to take care of him. If he did, then the immediate danger might have passed, but I didn't think it was over completely. My instincts told me that a man like that rarely gave up completely, and it was probably more likely for him to make his next move when Watson landed back in jail. If he were found not guilty and handed back his freedom, perhaps the attempts on his life would start a second time.

I was still thinking about the potential attacks during the first part of the morning when the judge, Hoffman, and I worked through the process of selecting the jury for the trial. Given a lack of sleep the previous night as well as the constant distraction of my overactive brain, it made the process feel so much more cumbersome than it should have. Thankfully, we finished just in time to still take advantage of a well-placed lunch, which I took with both Grace and my client at a nearby café.

When I walked back into the courthouse an hour later with my belly full and a genuine urge to wield justice, I felt like it was finally time to get to work. As a lawyer, the prep is certainly always needed, but it's a far cry from what I actually enjoyed doing. Standing in the middle of a courtroom with a defendant behind me, a witness before me, and a judge overseeing the whole show is where my heart sat. Convincing a jury of a client's innocence is a job I truly embraced, a role I saw as my ultimate calling.

Nothing can compare to the moment a lawyer first walks into a courtroom and prepares to deliver their opening statement in a murder trial. There is a certain level of focus needed in that moment, and it's rare for anything to wield enough power to break that focus. This was the day when all of our hard work would come into play, and I would go into battle for the father of my long-lost wife. Unfortunately for me, this also happened to be the day when I found a distraction sitting three rows behind my place in the courtroom, wearing a business suit and her usual smile.

I hadn't expected Elsa to attend the hearing, much less look as beautiful as she did. She gave me a bit of a wave when she noticed me looking in her direction, and I returned it via a quick smile before continuing on to my seat.

"Is that your girlfriend?" Watson asked when he sat beside me at our table.

"Just a colleague," I said, and immediately wondered why I felt a need to lie to the man.

I felt Watson stare at me for a few extra seconds before his attention diverted to the bailiff, who called for the room to rise. When Jenkinson walked in, he briefly ran his eyes across the room, finished with my client, and sat down, where he appeared to get himself organized in preparation for what came next. It took another few moments before he finally called for the jury to be brought out.

The courtroom watched in silence as each of the twelve members of the jury emerged from a side door and took their seats. I watched each of them with interest, knowing that it would be they who would decide the fate of my client, not a judge who might have been financially compromised. Those eight men and four women would listen to the facts presented to them, take those facts back to their meeting room, and deliberate for however long was needed before reaching a verdict. This was what true justice really came down to.

Once the jury members had all taken their seats, Jenkinson took a moment to address them with specific instructions. Again, it didn't matter that he'd been bought and paid for by whoever wanted to influence the court case; his speech was nothing more than basic instructions. When he finished with the jury, the judge turned to the main area of the court, looked from the prosecutor to me and back again, and started the wheels of justice with his next instruction.

"Mr. Hoffman, you may deliver your opening statement."

"Thank you, Your Honor," Hoffman said as he rose to his feet.

Cliff Hoffman wasn't an amateur when it came to prosecuting criminals. The man had worked the criminal circuit inside the Pennsylvania state lines for close to twenty years, starting with his first five years in Philadelphia before moving across the state to Pittsburgh. That's where he married his wife just a year later, a former prosecutor fifteen years his senior, who now ran a charity house for battered mothers. Hoffman took his role seriously, the kind of man who hardly smiled and often frowned when tempted by a joke told by one of his colleagues.

"Members of the jury," Hoffman began only once he had crossed the majority of the floor and stood directly before the twelve members. "While you might assume that a murder case such as this relies on evidence, the facts are often far more telling, and the facts in this case will prove the guilt of the defendant beyond a reasonable doubt." He turned to take a quick look in Watson's direction, using the moment to pull the majority of the jury's attention along with him. "The fact is, Brian Watson had an adulterous affair with his married neighbor, Mrs. Elizabeth Young. It's also a known fact that Mrs. Young had been married to her husband for more than twenty years, and the couple had raised a daughter who studied at UCLA." He paused long enough to take a couple of strides back and forth before continuing. "It's a known fact confirmed by the defendant himself that the pair had engaged in a nine-month-long affair. It's a fact that when Mrs. Young tried to break the relationship off, Mr. Watson got angry and tried to convince her to continue. It's a fact that the pair got into a heated argument the night before her murder, an argument overheard by several neighbors."

Again, he paused, looking down at the ground while he took a few extra steps and pretended to gather his thoughts, but he was just dramatizing his performance.

"It's also a fact confirmed by witnesses that Mr. Watson returned to the victim's home the very next morning, where he got into another argument and ultimately murdered the mother of one in cold blood. It's a fact, ladies and gentlemen of the jury, that the defendant then attempted to flee the country but was instead arrested at Pittsburgh International moments before boarding a flight bound for Switzerland."

That was when the prosecutor took a few more steps, this time directly toward the jury. He stopped when he reached the dividing wall fronting the jury area and gripped the top of it with both hands while meeting the gaze of each and every member sitting in the front row before continuing.

"Regardless of how you view this case, regardless of what faith or religion you choose to follow, regardless of whether this woman's actions conflict with your moral standards, the fact remains that Elizabeth Young was brutally murdered in her own home, a place where she deserved to feel safe." He pointed over his shoulder to the defendant without looking. "The facts of the case place Brian Watson at the scene of the murder just minutes before his lover's body was found, and it's the facts of this case that describe how this needless murder took place. It is my duty to prove to you beyond a reasonable doubt that only the defendant could have committed this heinous crime, and when I do, it is your duty to find the defendant guilty as charged." He again took the time to look at most of the jurors in turn before his final line. "Thank you, ladies and gentlemen of the jury."

I thought the prosecutor was going to shoot me a quick wink when he turned to go back to his seat and caught me watching him, but he only held my gaze for a second before reaching his chair and taking a seat.

"Mr. Carter, please deliver your opening statement," Jenkinson said and handed me the floor for the very first time.

"Thank you, Your Honor," I said as I too pushed myself out of the chair, but instead of immediately walking toward the jury, I remained at the table for a few seconds to let the suspense build a little. I could feel all eyes on me, including each member of the jury, the judge, and even the prosecutor. Just as I heard Jenkinson shift in his chair, about to call out for me to get on with it, I looked across at the jury.

"My name is Ben Carter, and I'm the lawyer hired to defend Mr. Watson. What many of you might not know is that Brian Watson isn't just a client; he's actually my father-in-law, or should I say my *ex*-father-in-law. His daughter, my wife, died in a tragic accident a few years ago, and I didn't hesitate when I heard about him being charged with this murder."

Using my own ability to dramatize the moment, I reached down and squeezed my client's shoulder. Watson looked up at me with an appreciative smile, and I nodded my affirmation back at him. When our moment passed by, I stepped around the table and headed for the jury, watching each of them in turn on my way to where the prosecutor had stood just moments before.

"The reason I believe that information to be so important is because it is another fact, and facts, ladies and gentlemen, do indeed make up the core of any case. The problem with facts, however, is that sometimes, they can be misrepresented by those presenting them and subsequently misconstrued by those hearing them."

I took a few steps to the left, turned, and took a quick look over my shoulder, and nodded at Watson before looking back at the jury.

"Misconstrued like right now, ladies and gentlemen. What I didn't tell you is that the defendant and I hadn't spoken in more than five years before him being charged. You see, we had somewhat of a falling out at the time, at the funeral, in fact. You see, facts mean nothing without context, and in a case as complicated as this, it's the context behind each and every fact that requires careful analysis by someone such as yourself." I took a couple more steps before continuing. "Did Brian

Watson have an affair with the victim, Elizabeth Young? Yes, he did. It's a fact he hasn't denied once. Did he have an argument with the victim on the night before her death? Yes, again, a fact nobody refutes. But this wasn't the first time Elizabeth Young took a lover outside of her marriage."

"THAT'S A LIE, THAT'S A DAMN LIE," somebody suddenly yelled from the gallery, and the judge immediately began to thump his little hammer onto any flat surface it could find. Colin Young launched into a tirade of abuse directed at me that was only cut off when a couple of court security guards dragged him from the courtroom.

While the interruption did cause somewhat of a distraction during my opening statement, it didn't stop me from finishing it. Once the commotion settled down again and a renewed silence fell across the courtroom, I continued with the final few lines of my prepared speech.

"My apologies for the interruption, ladies and gentlemen," I said with sincerity. "This is obviously an extremely emotional time for the friends and family of Elizabeth Young, which is why your finding in this case matters so much. Make no mistake that somebody did indeed murder this innocent woman in her home. It will be up to you not to blindly follow presented facts in this case but to carefully screen the context behind each and every minute detail so that you ensure that justice will prevail. Only by understanding the key evidence will you find the defendant innocent of this heinous crime. Thank you."

FIFTEEN

NOT WANTING to waste time with another recess so soon after the major break, the judge first confirmed that the prosecutor was ready to proceed and then gave him the go-ahead to call his first witness. I watched Hoffman's interaction with the judge, the man appearing a picture of professionalism, right down to the shine of his shoes. He'd straighten his tie whenever starting a new task or conversation and smooth down his hair whenever he finished. During a conversation, he had this habit of feeling the cuff of each sleeve in turn, some-times enough to fumble with the cufflinks.

"We call Officer Lance Gooch to the stand, Your Honor," Hoffman said with the fingers of one hand reaching for the knot of his menthol-green tie.

The cop who entered the courtroom did so with the kind of walk that conveyed purpose. With his shoulders back and his head held high, Gooch almost marched to the witness stand, looking like a man on a mission. He reminded me of the kind of officer who took more than the average pride in his job, the kind who spent extra time polishing each of the buttons on his jacket just in case of a surprise inspection that never really came.

The bailiff swore the man in, and it was obvious this wasn't the cop's first time in a courtroom. He followed each step of the procedure like a seasoned professional, almost mirroring the prosecutor's mannerisms, right down to the frown lines running across his brow.

"Officer Gooch, thank you for your time today," Hoffman said as he walked around the side of his desk and made his way closer to the witness stand. "You and your partner were the first on the scene, were you not?"

"We were, yes."

"And could you please tell the court what you found when you arrived at the home of the deceased?"

"We found a woman we believed to be the resident of the home deceased in an upstairs bedroom," Gooch said while looking out toward the main viewing gallery.

"Did you see any signs of a struggle at all?"

"Not initially, no," the cop said. "She had been stabbed a single time in the upper body, and she lay face up on the bed, which is why we could see that the weapon remained embedded in her chest."

"So no signs of a struggle. What about forced entry?"

"No, sir. When we asked the woman who called 9-1-1, she told us that she found the front door open when she arrived."

"This woman," Hoffman continued. "Did she happen to tell you why she entered the home in the first place?"

"Yes, she said she was a neighbor and had heard the home-owner arguing with a man the previous evening, and when she saw the same man again leaving the house that morning, she grew concerned and went to check on Mrs. Young's welfare."

"This man the neighbor saw, did she identify him?"

"Yes, she said he lived next door to the victim. Brian Watson."

"Officer Gooch, you mentioned that you *initially* didn't see any signs of a struggle. What about later?"

"Once we secured the crime scene and were waiting for back-up, I noticed a perfume bottle that appeared to have been thrown against one wall beside the bed with enough force to punch a hole in the drywall."

"And were there any prints found on the pieces?" Hoffman asked.

"Yes, sir, there was." Again, he looked at my client. "The defendant's prints, Brian Watson."

"Thank you, Officer Gooch," the prosecutor told the witness and then to the judge, he added, "No further questions, Your Honor."

"Your witness, Mr. Carter," Jenkinson said almost immediately, and I jumped to my feet.

"Thank you, Your Honor," I said and rounded the table. "Officer Gooch, I'm curious to know how warm the bedroom was when you first walked into it." The cop looked at me, puzzled.

"I'm sorry, how *warm* was the room?"

"Yes." When he didn't answer immediately, I expanded the question. "How warm would you say the bedroom of the deceased was at the time of your initial arrival?"

"It didn't feel noticeably warm," Gooch said, still looking puzzled. "I guess it matched the outside temperature. It was just a normal day, mid-seventies from memory."

"And the report indicates that you and your partner arrived within twelve minutes of the 9-1-1 call, is that correct?"

"It is, yes."

"We know from Mrs. Harrington's statement that she saw my client walk out of Elizabeth Young's home at exactly 8:25, the same time as the local school bus rolling down the street. Mrs. Harrington claimed to have entered the home within five minutes of seeing the defendant leave and made the 9-1-1 call about a minute later. Am I right so far?"

"Yes, I believe so," Gooch said.

"So that puts your arrival at around eight-forty that morning."

"Eight-forty-one," Gooch said.

"OK, then. Eight-forty-one. And when we check the coroner's report for the time of death as being somewhere between eight-fifteen and eight-twenty-five, it shows your arrival within approximately fifteen to twenty-five minutes from the murder. Is that right?"

"Yes, I'd agree with that."

I strolled a little past the witness stand, and then I stopped, turning to face both the witness and the jury, the latter the purpose of my little walk. It was the jury I wanted to see for my next question.

"When you found the broken perfume bottle, did you also happen to see the liquid on the wall or floor?"

"I'm sorry, I'm not following," the cop said.

"Mrs. Harrington was quite clear that she had concerns for the victim and went over immediately after seeing the defendant leave. By the time you arrived, barely minutes had passed by, which must have meant the liquid from the perfume bottle should still have been visible," I said. "The floor in the bedroom is carpeted, correct?"

"I believe so."

"The perfume should have soaked into the carpet and still been visible if the bottle had in fact been broken that morning, should it have not?" Gooch hesitated to answer, and so I continued. "I'd like to submit this analysis as evidence, Your Honor. It's a monitored test conducted three days after the murder under similar conditions to the morning of the incident. The temperature in the room, according to forensics, was seventy-three degrees, and when tested, the perfume in the bottle remained visible for exactly ninety-four minutes. I also have a receipt here showing the purchase of the perfume by the defendant the previous day, proving the bottle would have been near capacity at the time of breaking." I handed the receipt to the bailiff, who admitted it and the report into evidence. "Now, Officer Gooch, do you recall any visible moisture around the broken pieces of the bottle?"

"No, I do not."

"So would it be fair to say that the bottle might have been broken long before the events which took place inside the home that morning?"

"Yes, I would agree with that."

"Thank you. No further questions, Your Honor."

When the judge excused the witness and asked the prosecutor to call his next one, Hoffman's name turned out to bring a familiar face into the courtroom, one immediately recognized by almost everybody at once. I heard a subdued murmur roll across the room and felt Jenkinson's piercing blue eyes stare at the man as he crossed the floor toward the witness stand.

The trouble with Colin Young was that the man didn't look like the kind of person he really was. He appeared shy and withdrawn, a common trait for a man his size. He couldn't have stood much taller than around five-seven, his legs barely the size of my arms, and yet he had the kind of confidence more in line with a man twice his size. He could have been mistaken for a Marine with his shortly-cropped haircut, or any kind of military man, for that matter, but as far as I knew, he'd always been a baker.

When the bailiff finished swearing the new witness in, the judge didn't immediately hand him over to the prosecutor. He instead called for the man's attention and then reminded him of where he was.

"Rest assured, sir, I will not tolerate the kind of outburst this courtroom witnessed earlier today. Listen closely, Mr. Young. I promise you that if it does, I will have you removed from my court, and you will not be taking any further part in this trial. Do I make myself clear?"

"Yes, Your Honor, I hear you," Young said, and I noted how even the tone of his voice lacked any hint of its true power, a power I had now experienced twice before.

"Very well, then," Jenkinson, and only once he seemed satisfied that his warning had been understood did he hand the witness over to the prosecutor. "Your witness, Mr. Hoffman. You may begin your questions."

"Thank you, Your Honor," Hoffman said and immediately rounded the table to cross the floor. "Thank you for agreeing to answer some questions for us during this difficult time," the prosecutor began once he stood close enough to the witness. "I understand you know the defendant, is that right?"

"I do, yes," Young said, and I noted how he couldn't bring himself to look at Watson. He kept his eyes firmly cast down into his lap as he spoke.

"And from what I understand, the defendant met your wife through you, is that correct?"

Young nodded before answering. "Came over shortly after we moved in next door to him when he saw my classic in the garage." He looked up at the prosecutor and then at the judge as if needing to explain himself. "I own a 1964 Ford Galaxy that I've been slowly rebuilding over the last few years." He grinned to himself as his eyes returned to his lap. "Libby hated the car. Told me it was just a waste of good, hard-earned money, but I couldn't bring myself to sell it."

"I understand," Hoffman said. "So you met him through the car in your garage, is that correct?"

"Told me he owned one himself, something about it being his first car, although I didn't believe him. When Libby came out to check on who I was talking to, I saw the way he kept looking at her. Ever since then, it seemed like he would make up excuses just to come over."

"Were you aware of their relationship, Mr. Young?"

"Libby told me about the affair two days before she died. Told me she was tired of all the sneaking around. She said she even had him coming into our home to see if I would notice."

"And did you?"

Young didn't answer immediately, and I could see him fidget while trying to find a worthy answer.

"I might have ignored a lot of the signs. Didn't want to believe them, I guess."

"Has your wife ever been unfaithful before, Mr. Watson?"

"No," he suddenly snapped, this time looking up to meet the prosecutor's gaze before staring past him until he found me. "No, she has not," he repeated.

"Never?"

"No, and to hell with anybody who says otherwise."

I wanted to grin, but I knew if I did, then I'd be guilty of sending the grieving husband into another meltdown. I doubt he could have held it together.

"Did you love your wife, Mr. Young?"

"More than anything," he said, his tone noticeably quieter. "We had our ups and downs like any couple, I guess, but we always figured it out." That was when he began to lose control again. "And he stole our chance to fix things this time," he snapped and pointed to the man sitting beside me. I don't know whether Watson reacted, but something rubbed the witness the wrong way, and he immediately lost his self-control a second time. "HE STOLE OUR CHANCE TO FIX THINGS. THAT SON OF A BITCH STOLE—"

"MR. YOUNG, GET A GRIP ON YOURSELF," the judge cut in, but anybody watching could see that there was no coming back. Tears began to fall, the yelling continuing as Young launched into a tirade of abuse. His words quickly lost all legibility as he continued sputtering through his emotions before the security guards grabbed the man and led him out of the courtroom.

I will never understand why Hoffman brought the grieving husband to the witness stand in the first place. It wasn't as if his testimony was going to change the course of the trial. He didn't exactly have slam-dunk evidence to sink Watson, so why go through it?

Jenkinson ended up calling for a brief recess once Young left the courtroom, and just as I was about to head out to use the bathroom, Linda sent me a text asking to meet. I replied, asking when, and she suggested the Hose and Ladder after court finished for the day. I agreed, of course, anxious to find out what eye-opening information she had to share. Little did I know that the meeting would leave me with more questions than answers, answers I was beginning to think would elude me for the rest of time.

SIXTEEN

JENKINSON CALLED an end to the day just before five, and after following Watson out into the foyer of the courthouse, I watched him go with Hardy to head back to whatever hotel they had decided to shack up at. I did expect to find the grieving husband somewhere along my walk back to the Mustang, but the gods must have been smiling because there was no sign of the man I assumed wanted to have a word with me.

That first drink I had when I finally reached the Hose and Ladder half an hour later barely touched the sides. It wasn't that I needed it to quench my thirst but rather something to give me a distraction from the day itself, something like a double shot of bourbon to really smack me in the nuts. I was beat, and the next best thing to sleep would be a slight buzz.

"You look like you're enjoying that just a little too much," Linda said when she sat down beside me and nodded to the bartender for the same.

"Just a long day," I said, and swallowed the rest of it in one gulp. "What I really need besides this drink is some good news from my investigator. Tell me you've got something."

"I might have a *couple* of things," Linda said as the bartender set the bourbon before her. Not one to drag her butt, she downed the double as a single shot, squinted, then ordered a beer for each of us which we ended up taking to one of the booths.

"I've got Brody sitting in his car watching a certain building up in Wildwood," Linda said once we were alone.

"The gaming hall Watson told me about?" She confirmed it with a nod.

"Wouldn't call it a hall exactly, but then again, men do have a certain preoccupation with size."

"That they do," I said in total agreement and took a swig from my beer. Linda did the same, the silence temporarily falling over us before she continued.

"I was sitting out there myself for a good part of the day and happened to catch sight of someone who might give me a way in," she said.

"You already got a contact?"

"Possibly. A woman by the name of Dana Erickson." I'd heard the name before. "Used to work at a downtown strip club I once did a stakeout on. It's amazing how much a hundred bucks can change someone's day."

"Think she'll talk to you about Altera's operations?"

"I'm not sure, but if Erickson still lives at the same address as she did back then, then I'll be catching up with her later tonight."

We fell into another silence while watching a few moments of a ballgame being played on one of the screens hanging high behind the bar. I took occasional gulps from my beer, the cold liquid a little too pleasant to ignore, and ended up ordering us each another when I finished mine and made a quick bathroom stop.

"I might have something else," Linda said after I sat down again. This time when she spoke, I heard a hint of hesitancy behind her words.

"Go on," I said.

"It's about Bobby Markle." I felt something inside me shift. "I've been going through records pertaining to the car theft racket he was running back then." She paused again, taking an audible breath. "I..."

"Geez, Lin, spit it out already," I said.

"I came across an incident from 2013 that raised my interest. A man by the name of Xander Elliott was arrested for a hit-and-run in Dayton, Ohio. The victim had links to Henry Altera."

"What sort of links?" I asked as my insides kept tightening.

"Drug related."

"I need to know what Bobby Markle has for me," I said with a sense of nerves. "Keep digging. There's got to be something he's keeping up his sleeve. He wouldn't be playing with me unless he knew something, just like Costa knew something." I rubbed my eyes, the fatigue feeling more like a bad buzz. "If only he'd spilled what he knew before he bought his ticket," I whispered, more to myself than to my investigator.

"I'm sure I'll dig something up," Linda said. "I've got a few leads worth checking into, so hopefully I'll uncover the slam-dunk you're looking for."

We finished our beers and parted company when we reached the parking lot. It turned out that what I assumed to be just a bad buzz rubbing me the wrong way was, in fact, the fatigue I'd thought I felt mid-afternoon. Sometimes, it's difficult to detect when in the midst of cross-examination.

I don't think I lasted more than a few minutes by the time

my head finally hit the pillow after a very quick shower. The hot water only served to intensify my tiredness, and feeling like my legs would betray me at any moment, I shuffled into the bedroom and allowed myself to fall forward face-first onto the bed.

It felt like my alarm went off just a few minutes later, and I very nearly sent it flying across the room were it not for the sunshine streaming in through the open window. My first instinct was to shut my eyes again and believe it all to be some sort of realistic dream, but another glance proved to confirm my fears. Morning had indeed arrived.

"Ugh, you've got to be kidding me," I mumbled as I forced myself to sit up, where I remained for a few seconds, trying to blink my eyes open enough so they stayed that way. My eyelids felt like they had lead weights attached to them, and it must have taken all my might to finally keep them open.

This time, when I hit the shower, I barely turned the hot water on at all, allowing the coldness to steal my breath as the shock pushed away the final bits of sleep. Ten minutes later, I emerged with a renewed sense of purpose as I prepared for the new day ahead.

Grace messaged me just as I walked out of my apartment to say she had been delayed and probably wouldn't reach the courthouse until later that morning. Linda messaged me an update from the previous night shortly after I pulled out of the parking lot and joined the morning traffic. She advised me that the Erickson woman did indeed still live in the same building as previously and was more than happy to provide my investigator with information about her new place of work.

The third message came a few blocks from the courthouse when Jack Barnes sent through a thumbs-up emoji to a text I'd sent him an hour earlier. I asked if he could find me any information on the hit-and-run that Linda told me about the previous evening, a revelation I still couldn't get out of my head for obvious reasons.

I received a fourth text approaching the media pack waiting outside the courthouse, and so I wasn't able to check on it until I'd spent a few minutes answering their questions. Once safely free of the pack and inside the foyer, I found Elsa's good morning message waiting for me on my screen, the smiling emoji blowing me a kiss after she wished me good luck. I sent back a greeting of my own, wished her an awesome day, and added my own little smiling face at the end, just as Hardy and Watson approached me. The latter immediately pointed out my focus on the phone screen.

"Girlfriend?"

I looked at the man with an expression of annoyance, not because I had anything to hide but because it was...him. He grinned, just as I knew he would. The man wasn't the type to get butt hurt over someone taking offense at his comments. He had that kind of personality, right alongside the thick skin needed with such a sense of humor.

Ignoring Watson's comment, I thanked Hardy for delivering my client and watched as he headed back outside, probably happy to have a few hours to himself.

"Quite a guy," Watson said as we turned toward the courtroom.

"He's a good friend, yes," I said, suddenly not in the mood for talking.

Something about his comment rubbed me the wrong way, the comment about the girlfriend, I mean. It wasn't that he'd picked up something about Elsa. In actual fact, it had nothing to do with Elsa overall. It had to do with the ease with which he seemed to dismiss who I was in relation to his daughter. Maybe the anger from our years-long fallout hadn't quite faded away completely, and I continued hanging on to some sort of echo from it. Either that, or I really didn't get enough sleep the night before and was just in a pissed-off mood that Watson brought into the light.

He didn't seem to notice and followed me into the courtroom like it was just another day for him. Unlike most clients facing life in jail whom I had defended, this one seemed to take the pressure in his stride. He looked relaxed enough that the man could have been strolling down to his local café for brunch on a Sunday morning, unbothered by the slightest thing. I actually wondered whether there was something he knew that I didn't.

When we reached the courtroom, the gallery had already begun to fill with people anxious to observe the trial for themselves. Libby Young's death hadn't exactly whipped the media into a frenzy the way some murder trials did, but it still generated interest among the local community. Despite the attention, Watson walked through the group as if he was one of them and not the main attraction in this show.

I was surprised to see Arthur Clements sitting in a chair behind the prosecutor, the district attorney giving me a sideways glance before continuing his conversation with Hoffman, who had turned around to face his boss. The two looked to be in deep conversation about something, keeping their voices low enough to ensure that nobody overheard. Not missing a thing, Watson leaned in when we sat to ask about them.

"Since when does the district attorney come to watch a case like this?"

"I've seen him drop in from time to time," I casually said, but I knew what he meant. Again, Clements shot me a sideways glance before continuing the conversation.

"It bugs me just looking at that guy," Watson said from beside me before turning our attention to the back of the room. "I'm guessing she's going to be up on the stand some-time today?"

I followed his attention to where he was pointing, the woman standing in the doorway to the courtroom peering in the way I imagined she did through her own kitchen window. Hillary Harrington had that busybody kind of look about her, the kind of woman who needed fuel for her gossip machine and didn't care how she got it or who she hurt in the process.

"I'm guessing she will be," I said. "And do me a favor when she is."

"What's that?"

"Try not to wind her up," I said. "I don't want to see her follow in the footsteps of a certain husband."

"Hey, you were the one who pissed him off, remember?"

He was right, of course, but I wasn't about to admit it. A man trying to throw some humor into his morning doesn't take away the punchline when the joke falls flat. Instead, I grinned at Watson, who finally understood.

"I'll try not to egg her on," he said just as the bailiff brought the court to order. A moment later, the judge walked in, and not long after, Hoffman called his first witness of the day.

SEVENTEEN

"I CALL Hillary Harrington to the stand, Your Honor," Hoffman said when Jenkinson asked him to call his next witness, and a moment later, a woman walking with more purpose than a cop heading to a call for help entered the courtroom.

Hillary Harrington wore a strange smirk on her face when she walked through the open doors, scanning both sides of the gallery as she made her way toward the courtroom floor. Once on the stand, she stared at the bailiff while being sworn in, appearing to be relishing her moment in the spotlight. I couldn't help but wonder just how many times she'd daydreamed about this moment during the previous few weeks.

Hoffman waited until the bailiff finished before rising to his feet and slowly walking out onto the floor, where he thanked the woman for coming. Harrington introduced herself and shared her address and how she came to know the victim. I listened with intrigue, captivated by just how prepared the neighborhood gossip sounded.

"Ms. Harrington, is it true that you heard the defendant arguing with the victim the night before her murder?"

"Yes, that's right," the woman said. "It sounded quite intense, and I almost called the police then but held off."

"Whose home were they in?"

"Mr. Watson's," she said and then held a hand to the side of her mouth as she whispered, "I think they'd been drinking because—"

"Objection, Your Honor, hearsay," I interrupted, happy to jump in.

"Sustained," Jenkinson said.

"Oh, I'm sorry, did I say something wrong?"

"Just answer the questions as best you can, Ms. Harrington," Hoffman said. "No need to volunteer extra information."

"Of course, I apologize."

"How often would you say you saw Mrs. Young enter the defendant's home?"

"Oh, quite often. Sometimes maybe two or three times a week."

"And did you ever feel a need to perhaps let the victim's husband know his wife was having an affair with their neighbor?"

"I'm fairly certain he knew about the affair," Harrington said. "I'd seen and heard them argue as well, sometimes right after she came home from next door."

"Objection, Your Honor," I said for the second time in as many minutes. "How can the witness know what Mr. Young knew?"

"Sustained."

"Did I do it again?" The woman sounded genuinely surprised, but something about the grin told me otherwise.

To his credit, Hoffman did manage to navigate the witness for another ten minutes or so, asking his questions without another interruption from me. I did listen for any opportunity to intervene, but Harrington turned out to be a quick learner, evolving her approach to ensure her chance to share gossip on a much more important stage.

When the prosecutor eventually finished, Jenkinson handed the witness over to me, and I wasted little time getting to my questions after making my way to the witness stand.

"You've lived in that neighborhood for quite a number of years, have you not, Ms. Harrington?"

"Decades," she said. "Moved into the home in 1994 with my mother, but she passed shortly after."

"1994, wow, that's a decent amount of time. So you must know a great deal about your neighbors."

"I like to know who I'm living near, yes," she said, turning her focus from me to the public gallery each time she answered as if conducting a speech to an audience.

"Ever find them doing things that annoy you?"

"Sometimes, yes."

"Like what specifically?" I asked. She looked at me as if not understanding the question. "What specific reasons did you have for reporting your neighbors fifty-four separate times during the past seven years?" I heard a slight buzz rising from the crowd, but it didn't hold.

"Mostly about the noise, sometimes about where they parked their vehicles."

"So you're someone who really keeps an eye on things in your part of the world, then?"

"Yes, like I said, I prefer to know the people I'm living near."

I went back to my desk and picked up a sheet of paper from the pile before returning to the witness while reading it.

"You reported your neighbor, Roger Williams, living four doors down at 4254, just six months ago, for parking his vehicle in front of your house, is that correct?" I held up the sheet for her to see. "I have a copy of the police report if you'd like to refresh your memory."

"No, I don't need to see it. I remember," she said, again looking past me.

"You called officers four separate times that day, isn't that correct?"

"They were extremely slow in responding."

"But they did initially respond to your call, did they not? And according to the report, Officer Purcell advised you that due to the house fire at number 4254, it was fine for the young family's vehicle to remain parked in front of your house."

I continued to bring up various calls of hers until Hoffman finally intervened with an objection, pointing out the irrelevance, but by then, I had achieved my aim of discrediting the woman as much as possible. I couldn't prove anything she said about my client and his affair wrong, but as for her character, that didn't take much effort to highlight to the court. Hillary Harrington eventually walked from the witness stand with her grin a lot less prominent. I didn't think it was possible, but I think I may have achieved my aim of embarrassing the woman.

When Harrington finally left the courtroom, Hoffman called his next witness to the stand, a crime scene analyst named Roger Burrows. The bailiff did his thing in a matter of seconds, and the prosecutor began asking his first question from behind his desk less than two minutes after his previous witness left the courtroom.

"Mr. Burrows, could you share with the court your assessment of the body's position in relation to any possible struggle?"

"I didn't find any signs of a struggle, which is another reason why I believe the victim knew her attacker."

"Another reason?" Hoffman slowly rounded the table while engaging the witness.

"I couldn't detect any signs of forced entry, either," the analyst said. "From what I could ascertain, the assailant entered the home through the front door, went up the stairs to where Mrs. Young was in the bedroom, and subsequently stabbed her a single time in the chest. The victim fell back onto the bed and would have died within a matter of seconds."

Hoffman reached the very middle of the floor, where he stopped to consider his next question, pretending to delve deep into his mind to find one he would have already rehearsed well before calling his witness.

"There were, however, signs of a struggle in the form of a broken perfume bottle, were there not?"

"Yes, there was," Burrows said, "but after checking the area and finding that the liquid had already evaporated, I ran some further tests and concluded that the bottle would have been broken well outside of six hours before my arrival."

"What about prints on the murder weapon?"

"Only a single thumbprint was found on the handle of the knife," Burrows said.

"And did you find a match for the print?"

"I did. It belongs to Brian Watson."

That was when Hoffman turned the information dial to maximum, delving deeper into the possible connection between the murder weapon and my client.

"Mr. Burrows, did you happen to find where the murder weapon originated from?"

"Yes, it was part of a kitchen set. I found the rest of the knives in a block on the kitchen bench."

"So a person walking in through the front door would essentially walk past this knife block on their way to the stairs?"

"Yes, it's along the way," the analyst said.

"Going back to the victim, could you ascertain any physical evidence that might indicate the killer's identity?"

"After checking the entry wound and the weapon itself, I used the height of the victim's wound, together with the thirty-degree down angle of the blade, to surmise the height of the killer to be between five-eleven and six foot one."

"And do we know the height of the defendant, Mr. Burrows?"

"Six feet even, I believe."

The jury members looked on with intrigue, the twelve faces all focused on the prosecutor and his witness as the pair dissected more of the evidence. I wished I could have interjected to break their concentration, but given that the witness dealt in facts, any chance of me finding an opportunity to throw in an objection faded away as the prosecutor focused on specific aspects that didn't call for speculation.

When Hoffman eventually ended his questioning, Jenkinson handed the witness over to me. I knew I had my work cut out for me, but how does a defense lawyer win favor with a jury when the facts speak for themselves?

"Mr. Burrows, I'm curious about this print found on the handle of the knife. Could you describe its precise positioning?"

"Yes, as shown in the photo, you can see the thumbprint toward the back of the handle." I held up the image he referred to and pointed at it.

"And this would be the right thumb, correct?"

"Yes, it is."

"And yet my client is left-handed," I said as I neared the witness stand. "Doesn't it strike you as odd that a man about to murder someone would use his non-dominant hand to stab the victim?"

"I don't know whether he just did it that way because of a

spur-of-the-moment thing, but it's definitely his right hand that held the knife."

"You also mentioned that there were no signs of a struggle, so it was a single stab wound inflicted quite quickly, from which the victim died within seconds?"

"Yes," Burrows confirmed.

"I'm confused," I said. "Why would a man have enough time to grab a knife from downstairs, take it up to the bedroom to an unsuspecting victim, and then use the weapon with his non-dominant hand?"

"You'd have to ask your client that question," the analyst said as several people chuckled quietly behind me. I ignored the response.

"Unless, of course, the defendant had been in the home prior to that morning and left his prints in other places," I continued. "Like, perhaps on a perfume bottle he'd gifted the victim the previous evening, cutlery used in the past, maybe in the bathroom he'd used."

"I don't understand," Burrows said.

"My point is that one thumb print doesn't immediately prove a murder, does it? Isn't it possible that someone else could have handled that knife, wearing gloves, and that one print just happened to remain untouched?"

"Yes, it's possible," the witness admitted. "But I'm not—"

"Thank you, no further questions," I said, cutting him off before he had a chance to take back what little doubt I might have instilled into the jury. It wasn't exactly a win for me, but I figured small steps forward would be better than taking steps back.

The prosecutor and I ended up working our way through another two witnesses before Jenkinson called for our lunchtime recess. Watson joined Grace and me at a nearby café where we sat down for some food, me happy to stick with a simple turkey on rye and a soda. Grace opted for her usual salad, while Watson went for the cheeseburger and fries, adding a coffee to his meal.

We ate pretty much in silence for the most part until my former father-in-law began to share a story about Naomi's secret love for cheeseburgers.

"It was the only thing she would order wherever we went," he said with slight bemusement. "Anytime I'd take her to a new place, it was the cheeseburger she had to have."

"I don't remember her ever ordering one," I said, wondering whether he'd confused the memory with someone else. "I remember she had a thing for milkshakes at one point. This crazy obsession to constantly try new flavors." I tried to think back as I smiled through a textbook of memories. "What was that one she always asked for, and the vendors kept asking whether she wanted two milkshakes? Chocolate and banana." I laughed out loud. "I'd like a chocolate banana milkshake in the same cup, she used to tell them."

"She did have a thing for chocolate, too," Watson agreed. "Girl could have taken a bath in it and still not been satisfied."

We would have continued the conversation right through our meal were it not for my phone suddenly vibrating to life. When I saw Linda's name on the screen, I excused myself to answer her call. The second I did, I heard something serious in her voice.

"Ben, what time will you be finishing at the court today?"

"Around five is my guess," I said. "Why, what's the matter?" I sensed something but wasn't sure what.

"Nothing urgent," she said, her voice low and protective as if she was shielding it from someone standing nearby.

"Linda? What's wrong?"

"Nothing, just call me when you're done. I'll meet you in the courthouse parking lot."

It didn't sound like my investigator, not with the nerves I detected in her voice. There must have been something pretty significant happening for her to call me like that.

"Are you sure? Tell me now, and I can ask the judge for a continuance, if you need."

"No, it's fine, honest. I'm just stuck at the DMV, and it's seriously irritating me."

I wasn't really sure what could have been behind the call, given her usual confidence, but something had definitely affected her. At first, I thought it might have been another matter entirely, maybe her needing help for something of a more personal nature, but I should have known better. With my investigator being one of the most professional people I'd ever met, I should have known that it had something to do with the case. The seriousness I detected in her voice wasn't that at all, but concern—concern, I would soon discover, she had for me.

EIGHTEEN

I COULD BARELY KEEP my head in the game after the phone call from Linda, and the afternoon definitely dragged a lot more than I would have cared to admit. Hoffman brought three witnesses to the stand, which included a cop who had been called to my client's home for excessive noise a couple of months earlier, plus a fingerprint expert who tried to explain the validity of the print found on the murder weapon.

Given the state of my brain, considering everything that had been going on, particularly with the whole Bobby Markle situation, I'm surprised I didn't blow a heart valve during the course of the afternoon just from trying to maintain control of my anticipation. Truth be told, I wasn't exactly over the moon about my investigator contacting me like that and then not giving me the slightest bit of context behind the call. I know she had her reasons, of course, but that didn't help my situation in the slightest.

I felt like I was running on autopilot by the time the judge finally brought the day to a close. I first sent Linda a text to say that I'd be out in a few minutes. Watson headed out of the courthouse with Hardy shortly after, and I immediately hurried to my car with my brain now fully focused on whatever my investigator had in store for me.

It didn't surprise me to find Linda already parked next to the Mustang, and one look at her face told me enough to know that whatever she had to tell me was serious. She stood leaning against her car, and when I approached, rather than remain there, she climbed into the driver's seat after gesturing for me to join her. I first dropped my briefcase into the passenger seat of my car before climbing into hers.

For a second, we just kind of sat there with the silence hanging between us. Linda seemed to be searching for the words when I held out my hands in a what-now gesture.

"OK, I'm here, let me have it."

"Look, I know I turned this into a big deal, but I'm not sure whether this is actually worth it."

"I don't know what you're talking about," I said, wondering whether getting frustrated would help the situation. "Just tell me."

"I spent time watching the gaming hall last night, and right before I planned to leave, I saw someone walk out of there. Someone I recognized."

"OK, who?"

"Listen, Ben, before I tell you, I need you to just not jump to any conclusions," Linda said. "I know how crazy you've been getting with this lately."

"Linda, Jesus, just tell me."

"I saw Fabian Telford," she said, the name not hitting any exclamation marks for me. Or at least not immediately. What she said next changed the course of my day.

"I've had time to think about it," she began, "and when you add his story to the one about Bobby Markle and the..."

But that was as far as she got before the hammer dropped hard for me.

"Take me to him," I said without hesitation.

"Maybe we can just spend a few minutes spit-balling this around," Linda tried, but she was right about me jumping to conclusions and acting all crazy. The second I remembered Telford's story, the rest of the pieces just seemed to fall into place.

"Please," I said. "Just take me to his house. We can question him there, and if we're wrong, then so be it."

"Could we be wrong, though?" Linda asked while firing up the engine. "The more I thought about this, the more it just seemed to fit. Why else would Markle promise you information if he didn't at least know something about your case?"

"We're not wrong," I said. "Just drive and get us to his house so we can confirm our suspicions."

I wasn't demanding that Linda drive; I was just anxious to get to the man's house to get answers to questions I'd been carrying for far too long. A kind of buzzing filled me, my insides churning at the thought of finally getting to the bottom of a mystery stretching back years. When I pulled my cell phone from my pocket, I had to stop for a few seconds to catch my breath due to my fingers shaking so much. Linda noticed me looking at them.

"I'm hoping for your sake the man talks," she said as she pulled the SUV into traffic.

"I'm hoping for Telford's sake that he does as well," I said, almost fearing how I'd react if he decided to shut down and refuse to talk. I felt Linda's eyes still watching, and I turned to look out the window. "Was he alone when he walked out of the gaming hall?"

"There was another guy with him, but they left in separate

vehicles," Linda said. "I didn't get close enough to get the plate of the second car. Sorry."

"Don't be sorry," I said. "You got the one that matters most. If we can get Telford to talk, who knows where this could lead."

When Linda turned her SUV onto Telford's street, I had her pull up a few houses down to ensure that our arrival didn't spook him. I still didn't know his state of mind, and seeing a couple of official-looking strangers jumping out of a car in front of his home might set off his defenses. What I hoped was to make it to the front door and for the man to remember me from the cemetery where we'd first met. Maybe then I might have a chance to get inside his home without his walls going up.

"There it is," Linda said as she rolled to a stop and pointed to a house farther up the street. A familiar BMW sat in the driveway, indicating that the resident was home. Knowing the man lived alone, I assumed things were falling in our favor.

"OK, let's go." I unclipped my seatbelt and jumped out. Linda did likewise, eventually matching my stride as we mounted the opposing sidewalk like a couple of soldiers marching in a parade.

When we neared the house, music filled the air with the vocal talents of Freddie Mercury drifting out of an open second-story window. I didn't slow down when I reached the gate, barely breaking stride as I turned down the narrow path and headed for the door. Linda followed close behind and eventually took up position next to me when I pressed the doorbell.

The music continued echoing through the door as the final chorus of "Radio Ga Ga" came to a close. I waited until the melody faded away before pressing the doorbell a second time. Somewhere inside, a small dog immediately began to bark, announcing our arrival. The next song on the album never eventuated as I heard a familiar voice call for the dog to calm down. Linda and I exchanged a look when footsteps began to work their way closer before a shadow bobbed back and forth in the frosted window of the door.

When the door cracked open just enough to show the tip of a nose, a small ball of fluff suddenly shot out of the gap and immediately ran circles around my feet. Barking excitedly, the Pomeranian moved fast enough to look like nothing more than a blur as Telford opened the door the rest of the way.

"Geez, I'm sorry, folks. She just gets so excited by visitors," he said as he leaned down, trying to catch his pet. "Maisdy, come on, don't make me chase you again." He sounded almost frustrated, but not enough to get angry.

"Your dogs have a tendency to get away from you," I said with a hint of humor that I hoped he would notice, and when Telford looked up at me, he immediately grinned with recognition.

"Ben Carter, wow, I wasn't expecting to see you," he said as he finally managed to grab the dog by the collar and pull her into his arms. When he got the dog under control and stood up straight again, he held his hand out to me. "What are you doing here?"

"Good to see you again, Fabian," I said before diverting his attention to my investigator. "This is Linda, my assistant. I'm not sure if you remember her from the night at the comedy club." His demeanor changed slightly, but the smile remained, and he still shook with her.

"Yes, of course. How are you?"

"Good, thanks," Linda said, and looked in my direction to divert the man's attention back to me.

"So what brings you out this way?" Telford asked.

"Just a case I'm working on which I'm hoping you could help me with," I said.

"A case *I* could help you with? I'm not sure how," he said, looking from me to Linda and back again.

"Listen, Fabian, do you think we might go inside? I'd much rather talk in private, if that's OK." I looked over my shoulder to highlight a guy walking his dog passing by the front gate, and Telford took the bait.

"Yes, of course." He stepped back, held his door open, and waved us inside. Linda and I obliged and shortly after, we were sitting in his den where he finally released the dog in his arms, still struggling to break free.

"Ah," I said, suddenly spotting more movement near the back door where a beast of a dog sat watching us through the glass. "I was wondering where Jonesy was," I said, pointing to the St. Bernard.

"Yes, the horse is never far away when company comes around," Telford said but again changed the topic of conversation almost immediately. "Now you mentioned a case?"

"Yes, I'm wondering how long you've been gambling down at the gambling hall in Wildwood?"

It was obvious I caught him completely off guard, the question taking him back enough to stammer his response.

"The gam…gambling ho…house?"

"Yes, the one run by Riccardo Costa's crew," I added, ignoring his visible shock.

"I saw you leaving the place at exactly 10:04 this morning," Linda threw in, unperturbed by his embarrassment. "I have the photos of your car leaving the place, if seeing them would help jog your memory."

"No, I don't need to see them," Telford said but wasn't quite ready to admit his wrongdoing. "I'm not sure you have the—" he tried to say, but I wasn't going to accommodate any distractions.

"Cut the crap, Fabian, I know you frequent the place," I said, making no attempt to sound empathetic. "I'm just wondering how long you've been going there. Months? Years?" I leaned forward to get my point across. "I could just have my investigator here check out the place in more detail to get what I need."

"Seven years," he finally said, his voice barely loud enough to reach me. That was when I pushed myself off the couch and stood above him.

"How much did you owe them before they began threatening you?" I asked. He looked up at me wide-eyed.

"Owed them? No, never."

"I know the truth, Fabian," I said, telling my first white lie to get a response. "I'm just trying to see whether I can trust you to give me straight answers. Now how much did you owe them?"

"I honestly didn't..."

He paused, again looking from Linda to me and wondering which of us he would get pity from.

"Answer the question," I said, my tone flat and emotionless.

"Please," the man whispered. "Don't do this."

"Do what? All I'm asking is how big your debt was before they started threatening to hurt you." And that was when I took things further. "Or to hurt your son."

Telford froze, beads of sweat breaking out across his brow. His eyes grew wide enough for the balls to pop out as his mouth spasmed with unspoken words that never quite formed.

"We know about the car," Linda said, also leaning forward in her seat.

"Just fill in the gaps for us, Fabian," I said, before losing my cool. "TELL US HOW YOUR GAMBLING LED TO THE DEATH OF YOUR SON."

He first shrank back into the back of the sofa, and when he couldn't get far enough away, he pushed himself out and onto his feet.

"I don't know what you're talking about," he shrieked. "No idea what—"

"THEY MURDERED YOUR SON, DIDN'T THEY? RAN HIM OVER LIKE A STRAY DOG," I screamed, pushing my face into his until I could smell his breath. That was when he broke, all the resistance running from his face.

"OK, OK, you win," Telford said, and his legs finally gave out. He crumpled to the ground and let the raw emotions run free as the sobbing came thick and fast. He remained on his hands and knees while letting the humiliation take over. "They did it because of me," he whispered, his voice trembling. "They took my boy from me because of my debt...they *murdered* him. They mur-mur-murdered my sweet little boy."

I watched a long string of snot dangle from one nostril as the man completely lost control of his emotions, the tears dropping into a growing pool of grief on the floor beneath him. At first, I couldn't bring myself to move, not for a man who'd not only gambled his son's life away, but then wasn't man enough to face the truth, instead cheating the world into believing that he was the victim.

"How did they murder your boy?" I asked with a flat, emotionless tone as I remembered how the kid died. My blood physically chilled as a new sensation of understanding washed over me. It was not exactly the easiest question for a father to answer but one that needed to be asked just the same, and I was done pussy-footing around. "HOW?" I repeated with more intensity when he didn't respond, the hairs on the back of my neck standing to attention. Already suspecting the answer, I needed his confirmation.

"They ran him over," Telford whispered as he sat up and wiped at his nose. "At first...at first, I thought it was a genuine hit-and-run, you know? It had all the hallmarks of a genuine accident, and the cops did their interviews and stuff, but then Altera paid me a visit the very next day and confirmed my worst fears." Telford coughed and pushed himself off the floor and onto the couch, where he sat slumped with his head hung low. "He told me they liked to use that method as it took the cops down a completely different path and didn't raise any suspicions." Linda stood beside me, just as shocked by the revelation.

"You carried the lie for them?"

"They threatened to hurt more people if I didn't. I pretended that Zac died from a genuine hit-and-run. I even began a campaign to try and find his killer, all the while knowing exactly who was responsible." He shook his head in disgust. "My gambling was why he died. I owed them money, and when I couldn't pay, they followed through on their original threat. It's how they like to control people." And that was when he said something that caused every piece to fall into place. "They weren't going to stop with just me. They never do."

That was when I knew, the goosebumps breaking across my skin like a rash on steroids, the instant my brain connected the dots. The pit of my stomach churned with revulsion, phantom fingers squeezing the void inside me with slow, laborious spasms I felt powerless against. I looked at Linda with the same expression I'd seen on Telford's face just moments before and almost grinned at the irony. I could sense my own knees giving out, the strength escaping me as the truth finally settled over me. Naomi's death hadn't been an accident after all. She had been murdered, and I finally understood why.

NINETEEN

"GIVE ME THE KEYS," I said to Linda with an outstretched hand once we were outside again. I think she understood my frame of mind and didn't put up the slightest bit of objection. With my emotions riding on a razor's edge, common sense was the first to go, and while she probably should have driven, all self-control vanished as my instincts took over.

We drove in silence, Linda hanging on for dear life while I maneuvered the traffic like a crazed lunatic. Every second car I passed at speed must have honked at us, but I barely heard any of them, the fuel running my insides continuing to boil over. All I could think of was the lie I had lived with for more than five years.

"Just breathe," Linda tried to tell me when we eventually reached the hotel, but I was already too far gone. For me, the time to take a breath to calm myself vanished the second Telford confirmed the reason his son had died, the *real* reason his son had died.

"I'll breathe tomorrow," I told her as I brought the SUV to a stop in front of the hotel and climbed out.

My legs felt like they were operating on autopilot as I headed inside, turned right at the first junction, and continued down the corridor. Linda followed close behind, her boot heels clip-clopping on the porcelain tiles yet still not enough to pull me from my trance. I could feel the heat of my anger transform my brow, the beads of sweat prickling the skin, but nothing could have distracted me from my focus on walking.

When I reached Room 1014, I tried the doorknob, found it locked, and thumped on the door with a heavy fist. I assumed Linda stood behind me because I no longer heard the rhythmic clicking of her boots, although I could have been mistaken. Given that the pounding in my chest was almost as loud, I could have merely been listening to the wrong sounds.

When the door opened, I barely noticed Hardy looking through the gap, no doubt wondering why I would suddenly show up unannounced since I'd always messaged to say I was coming.

"Ben, hey," he said somewhere out of my comprehension as my eyes scanned the room for the other occupant, the only one who mattered at that moment.

Two steps into the room, I found what I was looking for. Watson stood at the bench in the small kitchenette, a kettle in one hand and a spoon held over the rim of a cup in the other. He looked up for a brief moment, saw me, and began to say something that he never quite finished.

"Geez, Ben, what a way to make an entrance," he said as he lowered his eyes to the cup and continued pouring. "Did you —" That is when I physically cut his words off, my fist connecting with the side of his jaw hard enough to turn the rest of the sentence into a gasp.

The moment before my knuckles made contact, I saw his

head begin to turn ever so slightly, no doubt due to him spotting the movement out of the corner of his eye. Unfortunately, speed wasn't on his side, and I was fueled by something unnatural and reacted accordingly.

I hadn't planned on hitting him, but a couple of yards from reaching the man, the sweat that had begun running down my face gave way to a single tear. That tiny traitor felt like a pressure relief valve failing, the soft, delicate trail it left as it slid from an eyelash and down the side of my face, willing me to flick it away. It took all of my focus not to, a primal need for violence proving the superior emotion on the day.

A single punch and his feet betrayed him as all two hundred and forty pounds went crashing into the bench before collapsing to the ground. Watson grunted in pain, one hand rubbing the side of his mouth where a thin line of blood traced its way down to his neck before blooming on the collar of his white T-shirt.

"What are you, crazy?" Watson managed to hiss, but I hit him again, the fist connecting with the edge of his right eye. He whimpered in pain, trying to turn away, and another punch skidded across the top of his head before hands suddenly grabbed me from behind.

"Ben, have you lost your mind?" Hardy called out as he tried to pull me back, but fueled by a kind of rage entirely foreign to me, I easily broke free to continue the beating.

I landed another couple of punches before both Linda and Hardy combined their efforts to drag me off enough for Watson to use his feet and push himself away. He eventually reached the wall and, with his back pressed against it, held his hands up defensively, calling for me to stop.

"IT WAS YOU," I screamed, my mind completely scrambled as the world turned red. The room appeared caught under some kind of filter, the light not natural, which seemed to be driving my anger further. "IT WAS *ALWAYS* YOU."

"What the hell are you talking about?" Watson cried out, and when I managed to break free enough to jump on him a second time, his panic pulled him into a fetal position that neutralized my attack.

I continued screaming and swinging, doing my best to cause as much damage as possible with little effect. It was only when Hardy finally swung an arm around my neck, twisted one leg around my waist, and raised his other that the two of us fell to the floor. My one leg couldn't support both of us, and with my rage-induced fuel on the decline, the adrenaline failed to make up the difference.

The image of Fabian Telford ran through my mind as I lost control of my emotions and began to sob. I wanted to run, to hide from the world and keep the pain between my wife and me. Watson had no business seeing it, and I hated the fact that he got to watch.

"I'm going to let you go now," Hardy whispered into my ear, the arm around my throat easing just enough so I could breathe normally. "When I do, Ben, you're going to roll over to the other wall and get yourself under control. Tell me you understand." I didn't answer him, the pain too great to let go of. "It's not happening until you acknowledge what I said," Hardy continued. "Tell me you agree."

"I agree," I said, ashamed of how weak my voice sounded. "I agree," I repeated and let myself go limp.

It took a couple of minutes or so before I managed to get enough control to be able to push myself off the floor. Watson remained at the far side of the room, still cowering low to the ground, when Hardy walked over to help him up. Linda helped somewhat, although I could see that she would have much rather left the room. The visible disgust on her face matched the emotional turmoil still coursing through me.

"Anybody want to tell me what the hell that was about?" Hardy asked when it appeared that the physical part of the conflict had ended. Watson looked over at me sheepishly, rubbing blood from his face, and part of me wanted to pick up the nearest object and throw it at him.

"Yeah, I'll tell you what that was about," I said, noticing a different kind of pain in my hand. I looked at my knuckles and found one to be sitting a decent way out of line. "Our friend here racked up a gambling debt he couldn't pay, which led to the crew he owed the money arranging a discreet hit-and-run THAT KILLED MY WIFE AND CHILD."

Just speaking the words tore me up a second time, and I lunged again for the man responsible. Hardy easily caught me well before I reached Watson, who again shrank back against the wall and held his hands up to shield himself.

"ADMIT IT, YOU SACK OF SHIT!" I screamed. "ADMIT IT!"

"OK, OK, you're right," Naomi's father finally managed, his voice barely audible as he slid to the ground and shook his head slowly from side to side. "It's true. She died because of me, but it wasn't gambling." He looked at me with a sorrow I couldn't bring myself to recognize. "It wasn't gambling, Ben, I swear."

"Why should we believe anything you say?"

"I'm not expecting you to believe me," he said as he tried to get up. I felt another urge to rush him but forced myself to turn my back and take a couple of steps the other way. Watson turned his attention to the others in the room and continued explaining. "It wasn't gambling. The IRS hit a couple of businesses hard, and Costa lost a considerable sum of money because of it. They blamed me, and despite trying to explain the reasons behind their ambushing us like that, they pushed for me to pay them back."

"How much?" I asked, turning around to face him again. "How much did they accuse you of losing? How much money did Naomi and our baby die for?"

"Nine million," Watson said, his shoulders visibly slumping. "Nine million dollars. I begged them, Ben. I got down on my knees in front of Costa and begged him to give me time."

"You should have begged harder," I hissed, pushing the words through my clenched teeth. "And when you knew they wouldn't listen, you should have told someone, *anyone*, to arrest them."

"You know I couldn't do that."

"No, of course you couldn't," I said. "Because if you did, you knew you'd end up in prison right alongside your buddies. You were too busy trying to save your own ass and hung your daughter out to dry."

"You got it all wrong," Watson said, but I'd reached the limit of listening to him. My hand throbbed, my head ached, and something inside me felt like it needed a hard shove to the side. I wanted to vomit, a sickening cramp reaching deeper than ever before.

"I need to get some air," I said and turned for the door. Just before I reached it, Watson called out to me.

"Altera was the one who drove the car, in case you're interested."

I stopped but didn't look back. Instead, I paused to give the information time to sink in. If I didn't, there was every chance I would turn back and launch another attack, and this time, I wasn't sure if I could stop myself. I continued walking after a few seconds and didn't slow again until I reached the outside of the building, where I stood next to Linda's car.

Watching the traffic pass by had a way of soothing my

mind. The constant drone of engines worked to drown out the screaming inside my brain. My hands continued shaking from the sheer amount of adrenaline dumped into my system, and all I could do was stare at them in disbelief.

The worst part about the whole thing is that it felt almost like an anticlimax for me. Something inside me felt as if I had known the truth all along, like I had carried it with me this entire time, and Watson spilling his guts was him merely pulling aside the curtain hiding the truth. Watson's proximity to the gang should have been a warning enough, if only I had dug a little deeper during those years of suffering.

"So Altera," Linda suddenly said from behind me. I continued staring at the traffic, letting the hum of traffic consume the name. "What are you going to do now?"

"I'm going to continue working this case," I said when she stepped up next to me. "And then, once I prove Watson's innocence and show that one of Altera's guys killed the woman, I'll make it my mission in life to bring him to justice." My answer seemed to surprise her.

"Justice, Ben? You're not going to go after him and torture his ass or something?"

"I'm a lawyer, Linda," I said. "The courtroom is my greatest weapon." I sighed, the sound almost as torturous as my emotions. "And as much as I'd love to break every bone in his body before putting a bullet in his head, I want him to suffer the way I suffered. I want his suffering to stretch across years, not end after a few measly seconds." I turned to face her. "I want to know that he's suffering in a prison cell each and every day, and only then might I feel some sort of closure."

Linda nodded and looked out toward the traffic again. I expected her to question my intentions, perhaps even convince me that the bullet-in-the-head scenario was a better option, but she never did. As far as I know, Linda accepted my plan because she knew it was the one area in which I excelled, and if I could somehow manage to get the gangster inside a courtroom, the chances of getting a conviction were almost a hundred percent.

TWENTY

WHEN LINDA DROPPED me back at my car after my run-in with Watson, I first watched her drive off into the night before considering the three possible destinations before me. The first option I had was to jump in my car, drive home, and sleep the rest of the night away. It was also perhaps the more sensible of the three, although I knew the chances of me falling asleep were slim to none.

The second option I had was also the toughest one to commit to, and that was to drive out to the cemetery and tell Naomi about my latest discovery. The truth was, I wasn't ready to make that drive, and I wasn't sure whether I would ever be capable of such a trip. And that left the third option, the one I knew I would choose all along.

What I needed was a quiet place where I could sit alone and drown my sorrows with a certain level of dignity. In other words, I wanted to grab myself a bottle of bourbon in some bar and find a dark corner where I could self-reflect on my life without judgment from anybody I knew.

The bar I chose also happened to be just four blocks from

my apartment building, which meant I didn't need to leave my car parked in some random parking lot overnight. I actually drove home first, changed into a T-shirt and jeans, and then called an Uber to take me to where I hoped to lose all sense of the day.

I was actually surprised at how busy the place was for a Wednesday night when I walked through the doors. Patrons filled most of the booths, and the bar sat somewhere behind a crowd stretched along its length. I actually considered leaving again, but a waving hand suddenly caught my attention, with Elsa calling out to me. It looked like she and a couple of girlfriends were in the middle of a conversation in one of the booths, and while company wasn't something I was looking for, it appeared as if I wasn't going to be able to avoid it.

"Ben, hey," Elsa said when I got close enough. "Surprised to see you here."

"Just thought I'd drop in for a quick drink," I said, the lie sliding off my tongue a little too easily.

"This is Kelly Winters," Elsa said as she gestured to the woman sitting opposite to her, and I shook with her. "And this is her sister, Josie. Kelly and I went to college together back in the day."

"Ah, nice," I said. "Nice to meet you."

"You want to sit with us?" Elsa slid a little farther into the booth to make room.

"Nah, it's OK," I said, doing my best to force a believable smile that Elsa was never going to buy. "You guys enjoy your night."

It felt awkward leaving them that way, but I knew it wouldn't take Elsa long to detect something wrong with me, and I wasn't sure just how ready I was to talk about it openly. Instead of trying to find a table, I made my way to the bar, managing to squeeze in between a couple of other patrons, and ordered a beer. I barely got my first mouthful before a hand slipped onto my arm, and I looked to see Elsa standing next to me.

"Why do I get the feeling beer isn't what you came here for?" she whispered into my ear.

Unsure of how to answer the question, I just stared at her, the urge to let my emotions go intensifying the longer I held it in. Elsa stared at me for a few seconds as if trying to read further into it before tightening her grip on my arm.

"Let's get out of here," she said and immediately headed for the door without looking back to see whether I was following.

Once outside, Elsa led me to her car, climbed in, and without ever speaking, drove us a few blocks before pulling up in front of an unfamiliar building.

"What's this?" I asked, but rather than answer, she only held a finger to her lips and climbed out.

Elsa grabbed my hand when we reached the sidewalk and led me to a nondescript door on the corner of the building. A man in a suit, who appeared to be guarding the entrance, opened the door for us with a welcoming smile. Elsa thanked him with a nod of the head and pulled me inside.

"I used to come here in the months after Marc passed," she said when we walked through another door and into a dimly lit room where soft piano music gently played in the background.

While the place did have a bar per se, nobody stood at it waiting for drinks. A dozen small tables sat scattered across the floor with people holding intimate conversations while leaning across them. A single candle in the middle of each lit up their faces, some holding hands, while others held their drinks. Several waiting staff stood guard around the outer edges, while a couple of others seemed to patrol between the tables, seeking out orders. I wasn't sure if this was the kind of place for me when I saw where the music was coming from.

"A piano bar?" Elsa looked at me and smiled while following one of the waitresses to our table.

"Not quite. This place runs different themes thanks to an owner who couldn't quite make her mind up about what she wanted."

She suddenly waved to someone standing in the doorway of what looked like an office. The woman signaled something to the waitress leading us across the floor, and I noticed her slightly change direction. Soon, I found myself climbing stairs before emerging on the second level, which looked even more exclusive with the balcony wrapping around the outer wall. From this vantage point, it gave guests a view over the lower floor, including the raised center stage where the pianist continued tinkling away on the keys. Just five tables were set up at even intervals in their own section of the space. Sitting at one with a female companion, I recognized Bodie Humphries, the recently retired 49ers quarterback.

"Surely you didn't just find this place walking the streets," I said as we took our seats.

"Extra dry martini with three olives, please," Elsa told the lady. I added a plain old shot of bourbon with ice to the order before we found ourselves alone again.

"Three olives?" I asked.

"It's bad luck to order an even number, didn't you know that?"

"You don't strike me as the superstitious kind, Ms. Schwarz," I said.

"There's a lot you don't know about me, Mr. Carter. Including my work as a public defender at one of the regional courts before transferring to the DA's office several years ago."

"I never knew you did PD work."

"Not many do. I don't exactly advertise the fact. For one thing, I've always been too busy, and then there's really no point when you're happy in your role."

"But you weren't happy," I pointed out just as the waitress returned with our drinks. Elsa waited for her to finish setting the drinks down and leave before continuing.

"Not in recent weeks, no, but I used to be quite content. That woman you saw me wave at before?" She took a tasting sip from her glass, gave an approving nod, took another, and lowered the glass again. "That's Denise Hasslebrock, the owner of this fine establishment. Eleven years ago, she barely survived an overdose courtesy of her then-boyfriend, who also happened to enjoy robbing convenience stores with her in the car. After I defended her in court, she turned her life around, and well, here we are."

"Isn't it great when a client's life completely turns around after a win?"

"It sure is," Elsa said. "Which is why I want to get back to working on the other side of the proverbial tracks." She took another sip before looking at me intently. "You didn't walk into Sandy's just now to socialize, did you?" she asked, referring to the previous bar.

"No, I didn't," I said, not sure if I was ready to open up.

"You know, after Marc died, there were days when I felt I just didn't belong in the world anymore. It was like I just didn't fit in, and nobody, I mean *nobody*, could pull me out of it. In those days, I just wanted to hide in a dark closet and disappear completely."

"Or find somewhere where nobody knew you and you could mix it with people who felt the same way," I offered.

"Yes, exactly, like the group. I assume you're still going tomorrow?"

"I am, yes. Maybe we could take the trip together," I said, not sure if I was crossing a line.

"We could," Elsa said without hesitation. "That would be great."

I still couldn't decide whether I was ready to open up and used the drink as a way of stalling the moment. Elsa followed my lead as I picked my bourbon up and began slowly sipping it, savoring each swallow as a silence descended over us. Subtle conversations continued around us, as did the soft piano music from below.

"Naomi must have been a special lady," Elsa suddenly said when she finished her drink.

"She certainly was," I said. "We had only just found out we were having a baby."

"What? Oh no, I'm so sorry. Please, I didn't mean to pry."

"You're not prying, and it's OK, honest," I said. "It's been a long time since I've spoken about her openly." I grinned, still holding the glass as I watched the remaining ice cube continue shrinking. "It's ironic to be telling you about her today of all days."

"Why, what's today? It's not her birthday or anything, is it? Because if it is, then I'm going to feel twice as—"

"No, it's not," I said with a grin, saving Elsa a potential breakdown. "It's not, honest. It's that I only just found out the real reason she died."

Elsa's expression instantly changed from mild amusement to clear shock. I don't know if it was because of my words or the change in my own demeanor, which I sensed the moment the words left my mouth. At first, I couldn't bring myself to keep looking at her, and so I used the glass as a distraction, rolling it between my hands and sending that remnant of ice spiraling along the outer edge. I could feel Elsa watching me and knew I couldn't leave her hanging.

"Naomi was murdered," I finally managed, the beating in my chest picking up pace.

I don't know if I said the words for Elsa's sake or my own, since I still hadn't admitted them to myself. It takes time for something that significant to sink in, but as I mentioned previously, I think in a weird kind of way, I had always known the terrible truth and just wasn't willing to admit it. Watson's confirmation only served as a nod to a truth I should have accepted from the beginning.

"Ben, you can't be serious."

"I am," I said with a forced smile that felt faker than the leather on my chair. "I wish it wasn't true, but it is. Riccardo Costa had her murdered."

That was when I knew I needed to unload, and unfortunately for Elsa, she just happened to be the person I felt comfortable enough with to reveal the truth. I don't know how long it took me to open up and share the entire tragedy, but three drinks later and with Elsa sitting on my side of the table, I finished the part about Watson finally admitting his part in the story. I swallowed the last bit of my bourbon after showing Elsa my knuckles that had turned crimson in the hours since the attack.

When I finished the story, a new kind of silence descended over us, and at first, we just sat there staring at each other before I reached for her hand and lightly squeezed it.

"I know it's quite a lot to take in," I said, and again tried to smile, but I gave up when it felt too unrealistic.

"Henry Altera," she said, almost whispering the name as if saying it too loud would summon a demon.

"He's the one," I confirmed.

"What are you going to do?"

"Like I told my investigator, I'm going to be a lawyer," I

said. "I'm going to do what I do best and find a way to bring him to justice."

"Elsa, hi," a new voice suddenly said from slightly behind me, and I turned to see the woman who had previously waved at us during our arrival standing nearby. "Sorry, I don't mean to interrupt, but I just wanted to make sure you guys were being looked after."

"Yes, as always," Elsa said, rising up and giving the woman a hug. "This is my friend, Ben Carter. Ben, meet Denise Hasslebrock."

"Pleased to meet you," I said, half-rising to shake her hand. She returned the smile.

"Likewise," she said before turning her attention back to Elsa. "Listen, I'm wondering if you're still thinking of going back to doing PD work. I have this friend who might need some help. Only if you're open to it."

"As a matter of fact, I am," Elsa said. "Is it urgent?"

"It can wait a couple of days."

"OK, perfect. Let me call you tomorrow, and I'll set something up."

"Great," Denise said and took a couple of steps back. "Thank you so much," and then to me, "Nice to meet you."

"And you," I managed to get out before she turned around completely and disappeared again. "Wow, look at you go," I said with a smirk. "Already picking up clients in bars, and you haven't even started." She playfully hit my hand and grinned.

"Just goes to show how popular I am."

Elsa suddenly leaned in without warning and kissed me, and not just on the cheek. With one hand curled around the back of my head, she pulled me closer, her lips feeling like the kind of comfort I had unknowingly yearned for. And when she eventually pulled back and looked into my eyes, I could see her needs matching my own, the kind that couldn't be met sitting in a bar.

TWENTY-ONE

"MR. HOFFMAN, CALL YOUR NEXT WITNESS," Judge Jenkinson said after the first one of the day left the courtroom, and to me, it felt like a win for all the wrong reasons. Let me ask you this. What sort of a man goes willingly out on a Wednesday night, has a few drinks, and then spends the next seven or so hours wrapped in the arms of a lover until almost sunrise before remembering he is due in court that morning? Picture me coyly raising my hand. Guilty as charged.

Not only was I surviving on just an hour and a half of sleep, but I also had to sit next to a man who, at that moment in time, I wished to have been located in another state, preferably another country on the opposite side of the globe. I can only imagine what people must have been thinking seeing us walking into the courtroom together, Watson sporting bruises on his face and me with a significant one across the knuckles of my right hand. Throw in the unshaven face, two-day-old suit, and you can just picture the scene for yourself.

Hoffman's first witness of the morning almost put me to

sleep with his droning voice and lack of emotion. The former employee of Watson, who testified about the temper of his former boss, dragged out his testimony for almost an hour, thanks to a prosecutor intent on being thorough. Much to my surprise, I did manage to throw in a couple of objections, but not enough to change the course of the testimony.

"I call Trudi Wagner to the stand," Hoffman said once the witness left the courtroom, and it was the first time I risked looking at Watson.

He seemed unperturbed by the name, his expression the same as when I'd first met him in the foyer of the courthouse. Hardy still looked on edge as if expecting me to launch yet another attack on my client, but to be honest, I didn't have the fight left in me. The revulsion, though, was another matter entirely.

Watson couldn't hide the shame on his face, and despite my anger still burning solidly inside my soul, I was surprised that I did feel somewhat sorry for him. Only a little bit, mind you, and there was no way I would have admitted to it, but I felt it just the same, a sliver of empathy just minding its own business. Fearing I might react in some way, I turned my attention back to the stand where the bailiff continued swearing in the new witness.

"Thank you for coming today, Ms. Wagner," Hoffman said once he got out of his chair. "Could you share how you knew the victim with the court?"

"Yes, sure," the witness said. "Libby was my friend. We met back in grade school and had been friends ever since."

"So a long time then. Would you describe your relationship with Mrs. Young as close?"

"She was my best friend, so yes, we were close." She tried to look in Watson's direction but stopped just short, instead lowering her eyes to the floor before turning them back to the approaching prosecutor.

"And during your friendship with Mrs. Young, did she ever tell you about her seeing the defendant?"

"Yes, she spoke about him often, although not so much in recent weeks."

"Can you say why?" Hoffman reached the point on the floor where he usually stopped and faced the witness front-on with his hands clasped together in front of his middle. With a different-colored suit, he could have been mistaken for door security at a bar.

"She grew fearful of him."

"Fearful?" Hoffman looked at the jury for a subtle dramatic effect before turning back to the witness. "Fearful how?"

"She wanted to cut things off with Brian, but she wasn't sure how. Libby had never been a confrontational kind of person, and the thought of telling him frightened her."

"Objection, Your Honor," I said. I don't think Watson expected me to jump up and visibly flinched when I caught him off guard. "Hearsay. The witness can't testify to what the victim was thinking."

"Sustained." Unworried, Hoffman immediately threw the next question.

"Did Mrs. Young ever tell you directly that she was scared of Mr. Watson?"

"Yes, she did," the witness said, and this time, she took the chance to look at the defendant. I felt Watson shift in his seat, clearly uncomfortable. It wasn't a good move with the jury looking on. "Libby told me with her own voice that she was scared of how Brian might react."

"Did Mrs. Young ever describe any physical altercation with the defendant?"

"No," the woman said, although she did sound kind of disappointed.

"Never?"

"No, never, although she did say that she was scared of what he might do if she broke it off with him."

Hoffman paused for a bit of theatrics, walking first a few steps toward the jury and then back again before asking his next question.

"Did you ever meet Mr. Watson yourself?"

"I did, yes, once. I was at Libby's house for a coffee when he showed up."

"Can you describe the moment for us? What was your impression of him then?"

"If I'm being honest, he chilled my blood. I could feel the tension in the room rise the second he appeared. Libby introduced him and immediately shuffled him outside again, where I watched them talk for a few minutes."

"Did you happen to hear what they were talking about?" Hoffman sounded hopeful as he took another step toward the stand.

"No, sorry, but I did see the way he grabbed Libby by the wrist while trying to tell her something. She didn't look too happy about it, just shaking her head."

"So they were having an argument?"

"Maybe," Wagner said. "It only lasted a minute or so before Libby came back in, and when I asked her about it, she said that it was nothing."

"Thank you, Ms. Wagner. No further questions."

"Your witness, Mr. Carter," the judge said once Hoffman had retaken his seat.

I could have accepted the offer, and I probably should have, given the state of the case from our point of view, but thanks to a certain impairment in my mental clarity, plus lacking the energy to chase something I didn't think existed, I did the unthinkable from a defense lawyer's perspective.

"No questions at this time, thank you, Your Honor," I said and retook my seat.

Jenkinson first checked the time on his watch before asking the prosecutor to call his next witness. I assume at his age, he would have needed regular recesses to take care of that old-man bladder thing most guys face. I watched the judge for a few seconds, his attention drawn to the door along with the rest of the courtroom when the new witness walked in. It's amazing how we sometimes think we know someone, only to be sometimes proven completely wrong by surprise twists.

I couldn't bring myself to believe the man took bribes. While the possibility definitely existed and seemed perfectly plausible, something inside me couldn't commit to the idea. Jenkinson just had this...this character trait that didn't fit the bill. If I had to name it, I'd say stubbornness would be the closest I could find to describing it. The man had a certain sense of selfish stubbornness to him that I didn't think would have allowed him to be bought.

"Thank you for agreeing to come today, Mr. Ploughman," Hoffman said as he pulled me from my thoughts. The new witness had already taken the stand during my distraction, Watson's former neighbor grinning with glee at the opportunity to testify. I would have put him somewhere in his mid-forties, a beer belly his most notable feature.

"My absolute pleasure," he said with a quick look at my client. Watson muttered something unintelligible under his breath, but a subtle elbow in the ribs from me stopped him from repeating it.

"You're a former neighbor of the defendant, is that right?"

"Yup, lived next to him for almost two years."

"And how would you describe your relationship with Mr. Watson during this time?"

The witness chuckled in response. "Ha, what relationship? The guy is a pest."

"Objection, Your Honor." The judge didn't need me to expand on it.

"The witness will refrain from making personal remarks and insults," Jenkinson snapped.

"Sorry, my bad," Ploughman said, lacking any hint of remorse. Hoffman, not wanting to lose momentum, repeated the question.

"Please describe the relationship you had with your former neighbor, Mr. Ploughman."

"It was hell. The guy lacked any sense of community. Mowing his lawn early Sunday mornings, working on that ridiculous car of his late at night." The witness shook his head in disgust. "And when I asked him to stop, the guy full-on attacks me."

"Mr. Watson attacked you?" Hoffman tried to sound shocked but failed dismally. His acting lacked a kind of spark, and it made his performance look more like a B-grade movie than a top-line prosecutor.

"Yeah, he did. I went to calmly ask him to turn down the music as his garage sat right next to my bedroom, you know? And instead of doing the civil thing, he pushes me up against a wall and threatens to stab me in the throat."

"Mr. Watson pushed you against the wall of his garage and threatened to stab you in the throat," Hoffman repeated.

"Yes, sir, he did." Ploughman seemed almost pleased at the prosecutor repeating his statement. "Had a screwdriver in his hand as well."

"What did you do?"

"What any other normal human being would. I apologized for the intrusion and got the hell out of there."

"Did you report this to the police?"

"Nah, I didn't think it was worth it," the witness said, trying to save face.

Watson and I exchanged a brief look, one where his eyes confirmed the man's story. I didn't need to ask him for the finer details to know that there wasn't much else to say.

"Thank you, Mr. Ploughman," the prosecutor said as he walked back to his table. "No further questions, Your Honor."

"Mr. Carter, your witness."

"Thank you, Your Honor," I said, rising to my feet but remaining behind the desk. "Mr. Ploughman, I'm curious as to why you wouldn't report such a confrontation to police."

"Like I told the prosecutor just now, I didn't think it was worth it."

"A man threatening to stab you in the throat while in possession of an implement capable of such a job, and you dismiss it as a simple altercation?"

"Yeah," Ploughman said, nodding as if I needed visual confirmation of his answer.

"Are you familiar with Ms. Hillary Harrington, Mr. Ploughman?"

"I am, yeah sure. Everybody knows old Harrington."

"Isn't it true that you reported her to the police for stealing a rose cutting from your garden?"

"I did, but that was only—"

"So you report an elderly lady for taking a cutting from a plant, but not a man threatening to stab you in the throat," I cut in, refusing to give the witness a chance to divert my intended path.

"Look, she reports everybody for any minor thing. I just wanted to give her a taste of her own medicine."

"But not someone threatening you with physical violence?"

"Obviously, I should have."

That was when I stepped around the desk and took a couple of slow steps toward the middle of the floor.

"Mr. Ploughman, may I ask what you do for a living?"

"I'm a shiftworker down at a processing facility."

"And what hours do you work?" I asked, posing my question in the direction of the jury, who watched me intently.

"Eleven at night until eight in the morning."

"Every night?"

"Six nights a week," he said to me, and then looked at the gallery. "Have been for almost four years," he added.

"And how do you get to your workplace?"

"I ride my motorcycle."

"A Harley-Davidson, is it not?" One of the jurors broke into a grin when they heard the brand of bike and appeared to predict my destination long before I reached it. I took it as confirmation I was on the right track.

"Yeah, so?"

"Can you tell me how loud your bike is?"

"Loud? I don't know, I guess it's louder than most. Especially those Japanese racing things the kids ride these days. Death traps they are."

"Yes, perhaps, but definitely quieter than your ride, which I personally measured during your departure three nights ago and found the noise level peaking at 102 decibels. That's even louder than the stock standard models, which leads me to believe you modified your bike to sound louder."

"So what? Most guys do it. It just sounds better."

"Perhaps so, but not to your neighbors trying to sleep at ten o'clock at night when you decide to rev your motorbike engine to the extreme, something multiple residents reported you to the police for, something that the police issued you tickets for, and something that you've been ordered to fix on your bike."

"Objection, Your Honor," Ploughman said as he interrupted. "Relevance? What does Mr. Ploughman's motorcycle have to do with the case?"

"Your Honor, it's very relevant when put into the context of the relationship Mr. Ploughman has with my client."

"Overruled, but don't stray for much longer, Mr. Carter."

"I won't, You Honor," I said before turning my attention back to the witness. "Mr. Ploughman, it strikes me as odd for a man who disrupts his neighborhood almost every night to take offense at a man fixing his vehicle in the privacy of his own home in the middle of the day."

"Yeah, well, I have to sleep through the day."

"And you expect the rest of society to make way for you, is that correct?"

"Objection, Your Honor," Hoffman threw out for the second time.

"I withdraw the question," I replied and turned back to my place at the table. "No further questions for this witness."

I had barely managed to take my seat when the prosecutor rose out of his and addressed the court with words that honestly sounded like music to my ears. They were the words that effectively handed the controls of the case over to me, allowing the defense to steer the ship finally.

"Your Honor," Hoffman said. "The prosecution rests."

TWENTY-TWO

I FELT like an actual zombie by the time the judge called for lunchtime recess, and I wasn't sure whether an average cup of coffee was going to do the trick. I almost messaged Grace to ask whether she could pick up a bottle of No-Doze and bring it to me, but just as I walked out ahead of Watson, I saw a familiar face smiling at me from the middle of the foyer holding a tray with two paper cups and a small white paper bag.

"There's your girlfriend," Watson mumbled behind me, but I ignored him, leaving the man to go off with his guard.

"What are you doing here?" I asked when I got close enough to speak at normal volume. Elsa held up the tray a little higher.

"Thought I'd bring you something special to get you through the rest of the day."

"Perfect," I said, reaching for one of the cups when she held the tray a little closer. The first sip sent a tingle all the way down into my toes, the bitterness of the double-shot more enjoyable than a brick to the head, which had been my other option to try and stay awake.

"How is it going in there?"

"As good as can be," I said and followed her out into the bright sunshine of a perfect Pittsburgh afternoon.

We walked for a couple of blocks until we reached a nearby park, a vacant bench under the shade of a tree, the perfect place to unwind for an hour. Once seated, Elsa opened the bag and pulled out a couple of sandwiches, which she held out to me.

"Where is yours?" I asked.

"I already ate," she said. "Besides, I'm not really a fan of eating in the middle of the day."

"I'm starving," I said, taking a smell of the first after pulling back the clear wrapping.

"I thought you might be, which is why I also picked up a couple of these," she said and revealed two chocolate donuts. "They go perfectly with the hot drink."

Despite the continuing drone of traffic punctuated by the occasional car horn, it felt almost peaceful sitting in that park with Elsa. Even in silence, I felt something different about her, the presence beside me just kind of supporting my sense of being. I'm not talking the classic Jerry Maguire you-complete-me thing here, but just comfort, if that makes sense.

When I finished the turkey and Swiss, I pulled out the turkey and mustard, made short work of it, and washed the final mouthful down with another mouthful of coffee. Elsa watched me work my way through the food, almost amazed by my progress.

"If I had known you were that hungry, I would have bought you a third sandwich," she said with a grin.

"Two is perfect," I said. "I'm just used to eating fast."

"Yes, of course."

The donuts went down just as well, but it was the ten or fifteen minutes after I finished eating that really hit the spot. We just sat there talking about nothing in particular while watching the city pass us by beyond the boundary of the park. Every now and then, a siren from an emergency vehicle would cause us to pause the conversation, but it would quickly resume when the incessant wailing faded away again.

"You know, I've been thinking," Elsa said after one such siren briefly interrupted us. "Maybe it's time for me to open up my own practice. Not just for taking on public defender work but branching out on my own to really stamp my brand on things."

"You should," I said. "I got this real estate friend who could shoot you through a few of the local listings."

"You have? That would be great," she said, patting my leg. "I know a lot of people, but funnily enough, nobody in real estate."

"Yeah, Jeff has been in the industry for years. He's the one who helped me with my current apartment."

"Hmm, an apartment I still haven't seen," Elsa said with her trademark smirk. It made me laugh.

"I haven't invited you around?" I pretended to look apologetic.

"No, Mr. Carter, you haven't."

"Then maybe it's time to change that." I checked my watch and pointed at the face. "But first, I have to get back to work."

"Then let me walk you to the courthouse," Elsa said, and after dropping our trash off, we headed for the nearest exit.

We got to a block from the courthouse when another siren approached from behind us. Given its proximity, I slowed to turn and look, finding an ambulance maybe a hundred yards off and approaching fast.

"They've been busy today," I said to Elsa, and then was surprised to see it stop at the front of the courthouse.

"That they have," Elsa said, also curious as to why it would stop where it did.

That was when we noticed a small crowd near the entrance to the building's foyer as two paramedics rushed inside with their gurney. The crowd parted just enough to let them through before filling the gap for better views. Elsa and I barely managed to make it to the top of the stairs before a second ambulance pulled up.

"What's going on?" I asked a nearby onlooker whom I recognized from inside the building. I think he worked as a courtroom assistant but couldn't quite place him.

"The DA collapsed in Judge Jenkinson's chambers," the kid said, his voice much too excited given the circumstances. Elsa exchanged a look with me.

"Excuse me," I called to those immediately ahead of me, and when they didn't move, I elevated my voice. "FOLKS, MAKE WAY. COMING THROUGH."

It took an effort, but I managed to squeeze a path through for Elsa and me to get inside. The usual buzz in the foyer felt eerily absent as many people stood silently in small groups while looking to the mouth of one of the corridors. I led Elsa toward it, turned the corner, and saw a group of people huddled together at the far end. The voices coming from two people in particular echoed down the corridor, loud enough for me to hear the paramedics furiously working on the district attorney.

"Oh, shit, Ben," I heard Elsa whisper from beside me when we came to a stop still a good distance from where the DA had fallen. I could see Jenkinson standing in the doorway of his chambers, looking sheepishly on.

Time seemed to stand still as no less than two dozen people watched the paramedics fighting to save the life of a man who saw himself as the unequivocal leader of the city's fight against crime. While not always the most popular, he certainly took his job seriously, and that didn't stop him from stepping on a few feet at times. I should know. My feet had felt his size twelve boots plenty of times.

Two more paramedics rushed down the hallway a few minutes later, pushing through yet another group of onlookers to get to their patient. After a brief vocal exchange between the rest of them, they eventually agreed to lift the district attorney onto the gurney and wheel him back to the ambulance so they could transport him to the nearest hospital.

The struggle was real. From where we stood, I could make out the strain on each of the men's faces as they did their best to lift all three hundred-plus pounds of the man. It eventually took seven men to do the job before the paramedics strapped him in and began wheeling the patient down the hall. People squeezed against the wall to let them pass, Elsa and me included. When it rolled us by, I saw the face of a man I'd opposed on numerous occasions, now looking ghostly white and lacking any hint of that fiery temper he was so renowned for.

The thing I remember most was the fear hanging in the air, not just from Elsa or me, but from practically every person in the hallway. I think that energy is universal, human nature sensing death's proximity and wanting to turn away to ensure it passes them by. It wasn't until the gurney rounded the next corner and disappeared from view that I noticed Elsa's hand squeezing my own. When I looked at her, I saw the exact same emotion I felt staring back at me.

"Mr. Carter," a voice suddenly called to me, and I looked over to see Jenkinson still standing in the doorway. He waved for me to approach.

"Give me a sec," I said to Elsa. "Unless you want to go, and I'll catch up with you later."

"No, it's OK, I'll hang around."

Given the circumstances and perhaps not putting too

much thought into it, I suddenly found myself leaning in and giving Elsa a kiss. We're not talking full-on tongue-swapping emotion here, just a firm peck on the lips that onlookers could see meant more than just a friendly gesture. We exchanged a brief look of confirmation when I pulled back before Elsa squeezed my hand a second time and walked away.

Jenkinson gave me a strange look when I walked past him and into his chambers, no doubt questioning the interaction he'd seen between a former prosecutor and me, but I didn't spare a second thought about it. What happened between Elsa and me wasn't anybody else's business, especially with her now officially a free agent, so to speak.

What surprised me more was finding Hoffman already sitting in the judge's office, albeit wearing a similar look of concern as the rest of the people currently in the building. He greeted me with nothing more than a head bob, the kind that went up before down.

"Cliff," I muttered as I took a seat beside him, not sure why I felt a need to verbalize the greeting. Jenkinson didn't give me much of a chance to think about it too long.

"Gentlemen, I summoned you to discuss a rumor I've just been made aware of," he began as he took a seat behind his desk. I wondered at what point he had summoned me, since the prosecutor appeared to have already been in his company.

"I wasn't aware of any rumor, Your Honor," Hoffman said, and I think it was the first time that I noticed something about him that I hadn't during any of our previous interactions. The guy was a kiss-ass. I detected it in his tone, the way he tried to sound as empathetic as possible. I nearly grinned at realizing it but managed to suppress the urge. Jenkinson ignored the comment completely.

"Some believe that I might be compromised, gentlemen.

Rumor is that I took payment to grant your client bail, Mr. Carter."

"I'm not sure how to respond to that."

"Well, the district attorney came to inform me that he would put it to you two, since it's your case. Well, that's what he said before the..." He stopped, simply pointing at the door without saying the words to go along with the gesture. This time, Hoffman decided to speak up.

"Are you asking us if we would like you removed from the case so you can be investigated, sir?"

I could have spoken up, I guess, since I had been harboring the very same thoughts myself, or at least *had* in the beginning. It appeared as if time had worked on me, in some degree, showing me a new truth that answered a lot of my questions. Both Jenkinson and Hoffman looked at me as if the decision lay with me. Perhaps, in a way, it did, since Watson was my client, and his future remained in question.

"If you're asking whether I want you removed, Your Honor, then my answer is no," I said. "I don't doubt your integrity in this matter, and I certainly don't doubt your commitment to our profession. I suggest we get back in there and do what this city expects of us and not let a few doubters disrupt the wheels of justice."

Rather than answer, the prosecutor simply nodded, a man of few words who didn't need to add to what I already said. The judge seemed to appreciate my words.

"Well, I thank you for your continued faith, Mr. Carter," Jenkinson said, and after shaking hands with both of us, said he'd see us back inside in ten minutes.

I wasn't surprised to see Elsa again standing where we'd watched the whole Clements thing earlier, but I did find her expression curious. It wasn't until I was just a few yards from her that I noticed the solemn face behind the slow-rolling tears, trying to keep it together.

"Elsa, what's wrong?" I asked, and when she responded, it felt like another revelation I had known all along.

"Arthur Clements has just been pronounced dead," she said, and I think speaking the words was the trigger that brought reality home.

TWENTY-THREE

IT'S amazing how fatigue works. One second, your eyeballs are hanging somewhere down near your knees, threatening to break free completely, and the next, they're back in their sockets, busily looking for the next thing to focus on. Despite the coffee and food from Elsa, I still felt the tiredness gnawing away at my insides, but hearing about the death of Arthur Clements changed all that. The fatigue left me so fast that by the time I walked back into the courtroom, I wasn't even sure it had been there at all. I felt wide awake, and more than that, I felt alive.

Watson was already sitting at our table when I walked into the courtroom. He greeted me as if nothing had changed between us, and rather than continue ignoring him like some spoiled brat, I returned the gesture with a succinct hello.

"Did I hear correctly that the district attorney just died?" he asked as I sat down next to him. I nodded. "Damn, just like that, huh?"

"Yup, just like that," I said. "And now, after all that's happened, we start our defense of your case, so I'm going to need you to keep your focus just like you have been."

"Cool as a cucumber," Watson said with an added thumbs up. "Count on me."

It was only after sitting next to him that I began thinking about my client in a new way. No, that doesn't sound quite right. Maybe it was me *expanding* my thinking of him that got me heading in a completely different direction. Anyway, whatever it was, something definitely rubbed me the wrong way, kind of like a bad itch that just won't go away. Something about his work and overall relationship with the Costa crew, which wasn't making sense.

I'm not sure how long I was caught up in my brain, but the next thing I knew, the bailiff suddenly called the court to order, and moments later, Jenkinson emerged from his chambers ready to continue the trial. He brought the jury out almost the second he sat down, and just like that, all the pieces were back in their places and the ballgame was ready to continue.

"Mr. Carter, are you ready to proceed?"

"Yes, we are, Your Honor," I said, feeling a pinch of relief at finally getting the ball rolling.

"Then you may call your first witness."

"Thank you, Your Honor. The defense calls Alison Booker to the stand."

When I sat back down to wait for the woman to enter the courtroom, Watson gave me a look I instantly recognized. It was the same one he had given me weeks before when I suggested bringing the woman in to testify on his behalf. Not only had he vehemently opposed it, but he had also effectively forbidden me from contacting her at all.

"Why the hell would my ex-wife want to get up on a witness stand and defend a guy she hates?" was how he began the negotiations for his opening witness.

"Oh, she's not going to want to," I told him, setting him straight. "I have no doubt she hates your guts, but this isn't about her, Brian. It's about you, and she's not the one wanting to get up on the stand. *I'm* the one who wants her up on that stand."

My argument worked, and he eventually agreed for me to make the call. Just as he had predicted, the woman at first ignored four of my calls, but when I personally showed up on her doorstep and persuaded her to talk with me, I got my way.

When she entered the courtroom, a person could have been fooled into thinking it had been two separate women who had walked in if they blinked long and hard enough. The expression she had for me compared to her husband changed in an instant, her face going from warm and friendly to cold and abrasive in the space of a second.

"Yup, there she is," Watson grumbled beside me when she passed us by, and I wondered what would have happened had she heard him.

"Yes, so keep your mouth shut unless you want to cost yourself a perfectly good character witness."

I didn't watch him pretend to lock his mouth with an imaginary key; instead, I focused on the woman being sworn in by the bailiff. She appeared quite pleasant, much like she did when I met her in her home that time, and definitely not the ogre Watson made her out to be. When she finished the process and turned to face the courtroom, I immediately jumped up and headed across the floor.

"Thank you for coming today, Mrs. Booker. I'm grateful for you making the time."

"That's quite all right," she said, still avoiding eye contact with her former husband.

"Could you share your relationship to the defendant with the court, please?"

"Yes, I was married to him for seven years."

"You were his first wife, is that correct?"

"I was, yes," she said, with still no hint of the venom I knew to be hiding just beneath the surface. I took it as a good sign.

"Now, Mrs. Booker, I don't want to pretend to paint a positive relationship you shared with your ex-husband."

"Good," she said. "Because it wasn't. Hence why he's my *ex*-husband." A couple of people in the gallery giggled but just until Jenkinson gave the crowd a stern look.

"Yes, of course," I said, acknowledging the hint of humor but happy to move on. "There were definite problems within the marriage, of course. Would you care to share what some of them were?"

"Oh, which ones would you like?" the witness said, still happy to hide her loathing behind a good dose of humor. "There are plenty to choose from."

"Just a couple will do."

"His drinking was a good one. Why don't we start there? Brian liked nothing more than to work all day and then come home to rip open the closest six-pack of beer he could find."

"He drank a *lot*, is that right?"

I walked close enough to put a hand on the railing of the witness stand, an intimate gesture that I hoped would simmer down some of the anger I knew to be raging inside the woman.

"He drank a hell of a lot. At least a six-pack every week-night and a few more religiously on the weekend."

"What other issues do you remember?"

"The way he relied on me for just about everything."

"Everything? Like what? Give us specifics." I made sure to sneak a look in the direction of the jury when asking a question so as to engage them a little more.

"I felt like what Brian *really* wanted wasn't a wife at all, but someone to mother him. Someone to wash his clothes, someone to cook his food. Do his laundry. You know, mother him."

"So would you say he was lazy?"

"Around the home, definitely, but calling him lazy would be doing him an injustice."

"What do you mean?" I asked, remaining close to the witness stand.

"Brian did work hard, I'll give him that. Never late, always the first to put his hand up for overtime, always ready to step in for a sick colleague."

That was when I did take a couple of steps back to keep the jury from falling asleep. I knew movement was key to keeping several senses engaged.

"Mrs. Booker, let me take you back to the alcohol for a moment. Would he get drunk from a six-pack of beer?"

"Sometimes, depending on how much food he had eaten. Weekends were a lot worse, though. He could go through four six-packs between noon and suppertime."

"Did you ever get into altercations when he was drunk?"

"Yes, we did," she said and took her first look in Watson's direction. I felt alarm bells go off inside me and took a few steps to my right to get between them.

"And during these arguments, did he ever get physical with you?"

"No, never."

"Not in the slightest? No arm grabbing or shoving?"

"No, I told you, never."

"Mrs. Booker, did your ex-husband ever cheat on you that you know of?"

"No, that's one thing I knew I didn't have to worry about."

"Why is that?" I asked, and that was when she took a second look in Watson's direction, this time with something I didn't think possible...empathy.

"His mother was cheated on when he was just a kid, and he saw the damage it did to her. Brian might have been a drunk back then, but he never touched me, and he never cheated on me. Brian respected women in a way I could never understand."

I left the answer hanging for a few moments, not wanting to interfere in the brief exchange between the two former lovers. The jury watched in silence, as did the rest of the courtroom, and I felt my purpose for calling the witness come to life.

"Mrs. Booker, I just have one final question for you. Do you think your husband is capable of murder?"

"To protect his family, sure, but not some helpless woman. Brian isn't like that." She looked at the judge as if he sat in judgment. "You got the wrong man, Mister. Brian is innocent. He ain't no murderer."

"Thank you, Mrs. Booker. No further questions."

"Your witness, Mr. Hoffman," Jenkinson called out to the prosecutor just as I reached my chair, and he didn't hesitate to take up from where I left off.

"Your ex-husband sounds like quite a man, Mrs. Booker," Hoffman said as he crossed the floor. "May I ask why you divorced him?"

"Did you miss the part about him needing his mother?" Laughter rose from the gallery but quickly subsided again.

"No, I heard that part, but that seems like a small inconvenience in the scheme of things."

"Yeah, well, you weren't there."

"You testified earlier that he never physically hurt you."

"That's right."

That was when Hoffman held up a slip of paper he'd been holding in his right hand and only then revealed its purpose.

"How about the time you called police for help back in…" He paused to read a line he would have already known off by heart. "November 7, 1998." He continued reading while walking closer to the witness stand. "It says here you wanted to press charges against your husband for pushing you into a wall."

"He never pushed me. I made it up to get him in trouble." Hoffman stopped to look at the witness, clearly overplaying his reaction.

"You mean you lied?"

"Yes."

"I'm confused. Did you lie then, or are you lying now?"

"Objection," I said, but Jenkinson was already ahead of me.

"Overruled," he said, keen to listen to the witness answer the question.

"Look, we had our differences back then. I was also drinking then, and that night was one of those times where we just had too much."

"And you got physical with each other."

"No, he wasn't like that," Booker tried, but Hoffman wasn't about to let her go.

"But you called the police, not once but twice, and both times—"

"I know why I called them," Booker cut in, "and it wasn't because he hit me." She turned to look at the jury. "Brian isn't a violent man; he never has been. Look, he didn't do this."

To her credit, Alison Booker tried her hardest to help, but in the end, I think Hoffman knew he would never get much better than he already had, and so he ended his questioning. Jenkinson dismissed the witness almost immediately, and just before she walked from the floor, she surprised even me by shooting her ex-husband a wink. I don't know if Watson returned it, but I do know he appreciated her coming at all. He never expected anybody to take the stand in his defense, much less someone who told me she wished him dead already.

TWENTY-FOUR

I COULD HAVE STAYED home if I really wanted to. Elsa gave me the option, but when it came time to make a decision, I couldn't let go of the idea of returning to the group that helped her beat the demons she'd battled for so long before finding them. I also felt a sense of need, an urge to see if they could do the same for me, and so I ended up agreeing to go, as long as Elsa drove and I got to sleep in the passenger seat.

"Yes, you can pass out in my passenger seat," she told me with a hearty laugh when I put forth the proposal. "I did, after all, manage to get some much-needed sleep, which is more than I can say for you."

I couldn't remember the last time I'd felt the way I did, especially after spending almost an entire night in the arms of a woman doing...stuff. It kind of reminded me of being a teenager, sixteen or seventeen years old, and breaking the rules to be with a girl. While I did lean against the B-pillar of the car with my eyes closed for the entirety of the trip to Canton, I definitely didn't sleep for any of it. Instead, I felt Elsa occasionally rest a hand on my leg as she drove, a sensation I definitely didn't complain about. I listened to her quietly sing along to random songs playing on the car stereo that she had connected to her Apple Music playlist. I imagined the road passing beneath us, each bump rocking me back and forth like a baby's cradle. On top of all that, I also let my mind run free.

My brain has never been one to just switch off, regardless of how tired I am. It has a way of readjusting itself based on the environmental influences surrounding me, like being in the car, for instance. With very subtle distractions, it seemed to draw extra bandwidth from whatever controlled the intricate pathways, and so the thoughts rolled on regardless. And what was I thinking of, I hear you ask? My client, of course, was a man whom I had begun seeing in an entirely different light.

A lot of the finer details of the case had raised questions, of course, just as you'd expect them to, but none more so than the ones surrounding him getting bail. It still didn't fully gel with me, despite the outcome benefiting my side of the case. It definitely kept Watson in a much better state than if he had been locked up in a jail cell, that much I knew. I'd had plenty of clients not quite so lucky, with many of them turning into bare shells of their former selves after spending time behind bars.

I imagined what it would have been like if Jenkinson had indeed denied bail and ordered my client to be held in custody until the trial. How would Watson have taken the news, and how would he have coped with being inside? And I believe that thinking about that very idea is how I suddenly came to open my eyes and sit bolt upright, not only scaring the absolute crap out of my driver but also pushing forth a new idea.

"BEN, JESUS, WHAT THE HELL," Elsa shrieked as I felt the car veer violently to one side before she regained control.

"Sorry," I said.

"Sorry? That's it? SORRY?" Elsa sounded angry, but in a

good-humored kind of way. "I could have killed us right now. What the hell was that?"

"I just had a thought," I said, still not entirely sure whether I was talking in my sleep or actually awake. Fatigue has a way of really screwing with one's perception sometimes.

"A thought about what?" I looked across and saw her hands gripping the steering wheel tightly enough for her knuckles to lose color. I expected to hear one pop from the force.

"About the case," I mumbled, fearing that if I didn't do something quickly, the thought would quickly fade into the shadows again, the way the best dreams always disappear moments after waking up.

Rather than first try to explain it to Elsa, I instead pulled out my cell phone, opened up the Notes application, and generated a new page. I could feel her watching me, taking puzzled looks in my direction every couple of seconds or so, but I knew I had to get it down on proverbial paper.

"Ben, are you OK?" Elsa asked me after a long stretch of silence. I typed several more words and then shut the phone screen before sliding it back into my pocket.

"I'm OK," I promised her, but was I? I couldn't quite decide, and so I let it go. "Have you ever had a case where you thought you knew the direction it was heading, only to find yourself facing the completely wrong way when the shadows cleared enough to show you the path forward?"

"All the time," Elsa joked. "When *hasn't* a case felt like that?"

"Well, the one I'm working on has been throwing me endless curveballs since I took it on, and I think I might have finally figured out one important clue."

I began to explain how Watson was granted bail after being arrested at the airport, already trying to flee the country. How the judge barely listened to the prosecutor's side of the argument, almost as if he'd made up his mind long before walking into the courtroom. Elsa listened as she continued driving, and when we reached our destination, before I had a chance to finish, she insisted that we stay in the car until I did.

"But we should really get inside," I said as several people walked behind the car on their way to the open doors. I could see several more standing near the table with the coffee machine.

"It will be fine," Elsa said. "Ronnie usually starts late anyway, and we still have at least ten minutes before the scheduled start time."

"You sure?"

"Go already. I want to hear the rest of this," she said, and so I did, filling her in on everything that had been happening.

I have to be honest, it felt weird to be sharing so many intimate details about a case with someone who technically worked for the opposing side. Yes, I know she had already quit, but Elsa still had plenty of contacts inside the DA's office, including Cliff Hoffman. If she wanted to, she could effectively share enough details to derail my case completely, something I knew she would never do to me.

When everything was said and done, we rushed inside before Elsa had a chance to respond, but a couple of hours later, she got her chance during the long drive back home. The meeting gave us a chance to step away from our hectic lives for sure, but it honestly felt good to step back into it at the first opportunity, if only to discuss things out loud with someone not connected with it.

"Firstly," Elsa began around three miles into our return journey, "let me just say that the chances of Crispin Jenkinson taking money to throw a case are a guaranteed zero."

"I gathered that much already," I said, although I still

appreciated someone else confirming my suspicions. I shared the details of the meeting I'd had in the judge's chambers alongside Hoffman.

"Wait, Clements was going to investigate him?" She went silent for a few moments, her eyes continuing to focus on the road ahead as she drove.

"Why does that surprise you?" I asked.

"Because Arthur was up for re-election soon, and I happen to know for a fact that Cliff Hoffman has been hoping to steal the job out from under him."

"Hoffman? Really?" The idea surprised me.

"Yes, really."

"Well, I guess he'll get his chance now with Clements gone for good," I said, then remembered Elsa. "Sorry, I didn't mean it like that."

"Don't be. I'm OK with it."

"I know it's none of my business, but were you close with him? I mean, professionally speaking?"

She didn't look at me, and when an oncoming vehicle briefly lit up her face with its headlights, I could see her lips pursed tightly while she mulled the question over.

"I respected him as a boss, you could say," she eventually said. "He wasn't always perfect, but who is when it comes to our industry?"

"Whoever follows in his footsteps is certainly going to have some huge shoes to fill" was all I could think of saying.

I think it was common knowledge that Clements didn't have the warmest of hearts for me, but then again, I doubt he shared coffee and war stories with anybody outside of his network. We were considered the other side, the opposing team, the people to be treated like the enemy. The people he dedicated his life to putting behind bars were the same ones I called clients and tried to save from people like him. No, we weren't so different, and allegiance was simply a matter of perspective.

I think it was somewhere near the halfway point of our return journey that the silence between us felt a little overwhelming. Elsa hadn't bothered switching the music on at all since our departure, and I again pretended to sleep with my head leaning against the B-pillar. The gentle rocking and hum of the engine should have been enough to send me off to sleep in an instant, especially given how little I'd had during the previous few days, but it continued to evade me.

Call it a second wind or just an overactive brain, but something kept pushing me back from the edge of even the smallest of snoozes. The good thing was that I had completely stopped thinking about the case and my client, but what replaced it felt even harder to process...Naomi. The meeting felt vastly different from the previous one I'd attended with different people sharing their stories. I chose not to speak on account of the fatigue and not trusting what would come out of my mouth. Neither did Elsa.

In a surprising move, it was the host, Ronnie, who opened up for the first time in my presence. Listening to her share the details of her tragedy really hit the room hard. I don't think I saw a single dry eye in the place as she shared the story of her daughter's illness, relentless bullying by classmates, and eventual suicide. Actually, I lie. There was someone in the room with dry eyes, and that was the person talking, the one who should have wept the most.

Ronnie showed such strength and resilience as she shared her story, and I wondered whether I looked as strong as she did when sharing my own. Grief has a funny way of holding people within its grasp in different ways, and she just knew how to deal with it.

"It was tough listening to Ronnie's story tonight," I said as

I slowly sat up and tried not to scare Elsa the way I had while driving to the meeting.

"She's one hell of a strong woman," Elsa said, again moving one hand from the steering wheel onto my leg. "That's the first time I heard about her daughter. It's usually her husband she talks about."

"She lost her husband as well?"

Elsa nodded. "He was a cop, shot in the line of duty. He was conducting late-night patrols and just happened to pull over the wrong car for a routine traffic stop." She reached up and adjusted the rearview mirror slightly as a vehicle with ultra-bright headlights approached from behind. "Man, I thought *that* story was heartbreaking, but geez. It holds nothing compared to the one tonight."

"I can't believe she went through *two* separate tragedies," I said. "I can't even begin to imagine how that must have destroyed her."

"It just goes to show that there's always someone in a worse position than us. It kind of puts our own lives into perspective, doesn't it?"

"It actually does." I leaned back into the seat as Elsa switched the music back on. She kept the volume low, but with so many things now running through my head, I barely heard it. Trying to imagine a woman's double tragedy was what eventually pulled me beneath the veil of consciousness, and with the comfort of Elsa's hand on my leg, I finally surrendered to the fatigue.

TWENTY-FIVE

ELSA DID SPEND the night in my apartment, but I can assure you that there was nothing physical about it. We walked from her car to my front door in perpetual silence, me mostly still asleep after she struggled to wake me after we finally made it back. The only diversion between the front door and the bedroom was a brief stop in the bathroom for each of us before we literally fell into bed. I remember feeling her lips on my cheek just before the light snapped off, but that's about it. Nothing else until the standard alarm jingle woke me the next morning.

I was surprised to find Elsa already up and in the bathroom, the sound of the running shower reaching out underneath the door. My eyes struggled to fully open after just six hours of sleep, but with me due in court for yet another day of testimony, it was the best I could manage.

"Let's do this," I muttered as I forced myself to roll over and swing my feet onto the floor.

The next hour or so went by with almost military precision as I prepared breakfast, myself, and the day ahead. Elsa had also decided to turn the day into something substantial by attending several appointments with real estate agents. Anxious to find a suitable office, she had arranged for five separate appointments spread right across the day.

When we reached the parking lot just before eight, we exchanged a kiss, wished each other good luck, and climbed into our respective vehicles. As I gave her a final wave through my windshield, I instructed Siri to send both Linda and Grace an urgent message asking them to meet me at the office. With the day's court session not due to start until ten, it gave me a little over an hour to get there myself and then share the details of my latest plan with them.

Being completely unpredictable, the traffic thankfully acted in my favor for once. It wasn't exactly midnight expressway pace, but it did continue flowing smoothly, eventually delivering me into the office parking lot where Linda already sat waiting for me.

"Must have something important for us if you're pulling us in before court," she said when I neared her car on my way to the main entrance.

"It's *always* important when I call for your attendance," I said with a smirk, but I quickly lost it when she asked her next question.

"How have you been since your run-in with Watson?"

"Still trying to fully absorb it," I said, and I wasn't lying. For the first time in years, I had answers to the questions that had tortured me since the night of the accident.

"I bet," Linda said and waved as Grace passed in her car.

When the three of us eventually sat down in my office, each of us held a coffee cup in our hands, courtesy of my assistant, who had stopped at a nearby café on her way in.

"Thanks for coming in early, guys," I said once we got the initial chit-chat out of the way. "I wanted to run something past you before committing to this new line of thinking."

"Is this about Watson?" Linda asked. I nodded.

"About Watson in a roundabout way. I've been continuing to go over the whole bail situation and how we managed to get him freed."

"Something definitely fishy about it," Linda said.

"Yes, and for weeks now, I had assumed that it was most likely because of the judge getting paid for the decision."

"Makes sense," Grace said, looking from me to Linda and back again.

"Yes, which is why I couldn't bring myself to consider any other reason. I stupidly put on blinkers and saw very little else," I said when Linda looked at me with surprise.

"Wait, are you saying the judge isn't getting paid off?"

"No, I don't think so," I said. "I've pretty much heard from the man himself, plus Elsa is a pretty good judge of character, but..." I paused to try to emphasize my next words. "But here's the thing that I've been thinking about." I looked from one woman to the other. "Who would want to pay for the judge to let Watson go free on bail?"

At first, Linda and Grace looked at each other as if I'd gone crazy, asking a question whose answer I should have already known.

"I thought we already established that," Linda said. "Henry Altera. The Costa crew."

"Yes, we had, but why would he pay? What's the purpose?"

"So they could kill him, of course," Linda said with a tone sounding as if I needed reminding.

"They would know ahead of time that we would take measures to protect him, like we have. It's also a big, wide world, and who's to say that Watson doesn't jump bail and disappear to some country?" I shook my head. "No, they didn't pay, and the reason I know they didn't pay a bribe to the judge is because they would have been much better off with Watson inside if they wanted him dead." When it looked like they weren't following my logic, I continued, throwing in the very bit of information that had unlocked it for me. "Think about it, guys. Altera organized a hit on his own boss while inside. He's got the connections. He knows how to get people stabbed, so why would he risk losing Watson by trying to get him *out* of jail?"

I stood and slowly walked to the window while running the previous few sentences through my head a second time.

"No way, I don't buy it. My guess is that they expected Watson to get denied bail, end up inside, and *then* get stabbed."

"If their intention was to murder him all along," Linda added.

"Correct," I said, confirming her addition.

"Wait a second," Grace said. "If we no longer think that they paid the judge, are we still working on the premise that they murdered Libby Young to implicate Watson in the first place?"

"That's the question I've been asking myself for a while now," I said. "The way I see it is that they organized the murder to get Watson into court and then have him remanded into custody. Once in jail, they arrange the hit and, well...job's done."

"If that's what you're going with," Linda began, "then why do you not sound convinced?"

"Because I'm not," I said. "Something still feels off."

"In what way?" Linda asked.

"It just doesn't feel right," I said. "The supposed robbery on Rhett and Watson by those two junkies, the bail hearing, Watson ending up a suspect when he did, the arrest at the airport. None of it makes sense. They look like pieces of a puzzle, just *different* puzzles."

We sat in silence for a few moments as each of us considered the previous few minutes of conversation. Linda finally broke it with probably the only question that really mattered.

"OK, then, if Altera or his crew didn't murder Libby Young, then who did?"

"That's the question we should have been asking ourselves since the very beginning," I said. "Now we're so many weeks into this case, and who knows how many of the leads have gone cold?" I looked at Linda for help. "I'm hoping you're going to be able to weave some of that magic I know you're capable of."

"I'll go through the witness list again," she said. "Maybe I'll try to have a chat with Hillary Harrington. God knows that old battleaxe certainly has a handle on the goings-on within her neighborhood."

"Maybe she can remember any arguments the Young woman had with neighbors," Grace added.

"Or previous lovers coming and going from the home," I threw in. "We just need *something*. One tiny little break." I checked the time on my cell phone. "Damn it, I gotta run," I said and grabbed my briefcase. "I'll leave the two of you to get on with finding me answers. I don't care how you find them, just find them."

I gave Carol a quick wave hello as I walked back through the reception area and continued on to my car. Once back in traffic, I turned the radio on for a bit of background noise, if only to break up the monotonous loop of questions continuing to roll around my head.

When I eventually reached the courthouse, the small media pack standing around near the entrance barely noticed my approach. When one of the reporters looked in my direction, I gave her a smile and expected them to come for me, but instead, she ignored my gesture and continued chatting on her phone.

"Yeah, they didn't speak with Hoffman either when he arrived a few minutes ago," Hardy said when he approached me from behind. "I think I heard one of them talking about the mayor coming to speak to them about the district attorney's memorial next Thursday."

"Oh yes, of course," I said. "Guess a young mother's murder trial isn't really cutting it for the six o'clock news headlines these days."

"I'm sure you'll get top spot again when you prove my innocence," Watson threw in before the three of us headed inside.

When we reached the foyer of the courthouse, Watson needed to break off for the bathroom, leaving Hardy and me standing near the entrance to the courtroom. Given how busy I had been during recent weeks, I suddenly realized how little time I had spent with my friend, someone with whom I shared quite a history.

"We need to catch up for some drinks sometime soon," I said while we waited for my client to return. "Things have just been so hectic."

"Hey, I get it," he said, sounding nonchalant about my excuse. "There's no rush. I've got news that I've been meaning to share with you anyway. Just time is always a factor."

"Oh yeah? What kind of news?"

"The kind that needs a couple of buddies to sit down with a beer," Rhett said, and I saw something in his eye, a kind of proud twinkle that guys usually got when they were about to announce landing a new job or getting a promotion.

"Well, OK, then. I look forward to the big reveal," I said. "How about we tee up something for tomorrow night? We can bring Brian along, if that's OK with you."

"Bring Brian where?" Watson interrupted before Rhett could answer.

"We were just making a time to catch up tomorrow night," Rhett told him, and his face immediately lit up.

"Good. It's about time you guys took me somewhere other than these damn hotel rooms."

"We're just ensuring you make it to the end of the trial," I said. "Wouldn't want your old friends paying you a visit now, do we?"

"All right, well, I'll catch you guys later." Rhett shot us a wave and headed back to the courthouse entrance, where it looked like the mayor had finally fronted the media pack.

It wasn't the mayor I paused to watch. Instead, I followed Rhett as he pushed his way through the front doors, walked past the media conference, and headed in the direction of the parking station one block over. If I had known then what I know now, I would have run after him and made him tell me the news right then and there. Sometimes, the universe isn't our friend, and as it turned out, I never got to hear him tell me the news. What we didn't know at the time was that our fate had already been sealed.

TWENTY-SIX

THE FIRST WITNESS I called that morning was a forensic pathologist named Dr. Melissa Yumiko. I'd worked with her through several cases over the years and had always found her to be not only reliable but also a confident witness. The thing about expert witnesses is that, just like regular witnesses directly related to the case, experts have to hold up under cross-examination. If they didn't, then any prosecutor with a confrontational nature had the potential to upend cases just through questioning alone.

"Thank you for attending this morning," I said to the witness once Jenkinson handed me the floor. "Could you state your qualifications to the court?"

"Seventeen years in forensic pathology working for Dexter's Medical Facility here in Pittsburgh."

"And during those years, Ms. Yumiko, how many murder cases, in particular stabbings, would you have undertaken?"

"Approximately nine hundred, I believe."

"That's quite a number of homicides," I said, reaching a point on the floor where I could see both the witness and the jury before me. "And can you tell me some of the details you look for when assessing a victim's injuries?"

"We look at the injuries for information that will help us identify the murder weapon, if it's not already located, usually from the width and depth of the wound or wounds."

"Anything else?"

"Yes, we can also determine the height of the attacker if we can determine the positioning of the victim at the time of the attack. The handedness of the attacker. It really just depends on what law enforcement needs us to check on the victim. A body can divulge quite a lot of information when you know where to look and how to interpret that information."

"You spoke of handedness," I said, finally reaching the part where I needed the witness to go. "You can actually determine which hand a suspect used?"

"When we have enough supporting evidence, yes, although it's still only a professional assumption."

"What sort of supporting evidence are we talking about here?" I asked, closing the distance to the witness stand and resting a hand on the railing.

"The type of weapon used, how deep it penetrates, the angle, it's a whole lot of different parameters that lead to a determination."

"You've looked into the details of *this* case, have you not, Doctor?"

"I have, yes."

"And did you find any of these supporting parameters within the injuries of Mrs. Young?"

"I did."

"Could you describe them for us?"

The witness gave a nod to the bailiff, who in turn arranged the screen to be positioned and then switched on the projector. An image of the victim's body still lying at the crime scene appeared. I heard a couple of people in the gallery react to the scene but not enough to cause a disturbance. It wasn't exactly gory. The photo had the victim's face cropped out and focused more on the actual knife protruding from her chest. Blood stretched across the floral blouse she wore, and some of the colors hid the true extent of the wound.

The doctor, using a laser pointer, began to point out different aspects a normal person might not notice. She went through a total of three images, the final one of the body lying on the metal table in the examiner's facility.

"You'll notice that the knife had been pushed deep enough for the guard of the weapon to leave a significant bruise on the surrounding tissue," Yumiko said while pointing to the accompanying image. "The blade itself penetrated through the costal cartilage here, which would have also taken considerable strength to achieve, the tip of the blade also causing damage to the opposing spinal column. You can see the damage here on the T3 vertebrae."

"How much strength are we talking about?"

"Considerable," the doctor said. "I know I wouldn't be able to achieve such an injury, and I consider myself fairly fit."

"Looking at the defendant, Doctor, would you consider him capable of such an injury?" I took a couple of steps to the side, hoping for my movement to alert any of the jury members whose attention had been waning.

"Dominant hand, yes, but I'd hazard a guess he'd need to be in a heightened state of excitement to cause it."

"What about his non-dominant hand?"

"I highly doubt it."

The witness turned back to the screen and brought up the original image of the victim with the knife handle sticking out of her.

"You can see the angle of the handle quite clearly, as well as the positioning of the body and where she fell. Given the height of the victim, if her positioning during the attack had been facing her killer, and he came directly at her, then we can clearly make out a right-angled arc from top to bottom with a twenty-three-degree lean to the right on the blade."

"So like this," I said, mimicking the action with a visual demonstration for the sake of the jury.

"Yes, correct." To ensure there was no confusion, I added other iterations.

"And not like this," I said, pretending to be stabbing someone from behind, or standing differently, and then with my other hand.

"Definitely not with your non-dominant hand, no. It would be virtually impossible to generate that kind of strength."

"Thank you, Doctor, you've been very informative," I said, and then to the judge, "No further questions."

"Your witness, Mr. Hoffman," Jenkinson said, and the prosecutor immediately pushed himself up using the table for support.

"Doctor Yumiko, I understand that you calculate various measurements from the injuries, but do you expect this court to believe that you can correctly identify which hand a suspect might have used to stab someone?"

"It's not an exact science, no, but sometimes science requires a best guess to help validate a theory."

"So you're guessing?" Hoffman looked at the jury, ensuring his grin was wide enough to show teeth.

"Guessing based on supporting evidence, yes." I admired how Yumiko lost none of her confidence, even under direct questioning by an overzealous prosecutor.

"And what if this supporting evidence isn't confirmed as credible?"

"Like what exactly?"

"You say the body landed on the bed after being stabbed. How do we know that for sure? I mean, isn't it possible that the victim could have been carried to the bed after death?"

"It's possible but unlikely," the witness said.

"How so?"

"Because after analyzing more than nine hundred crime scenes involving a stabbing, I can confidently say that it's not a normal thing to do."

"You've never encountered a victim moved onto a bed after being stabbed?"

"Yes, once."

"So it's possible?"

"Yes, it's possible," Yumiko said. "But in that one instance, the victim was still alive, and the blood trail confirmed it. She died minutes after being found by a family member."

"OK, so let's say the victim did happen to fall on the bed. How do we know the attack happened front on?" Again, Hoffman looked at the jury to engage them in his acting. "How do we know the victim wasn't facing away from the door and the suspect came up behind her, swung the knife in this direction?" he said, demonstrating his theory. "And then once he stabbed her, he rolled her around onto the bed."

"Again, it's possible but unlikely given the strength needed to generate the power for the blade to reach all the way to the thoracic spine."

"What if the suspect was in a heightened state of panic?"

"Maybe, but Mr. Watson's physical state doesn't support such a theory," Yumiko said and then looked at my client. "No offense."

"None taken," Watson replied with a hint of amusement. A couple of people behind us giggled, causing others to join in until a look from the judge silenced them again.

"What about if the defendant had something else in his system besides just adrenaline? Some type of drug, perhaps," Hoffman said, and that's when I put an end to his fishing trip.

"Objection, Your Honor. There's no evidence that my client has ever used illicit substances, and the prosecutor suggesting such a thing is reaching at best."

"Sustained."

"I withdraw the question," Hoffman said. "Nothing further of this witness, Your Honor."

The doctor and I exchanged a brief smile just before she left the courtroom, more so from me as a sign of gratitude. Dr. Yumiko added value to my case, just as she always did, and I wanted her to know it. It was while watching her leave the courtroom that my client suddenly whispered something to me that caught me by surprise.

"Put me on the stand" was what he said.

I had to look at him to confirm that I had actually heard the words he'd just spoken, and given the way he was looking at me, I could see he was serious.

"Absolutely not," I said. "Are you crazy?"

"I'm the one who knows what happened between Libby and me that morning. It only makes sense for me to go and defend myself."

"The answer is no," I said, my tone a little too loud, and I looked around to make sure nobody had heard. "This isn't something I'm willing to negotiate on. The answer, Brian, is no."

"Look, just—"

"Mr. Carter, whenever you're ready to call your next witness," Jenkinson called down with an air of impatience.

"Just do it," Watson said, trying to get his words above those of the judge. Caught in a situation, I took the only logical course of action.

"I apologize, Your Honor, but might I request a brief recess?"

He could have denied me, of course, but maybe due to his own bladder needing relief, he granted my request.

"Let's make it ten minutes," he said, and confirmed it with a strike of the hammer. The bailiff brought the room to its feet, and the judge left the rest of us to do as we needed.

"Let's go," I told Watson and immediately headed for the exit, turned left down the corridor, and found the first available interview room. Once Watson joined me inside, I closed the door.

"Ben, you know this makes sense."

"Listen to me," I said, taking a couple of steps toward him and holding a finger up as if about to make a point.

I had to pause for a few seconds as my mouth felt overwhelmed by the flood of words I was lining up to fire at him. Pursing my lips, I took a deep breath to calm myself.

"When I agreed to take you on, I made it clear that I would run this show. Putting a defendant on the stand at their own trial is probably one of the dumbest moves any defense lawyer could make. The prosecution would have a field day tearing your testimony apart—a *field* day."

"You can call all the witnesses you want, but nobody is going to be able to prove my innocence. You know it, and I know it. Putting me up there is the only way."

I was about to raise my voice to get the point across when my cell phone began to vibrate. Pulling it out of my pocket, I found Linda trying to reach me and asked Watson to hang on while I answered the call.

"Lin, hey, what's happening?"

"Sorry to interrupt your day, but I just received a call from Wendy Cole."

"I'm sorry, who?"

"I think she's a friend of Libby Young. I've been trying to get in contact with her for a few days. Not an easy woman to get a hold of, but she's agreed to meet me this afternoon."

"OK, go and meet with her. I don't think I'll be able to get out of court. I've got witnesses for most of the afternoon. Keep me updated, OK?"

"OK, will do," Linda said and ended the call. I checked the time and saw that I had run out of room to negotiate further.

"And this argument is over," I told Watson as I opened the door again. "Lose the idea of me putting you on the stand because it is never going to happen."

Despite griping, Watson agreed and followed me back into the courtroom, where the bailiff looked ready to proceed. He waited until we reached our table before calling the rest of the room to their feet. Watson stood quietly beside me, but I could tell he wasn't happy with me. He wasn't the kind of man to sit back and let others decide his fate. Unfortunately for him, this wasn't one of those times where he had a choice.

TWENTY-SEVEN

WE CONTINUED with another two witnesses before Jenkinson called for lunchtime recess. The last one before the break turned out to be a bit of a fizzle for me, and so I welcomed the break with open arms. There's nothing quite like an expert who changes their mind when under pressure and effectively flatlines our argument in one go.

Watson and I met Hardy out in the courthouse foyer and decided to get some food at a nearby café. We sat around a table for most of the hour just talking crap, the usual topics men speak about when in a group. Sports, movies, stuff like that. Just before one, I suggested making our way back to the courthouse so I wouldn't risk running late, something I knew Jenkinson frowned on.

We would have made it with plenty of time to spare, were it not for my spotting someone suspicious hanging around my car. I had to park it in a nearby parking garage that morning on account of no available spaces where I normally left it. Sitting up on the first level, I could make out its roof through the opening in the wall, along with some guy appearing to be leaning down and tampering with the driver's side door.

"You guys see that?" I asked, slowing my pace to get better focus.

"Is that your car?" Watson asked, and I nodded.

"It is," I said and immediately found a gap in traffic wide enough for me to cross the street.

I broke into a run when I reached the sidewalk, followed it to the garage entrance, and found the nearest stairwell heading up. I heard both Hardy and Watson following, although the latter wasn't exactly a fitness guru and a few steps behind. Scaling three steps at a time, I just about gave myself a hernia with the effort to make it up at speed, while at the same time trying to keep the echoes of my boots on the concrete down to a minimum. I didn't exactly want to announce my arrival.

Hardy did well to keep up with me, and by the time I hit the top of the stairs, he was less than a second behind me. He pulled his handgun out of its holster just as I rounded the corner and entered the parking area and saw the front of my car poking out from behind a much larger SUV. The problem was that by the time I finally reached it, the would-be thief had disappeared.

"Where the hell did he go?" I asked, spinning around and trying to see in every direction at the same time. Hardy did the same, but neither of us could spot the guy.

The only sound aside from the passing traffic on the nearby street was Watson's boot heels on the concrete. He'd finally managed to catch up to us with his face almost as red as the Camaro's hood that he leaned on while trying to suck air into his lungs. The man looked close to a heart attack.

"He's gone," Hardy said as he reholstered his weapon and walked to Watson to check on him. I would have, too, were it not for my cell phone suddenly coming to life. I pulled it from my pocket and began to walk toward the other two as I answered Linda's call.

"Linda, hey," I said, still trying to find where the guy was hiding.

"I just met with that woman," she said, her voice low but clearly echoing.

"Are you in a bathroom?"

"I am, yes. She's out in the kitchen making us another cup of tea."

"Did you find out anything of interest?" I had high hopes as I reached the other two and watched Watson trying to wipe the sweat from his brow with the sleeve of his shirt.

"You're going to want to come down here and speak with Wendy for yourself," Linda said.

"Why is that?" I asked as both Hardy and Watson suddenly looked at something behind me.

"Because she knows who murdered her friend" was all I heard before two men suddenly stepped around me with guns drawn. I lowered the phone and turned to find Henry Altera standing right behind me. The second my eyes fell on him, I knew the whole thing had been set up.

"Well, well, looks like we have quite a meeting here," he said with a chilling grin. His two goons remained a few steps to either side of us with their pistols aimed at the three of us.

"What do you want?" I asked, refusing to be intimidated, unlike Watson, whose face had completely drained of color.

"To have a talk," Altera said. "Only this isn't the place for it." He nodded to one of his guys, who immediately gestured for Rhett and Watson to walk to the SUV parked next to my car, where two other men stood waiting. I was about to follow, but Altera had other ideas. "No, not you," he said as he held a hand out for my phone. "Let's get rid of this, shall we?" He ended the call I suspected was still active and flung the cell phone away like a Frisbee. It skittered across the concrete as the second guy stepped closer and gave me a push.

"Go to your car," he mumbled, Altera stepping aside as he gestured in the same direction with his own pistol. "After you," he said with the same grin.

I watched as both Hardy and Watson were bundled in through the same side of the SUV before it took off toward the ramp leading to the lower floor. The guy with the gun directed me toward the passenger side of the Mustang, and once he climbed into the backseat, I sat in the passenger side before Altera shut the door and climbed into the driver's seat.

"I never quite understood the attraction with these things," he said as he hit the Start Engine button. His grin did widen when all eight cylinders came to life. "Prefer the European sports cars myself."

"Look," I said as we rolled out of the spot and followed the SUV down a level. "I don't know what you want from us, but I'm sure we can work something out."

"That's why we're here, counselor," he said. "To work things out. Just need a little more privacy, though."

With the gun trained on me from the backseat, there wasn't a lot I could do, a virtual prisoner in my own car. The knowledge that the man responsible for the death of Naomi was sitting right beside me wasn't lost in the moment, believe me. I had a gun in the glove compartment, the weapon mere inches from my hands, but I knew the chances of my getting to it before being cut down by a bullet were virtually zero. It appeared as if Altera read my mind.

"If you're getting any ideas about jumping out of the car or grabbing a weapon from wherever you've hidden one, I strongly suggest you don't. Sven isn't one for playing around, and he has a *very* itchy trigger finger," he said.

"Then tell me something," I said. "Did you organize the murder of Libby Young?"

"Who?" Altera looked at me with confusion.

"Elizabeth Young, the woman Watson is charged with killing."

"What makes you think I had anything to do with that?" He looked at his colleague in the rearview mirror. "Can you believe this guy? Blames me for it."

"Just tell me if you did so I can scratch your name off the list." He laughed at that, genuinely amused by what I'd said.

"Why the hell would I go to the trouble of killing some random broad?" Altera asked but didn't bother waiting for an answer, an answer I wished I could have given him. "Watson is a crazy guy, maybe he did it. Any man dumb enough to sleep with a married broad living right next door needs his head examined."

There was something in his tone that told me he wasn't lying. He didn't have a need to. It wasn't as if anybody was coming after him, but more than that, he was right. Why did he need to? He could have reached Watson at any time he wanted. I began to wonder whether the murder had simply thrown a wrench in the works for Altera, a temporary speed-bump which he was about to rectify.

That was when he looked at me again and grinned wide enough to flash his gold tooth.

"You ever wonder why that Young woman had so much time to play around? Ask yourself what her husband was doing."

"What?" Instead of answering, he just looked at me, that same expression of superiority behind it.

"Where are we going?" I asked, but reaching the express-way, Altera suddenly brought the engine to life, the raw power drowning out my words.

"Whoooo, would you feel that?" Altera yelled, gripping the wheel tightly as he opened the throttle further. "Maybe I was wrong about these poor man sports cars."

We continued on for what felt like maybe twenty minutes until we took a turnoff right before State Route 51 reached the Monongahela River, Altera maneuvering the Mustang along a narrow dirt road until it opened up at a holding yard. A huge kind of warehouse sat along the left fence line, and I spotted the SUV holding Rhett and Watson parked in front of it.

"Looks like the boys are waiting for us," Altera said as he pulled up nose to nose with the other vehicle and immediately climbed out.

Two guys came to get me out before the one in the backseat followed. They escorted me to where Hardy and Watson stood in front of a couple of thugs guarding them.

"Let's get them inside," Altera called over his shoulder as he walked inside.

"Move it," one of our escorts demanded, and the three of us slowly made our way inside, closely followed by three men holding their pistols on us.

Escape seemed impossible, although I never stopped looking for an opportunity to do just that. Ahead of us, Altera kept walking into the building until he reached the large open interior holding a couple of tractors at the far end, plus something huge hidden under a large tarpaulin that hung suspended from a hook attached to the central ceiling beam.

"All right, here...we...go." Altera turned around and waited for us to reach some nondistinct spot on the ground. One of the guys still guarding us began to circle around until he stood next to his boss. "Now," Altera continued, "we have a couple of things to go through, and time is of the essence."

He suddenly grabbed the gun from his closest colleague, aimed it at our group, and fired. Time slowed as the gunshot sent a wave of painful ringing through my head that I immediately tried to jump away from. I heard Watson cry out in shock from somewhere beside me before realizing the sound included my own cry of disbelief.

When I looked down to find Hardy collapsed on the ground beside me, disbelief washed over me. The man appeared to be looking up at me as if asking me for help through his expression alone, but the glazed eyes lacked any hint of life. In one split second, Henry Altera had taken another soul from my life. I swore to myself that there wouldn't be a third.

"What the hell did you do?" I cried out as I dropped to my knees and tried to stem the flow of blood coming from Hardy's chest.

"Don't bother," Altera said as two of his men picked Watson up off the ground and dragged him to a nearby doorway. "I can tell you from experience that he's gone. That sort of wound is always fatal." With another two men standing behind him, Altera suddenly leaned down far enough to grab a handful of hair. The pain was electric, white heat ripping through the top of my head as it felt like my scalp was about to come apart. "Don't think I don't know who you are, Benjamin Carter," he hissed into my ear. "I already stole Brian's daughter from him. When I come back, we'll talk about how you'd like to avenge your wife."

He let go and turned to follow the two men dragging Watson out, while the other two each grabbed one of my hands and dragged me over to one of the roof supports, the pillar a stable place to tie a prisoner to. They used rope, binding my wrists tightly enough for my fingers to start tingling almost immediately.

When they were done, one of the men walked to where Altera and the two others had taken Watson. The last guy took a few steps back, leaned against an opposing pillar, and lit a cigarette. He was the one who would watch me until his boss returned to make sure I didn't try to escape. I understood that whatever method I planned to use to exact my revenge on Altera would need to be reworked. I had a faint suspicion that one of us wouldn't make it to the end of the day. The only question was who.

TWENTY-EIGHT

IT WASN'T long before Watson's agonizing cries filled the air of the warehouse, his torturers unperturbed by the noise. That told me we must have been far from any possible neighbors, which meant time wasn't a factor. They would stretch Watson's suffering out to however long they needed and not worry about anybody coming to investigate.

The worst part for me, aside from not knowing what they had in store for my ass, was still seeing Hardy's body where it had fallen. Nobody seemed to care for him lying there twisted up with his leg skewered out in an unnatural position. The blood I initially tried to stem must have continued flowing until the final bit of pressure from his heart eventually faded out completely. Most of it pooled into a near-perfect circle of death that still appeared to be somewhat glistening from the overhead lights, all except this one tiny trickle that had carried itself almost half a dozen yards toward the nearest wall.

It's amazing what goes through your mind when faced with the very real prospect of death. I must have stared at that faint trail of blood more than anything, the very life it once carried now nothing more than sustenance for whatever bugs found it. Rhett Hardy hadn't been the closest of friends in recent years, but we had still shared enough time together for him to qualify as near family for me. He had dreams, goals, and people in his life. I wondered about the secret he'd wanted to share with me, the news he seemed excited about. In the blink of an eye, a completely random event had robbed him of the chance to not only tell me, but also to experience whatever it might have been. A new girlfriend? A marriage proposal? A new baby?

"Damn, that is one stubborn son of a bitch," Altera suddenly mocked as he walked out of the room wiping his hands on some rag. He inspected his knuckles and grinned. "Got a head as hard as a plank of wood, too."

"What the hell do you want? Maybe it's something I can help you with."

"Nothing you can help with, Benny boy," he said, the name immediately stirring something inside me. "Not unless you know where that son of a bitch is keeping the seed phrases to our crypto wallets."

"That's what this is all about? Money?" Why did it surprise me so much?

"Of course it is. What else could it be? You think I like his company? Asshole stole nearly forty million dollars of our money. Did you really think we were just going to let him walk away? Prison or no prison, we were going to get the information out of him one way or another."

That's when the penny finally dropped for me, the reason why they hadn't just killed him and been done with it. Watson had told me they just wanted to save face for him stealing money, but he'd laid the groundwork to take a lot more than that. Far more than I could have ever imagined. Altera must have noticed my expression change.

"I'm guessing he didn't tell you, huh?"

I just shook my head. "Why did you have to kill Rhett?"

"Who? Your friend here?" As if to remind himself of who Rhett was, he walked over to the body, leaned down, and pointed at it. "This guy?" And then, as if needing yet another opportunity to exert his power, he kicked my friend, not once but twice, both times in the chest. The impact shifted the body enough to straighten the aforementioned leg, making it no longer appear broken. I felt the heat of anger, of course, but continued pushing it down as far as I could possibly keep it contained.

Altera returned to the room, and not long after closing the door, the painful screams of my former father-in-law resumed. I could hear the wailing intermittently jump like a needle stuck in a groove on a record, no doubt from the fists and boots impacting his body. I closed my eyes and tried to block out the sound, but no matter how tightly I squeezed them, nothing could stop those godawful cries.

"Your friend will be dead soon," the guy watching me suddenly said as he flicked his latest cigarette into Rhett's congealing blood. It bounced across the surface once before getting stuck at the next landing. I could hear the slight hiss as the partially congealed substance absorbed the heat. "And when he is, it'll be your turn." He grinned, maybe trying to impersonate Altera, but it lacked the intensity of his boss by several degrees.

"Yeah, it's always such a sign of strength when five guys with guns tie up a man and beat him up," I said, almost tempting the guy to come closer. "Such heroes."

"I say always play your advantage," the guy said and fired up another smoke.

I'm not sure how much time passed before my legs lost their will to stand, and I gave in, allowing myself to slide to the ground, using the pole as support for my back. The previous aroma hanging in the air of cigarette smoke and oil from the machinery had also been slowly pushed into the background by the distinct smell of death. Given the heat of the day being intensified by the tin roof of the warehouse, Hardy's blood seemed to have begun evaporating, or reacting, or whatever the hell it did. Either that, or I just imagined it, since I was already sick from seeing him shot.

"Can I have some water?" I asked when the guy watching me returned from wherever he'd disappeared to, but he only shook his head. "Look, I can't sit here in this heat. I'll pass out from—"

"I ain't getting you water," he cut in, "so just sit there and shut it."

I'd felt for any hint of weakness in my bindings several times already, but feeling the rope bite into my wrist confirmed my worst fears. There was no escape for me, not while those ropes remained tied the way they did. Even if I did manage to untie them, I still had the guy sitting in front of me with his pistol. If I managed to break free and charge at him, he'd pop a cap in me and still have time for a cigarette before I could reach him.

On and on the beating went in the other room, and all I could do was listen as Watson's life must have been slowly draining out of him. There were moments when the cries stopped for several minutes at a time, and I wondered whether he had passed out while his tormenters either took a break or tried to revive him. Either way, the suffering he was going through must have been immense.

"Forty million," I whispered to myself, still trying to comprehend the sum of money Altera had mentioned. It sounded like an unrealistic sum, and yet one that was also quite achievable given the volatility of crypto.

I once had this friend who, in 2021, threw five hundred bucks into some random coin his cousin told him about and, within just two weeks, turned it into a little over four million. Just imagine that. Four million freaking dollars from less than a week's wages for him. And the funniest part is, he wasn't even surprised when it happened. If he could make four million inside two weeks, then I had no doubt about Watson holding on to forty million. It all came down to time and initial investing capital.

I was still trying to wrap my brain around the idea of making four million dollars in a couple of weeks when the smoking dude's head suddenly snapped hard to the left after something mechanical popped audibly from the doorway leading outside. His own brain partially sprayed the wall behind him before he slid off the stool he'd found for himself and landed in the dirt face down.

A shadow suddenly appeared, partially hidden behind the bright rays of the sun shining through one of the skylights. I pulled myself up using the pole for support and tried to twist myself behind it, but my arms wouldn't quite bend enough.

"Ben," a voice whispered to me, and imagine my surprise when I saw Linda creeping out of the shadows, the silencer fixed to her pistol trained on the door where Watson's cries had resumed.

"How did...what...what are you doing here?" I asked, nearly so overwhelmed from the shock of seeing her that I couldn't speak properly. Just as she was about to cut me loose, the door to the torture room opened, but instead of someone walking out, I only heard Altera calling for water.

"Bring us the bottles from the other room," he yelled out.

"Quick, we don't have much time," Linda hissed at me and began cutting the ropes with a knife.

Time never felt as precious to me as it did at that moment.

All it would have taken was for Altera or one of his men to look out through the doorway and see their colleague dead on the ground, and all hell would have broken loose. Instead, Linda kept herself together and calmly cut through my bindings before handing me a pistol and waving for me to get to the other wall.

"How the hell did you find me?" I asked once we had a bit of cover separating us from a potential confrontation.

"I don't know how to tell you this, Ben, but I'm not just your investigator, and it's my job to keep an eye on you in case something like this happens."

"How?"

"I put a tracker on your car some months ago." She held up her phone. "It's amazing the technology we have these days," she said with a smile, but that was when things took a turn.

"Boss, check it out," someone called, and a second later, one of Altera's guys appeared and leaned down to inspect his colleague. It was all the opportunity we needed, and Linda finished him with two quick shots to the torso. He dropped to the ground with an audible thud before someone suddenly reached around the corner with a handgun and opened fire.

What followed was a gunfight like you might see in a Hollywood action flick. Both Linda and I kept our cover behind some crates, giving Altera's men a chance to go through their supply of ammunition and occasionally returning fire. Unlike what we knew about their amount of ammo, we had a limited number of bullets and had to exercise caution.

"Drop your guns," Altera called. "You know you've got no chance of getting out of here alive."

"We'll take that under advisement," I called back and received several shots as a reply.

"Don't be an idiot, Carter. Nobody else needs to get hurt.

We only want the information we came for." Linda looked at me and shrugged her shoulders.

"Yeah, it appears that Watson's been holding out a lot more than he's been letting on."

"How much?"

"Forty million," I said, but before I could say anything else, another volley of gunfire echoed around us, threatening to continue nonstop, but that was when a new noise suddenly began to blend into the background. At first, I wasn't sure I was hearing correctly, but when I looked at Linda and she nodded, I understood the sirens to be real.

"I called them before I left," she said over the top of several gunshots. "Didn't think I was going to attempt a solo rescue, did you?"

Altera suddenly ran from the room, followed closely by the two remaining guns, one of whom Linda managed to shoot before he reached the exit. He stumbled several feet and careened into the wall with a significant hole in his neck before collapsing. I didn't think twice, immediately taking off after the would-be escapees.

"Check on Watson," I called over my shoulder before giving pursuit.

The bright sunshine briefly blinded me when I hit the outdoors, but it didn't take long for my eyes to adjust before spotting Altera climbing into the SUV. With the key fob to the Mustang still in my pocket, I ran for my own car, jumped into the driver's seat, and fired up the engine just as the massive Suburban began to roll forward. Knowing that any chance of stopping it would disappear if the monster of a vehicle built up enough momentum, I did the only thing I could think of: I hit the accelerator and aimed for its front.

With the Suburban weighing twice as much as my car and needing to do a U-turn to get out of the yard, it was always going to be a tough ask for it to escape. If he had been smart, Altera would have demanded the key fob from me when he first drove the Mustang. He could have then jumped into it during his escape and probably would have had half a chance. Not so with the behemoth he probably once considered all-powerful, much like himself.

I built up quite a bit of speed while closing the short distance between us and managed to hit the Suburban hard enough for the front end to veer sharply to the left and crash into a parked truck. I quickly reversed as much as I could before throwing the car into gear and crashing into the passenger-side door, effectively blocking that side for any escape attempt.

With wailing sirens announcing their arrival, four police cruisers came racing into the yard as the two occupants climbed out through the driver's side door and began running for the nearest pile of shipping containers. The police called for both men to freeze, and when one slowed and pulled his weapon around to shoot, they opened fire, cutting him down with close to a dozen bullets.

Altera could have kept running, but he chose to stop, his hands held high as he turned to face the cops. I kept my own gun trained on him when Linda ran up beside me. Unlike the rest, who were watching the criminal boss, she had her eyes on me and for good reason. With my trigger finger struggling to squeeze a round off and send a bullet into the man responsible for the murder of my wife, she knew I was on the edge.

"Ben, think about it," she said, her voice calmer than I'd ever heard it before. "You shoot him and they're going to be arresting *you*."

"But he killed her, Lin," I said, the beads of sweat rolling down the side of my face as if masking the tears. "I can end him finally, right here and now."

"Yes, and effectively bring an end to his suffering as well." She reached out and touched my arm. "Or you can see him face justice and then suffer inside a jail cell for as long as God wills it."

It felt like a bubble had come down and enveloped the three of us, the rest of the world disappearing behind a wall of self-doubt and the deepest grief imaginable. The worst part about the whole thing was the overwhelming sense of failure if Altera walked from that yard alive. No, not failure—betrayal. I felt like I was betraying the memory of my wife, my unborn child, and our family if I let that son of a bitch continue breathing.

I don't know how long the cop stood there with his gun trained on me, but I only noticed him when I saw Altera look in his direction. He knew just as well as I did how close he stood on the verge of meeting his judgment. Was I really going to just lower my weapon and walk away from something I had dreamed of doing for five years? Was I going to forget about the countless nights lost in a whiskey bottle or the many hours spent weeping beside the final resting place of my wife and unborn child?

"Ben," Linda repeated, her voice completely empathetic like a nurturing mother saving her youngest from ultimate doom. "Ben, you don't have to do this."

"Shoot me, you weak coward," Altera suddenly called out, tempting me to take the shot. "I still remember the look on your wife's face when I smashed into her," he said, all the while grinning enough for me to see the single gold tooth. "Man, she squealed like a stuck pig when the car bounced over her."

"Ben," Linda repeated, and as much as I wanted to listen, I squeezed my eyes shut, feeling every inch of my soul focusing on the trigger finger. That was when Altera said something that changed everything.

"Wait until this guy finds out about where Libby Young's deadbeat husband spends his Friday nights."

When he began laughing, I opened my eyes and lowered the gun. The cop, with his weapon still trained on me, briefly held his position before turning toward the real threat. Four cops approached Altera and ordered him to get on his knees. Part of me prayed for him to resist, to pull some pistol he'd been hiding in his pocket and try to use it. Part of me wanted to see him finally go down the way he deserved, but Linda was right. I am and always will be a lawyer. Justice is in my blood, and it is that justice which will ultimately bring me closure.

TWENTY-NINE

ALTERA DIDN'T GO QUIETLY nor easily. First, he refused the officer's demands, and then, after getting tasered multiple times, he ended up hogtied and carried back to one of the cruisers. His screams eventually cut off when one of the officers slammed the door on him. Linda and I didn't hang around for the final part as we went back inside to where the paramedics continued treating Watson. He was a complete mess, blood leaking from multiple cuts to his face. Altera had broken four fingers on his right hand, removed two fingernails from his left, and stubbed a cigarette out on his forehead. He'd been punched so many times that his nose looked almost smeared to the left, and yet despite all of his injuries, he grinned at me when Linda and I walked into the room.

"I hope they'll be able to straighten my nose again," he joked, and none of us could hold back our laughter.

"You look just as beautiful as ever," I said, stepping back as the paramedics helped him onto the gurney and slowly wheeled him out.

Linda and I remained at the warehouse long enough to watch the ambulance drive off, leaving just a couple of the original police cruisers behind. Jack Barnes eventually showed up, and we spent another hour or so filling him in on what had happened. He listened intently, and then just as we were preparing to leave, he had to point out something I still hadn't noticed.

"Guess you'll be needing a new car," he said, pointing to the mangled front end of my Mustang.

"I might just start leasing them," I said, making him laugh.

It was during the drive back to the city that I remembered Linda's original phone call from when Altera first surprised us.

"What were you going to tell me about this Wendy lady?" I asked.

"Oh, yes, of course." Linda smiled and shook her head. "I wish you could have been there when I spoke with her. She isn't a friend of Libby Young after all."

"Then who is she?" I wasn't following.

"A former lover of *Colin* Young."

"The husband?" I didn't think I'd heard correctly. "Why would she be calling us?"

"Yup, the one and only," Linda said. "That last part Altera called out to you about the Young woman's husband?" She paused to take a turn. "Turns out he's been gambling at Altera's gaming hall. I heard from Dana Erickson that he's got himself into quite a bit of debt down there."

My mind began to race as multiple theories suddenly collided, while new ones formed and tried to take over.

"Young gambled down there?"

"That's not all," Linda said as she slowed for a red light. "Wendy saw him take out a life insurance policy for two million dollars on his wife just two months ago."

It all suddenly came together, each piece of the puzzle neatly falling into place. The multiple scenarios I had been playing through my head throughout the trial faded away as a new one came to mind, one which made a lot more sense than anything I had been envisioning.

"I need to make a call," I told Linda and pulled out my cell phone.

While people often believe that most murder trials come to a climax when some random witness breaks down in a massive Perry-Mason kind of meltdown and confesses, the truth is that it rarely ever happens that way.

Less than four hours after Henry Altera's arrest, Linda and I watched Colin Young being taken into custody by Jack Barnes and a number of officers. Unlike the previous times when I had seen him exploding with emotion, the husband and killer submitted without fanfare, eventually breaking down in tears when the cops led him out of his home. I saw Hillary Harrington watching out of her kitchen window, and when I gave her a wave, she quickly pulled the blinds down. Just before the cop closed the door on him, Young looked in my direction. In that brief moment when our eyes met, I could see that he welcomed his fate, probably relieved that he no longer needed to hide.

Linda eventually dropped me off at Elsa's, and together, we drove down to the hospital where Watson had been admitted. He was still in surgery, the doctor describing his condition as stable. What we didn't know at the time was that he wasn't just suffering from the visible injuries. Multiple kicks had broken most of his ribs, and he was lucky to be able to draw a breath at all.

Elsa refused to let my hand go as we sat in the waiting room, waiting for Watson to come out of surgery. She looked genuinely scared when I told her the story, including the part where Altera shot Rhett Hardy right beside me. I felt her fingers tighten each time I reached some critical part of the story.

When I eventually finished sharing everything, she leaned in and kissed me, first on the hand, then on the cheek.

"I'm not sure which part frightens me more," she whispered to me. "Them tying you up and telling you that you were next, or you in the car with that psycho, not knowing where they were taking you."

"It was pretty scary," I said. "But it's over now."

"And I'm glad it finally is," she said and planted a third kiss on my lips.

That was when the doctor walked in, a medical cap still on her head as she made her way over to us.

"He's out of surgery and doing as well as can be expected," she said.

"Any permanent injuries?" I asked.

"None that we know of," she said. "He's just being taken to Recovery. Maybe give it thirty minutes or so, and then you'll be able to go in and see him." She was about to go again but stopped. "I'm sorry, but just you for now. You're his immediate family, right?"

"I am, yes," I said.

"We just have rules, that's all."

"Understandable," I said, and watched as the doctor walked through the opposite door to the one she'd walked in from.

"Oh, that reminds me," Elsa said as we returned to our previous seats, which looked like we would be remaining in for the next half hour. My butt ached from just the thought.

"What's that?"

"You're not going to believe me when I tell you who Arthur's temporary replacement is."

"Oh geez," I said. "Don't tell me Hoffman is already gloating about his new role."

"It's not Cliff," Elsa said, surprising me.

"Hoffman didn't get the tap on the shoulder? Who then?"

"It's Xavier Bartell." Just hearing the name brought a smile to my face.

"Xavier got it? That's awesome," I said. "I bet he's happy."

"Surprised, actually. He told me he expected Cliff to get it as well."

"How long until the election?"

It's next month," Elsa said, "and I think Xavier will be a shoo-in."

"So do I," Elsa said and retook her seat.

We sat in that hospital waiting room for another hour before a nurse finally came to get me. Elsa assured me she was fine waiting for me, holding up her near-fully charged cellphone and her finger over the TikTok app icon.

"I won't be long," I promised.

"Take your time," she said and immediately opened her entertainment.

It felt weird walking into that hospital room alone, not because of who was lying on the bed but because of the unbearable sense of déjà vu gripping me. It didn't hit me until that very moment that this was the very same corridor I had walked down the night Naomi was brought in barely alive. She ended up in a room two doors down from where her father now lay, the scene almost exactly the same. Even the beeping from the monitoring machine seemed to keep the very same rhythm I remembered. The only difference was that this time, the patient was awake.

"Ben, I didn't expect you to be here still," Watson said when he saw me walk in. "It must be late."

"It's just after nine," I said and stood next to the bed.

Standing there, I felt my insides gripped by a sudden rush of nausea when I saw the face staring back at me. Not only did Naomi share a lot of her father's features, but her injuries matched what I now saw looking back at me, the bruising running down both sides of the face, the one open eyeball's white turned completely red with gruesome bumps from the broken blood vessels. Watson must have seen my reaction to seeing his face.

"Never mind, kiddo," he said. "Nothing a few weeks of rest and relaxation won't fix." I wasn't so sure but didn't say so.

"Listen, I won't stay long. I've got Elsa out in the waiting room," I said.

"Why is she out there?"

"They only allow immediate family in and, you know." He looked at me with his one open eye.

"Listen, Ben, why don't you take a seat for a moment?"

I wasn't sure whether I should, not because I didn't want to but because I feared the nausea I continued trying to hide would overwhelm me to the point of launching my lunch across the floor. Reluctantly, I did as Watson asked, pulling a nearby chair closer to the bed.

For the first few minutes, we just sat there silently with the incessant beeping loud enough to cause a blip of an echo, a split second after the main one. I'm not sure whether Watson had anything specific he wanted to say or just wanted a bit of company before facing a night alone. When he did eventually begin to speak, he did so staring straight up at the ceiling as if unable to look at me.

"You know, I almost came to see you about a year to a year and a half ago," he began. "I remember driving over to your apartment and wondering why the hell it had taken me so long to build up the courage to do it. And then when I got there, I realized I didn't have the slightest clue what to say to you."

"Brian, you don't have to—"

"No, I want to," he said, cutting me off. "Sure, there are some things better left unsaid, but then there are other things that sometimes *need* saying." He tried to take a deep breath, must have felt the pain, and immediately held his breath before carefully releasing it again. "Damn that hurts," he muttered, more to himself than me.

"You want some more pain relief? I can get the nurses to bring you something."

"No, it's fine," he said. "Maybe it'll do me good to feel some pain for a bit. Maybe it will help me feel alive again."

I waited for him to try and take a couple more noticeable breaths, each time, his chest heaving slightly before slowly settling down in carefully controlled stages.

"Where was I again?"

"You had driven to my building."

"Ah, yes, of course. So anyway, there I was, sitting outside your building, not sure what to say. I didn't even know what time it was. I'd been so disconnected from life that I hardly knew where I was most days. I just seemed to float from one moment to the next, sometimes inside a bourbon coma, sometimes tequila. I don't even know how long I sat outside your building for that night, but then I saw you." He paused, closing his good eye as if visualizing the moment. "You and that investigator of yours. At the time, I thought she must have been your girlfriend and the kid hers. I remember feeling so angry, but then not sure whether I had any right to be, since it was my fault you lost your first family."

"Wait, you saw me with a kid? A kid and Linda?"

"Yes, you and her and the kid."

He caught me off guard, my brain briefly blocking the moment he was describing, but then I remembered the case with little Max Dunning, a kid who temporarily captured my heart.

"You saw me with him?" I couldn't remember the exact moment, but I felt something familiar about the scene he described, remembering some late night or early morning trip where we snuck Max out of my building.

"I did," Watson said. "I remember it clearly because I ended up punching the steering wheel hard enough to break a finger."

He went silent again, no doubt reliving the moment and trying to revisit the emotions surrounding it. I watched him from my seat, unsure what to say, but then he broke the silence for me.

"I think that was the night, the *first* night, where I truly believed that you deserved to move on with your life. I hated myself for what I had done, but up until that moment, I wanted to keep you inside the bubble of grief with me. You were the only one who I knew shared the same pain as me and..." A tear escaped the side of his eye. "And in my selfish state, I didn't want to be alone inside it. If I was going to suffer, I wanted to know that...that...that I wasn't alone."

That was when he looked at me, his one good eye studying me as he considered his next words.

"Brian, it's..."

"No, I need to get this out," he insisted. "That was the night I finally understood that you had no business needing to keep the pain of Naomi. I drove away that night, finally able to get on with my own life. I no longer felt the need to hang out at the cemetery, watching to see if you still visited my little girl. I no longer felt a need to stalk the man whom I had destroyed through inaction." He suddenly held a hand out, the wrapped fingers barely able to move. "I'm sorry, Ben. I'm sorry for what

I turned your life into. I'm sorry for robbing you of what would have been an amazing life with Naomi."

We shook hands, in a roundabout kind of way, and moments before stepping through the doors where Elsa would still be waiting for me, I had to wipe the tears from my eyes. Closure can come in so many unpredictable ways, and I never expected to find mine two doors from where the nightmare began in the first place.

THIRTY

WHEN I WOKE up in Elsa's arms the next morning, it didn't just feel like a new day. It felt like a new life, an awakening, if you will, after one of the most eventful days in living memory. With so many aspects of my life coming to a close at once, it was hard to believe that I would make another life-changing decision just an hour before midnight after a lengthy discussion with my new partner.

The idea for change had been weighing on my mind for weeks, and before you go blaming Elsa, I want to make it clear that the decision was mine and mine alone. There might have been some level of influence from her, but the truth is, I needed to make the call, and I chose action.

Elsa did ask if I wanted her to go with me, but I declined her offer and told her that it was probably best if I went alone.

"I'll meet you in a couple of hours down at Jeff's," I said, referring to my friend who owned the real estate office we intended to use.

"OK." Elsa gave me a kiss and then handed me her car keys.

"Just remember that it doesn't have as many cylinders as yours."

"I'll take care of it," I said and smiled.

It felt weird driving her car, but not nearly as weird as when I walked into work that morning. Carol greeted me just as she normally did, and Grace was sitting at her desk doing some online shopping. She looked up when she saw me approach.

"How is Brian doing?" she asked when I got close enough.

"He was OK when I saw him last night. He has a lot of recovering to do, but I think he'll be OK."

"The news hasn't stopped about Colin Young's arrest. He confessed to police early this morning."

"Yes, I heard," I said, and while I would have loved to continue talking about a case I had effectively won, I had more pressing issues to deal with. "Grace, is Dwight in his office?"

"He is, yes."

"Would you mind joining me for a few minutes?"

"Is everything OK?" She looked concerned.

"Yes, everything is fine. I just wanted to have a quick chat." I felt that familiar phantom hand reach into my stomach and squeeze.

"Yes, of course," she said and got up from her chair before leading me down the corridor to her husband's office.

Dwight sat sideways behind his desk with one foot resting on the edge, staring at a picture hanging from an opposing wall of a yacht he once owned. He moved the foot off the desk the second Grace walked in.

"Hey, hon, what's up?"

"We're not buying another boat," she whispered before gesturing for me to sit. "Ben wants to see you."

"Ah, the man of the hour," Dwight said and half stood with an outstretched hand. "Good job on solving the Young case. I heard the husband confessed this morning."

"Yes, I heard." I shook with him and sat down. "And I also heard that Winthrop Curtis refused to represent Henry Altera." Dwight seemed surprised.

"Really? Wasn't the mob his only client?"

"No, I heard he has a case currently in Cumberland County. A retrial, I heard."

"And I know it's not easy, but I'm glad that Altera fellow is in custody. Hopefully, he ends up doing some serious time."

"I hope he suffers each and every day he's in there," I said and decided that was the moment to bring up the reason for my visit. "Listen, I know it probably feels like the wrong time, but I have something to tell you guys."

"Is this where you tell us about your new girlfriend?" Dwight said and immediately felt the wrath in the look Grace gave him. "What? He's got a cute girlfriend."

"Yeah, she's very cute," I said. "But Elsa isn't the reason for me stopping in." I paused, unsure how to say the words I'd rehearsed since the previous night. "Look, I'm just going to come out and say it," I finally managed. "I want to resign my position with your firm."

It honestly felt like all the air had been sucked from the room, both Grace's and Dwight's jaws hanging partially open at hearing the unexpected news. They exchanged a brief glance with each other before looking back at me. Grace sounded more shocked than her husband.

"You're leaving us?"

"I'm so sorry, but I just have this urge to open my own practice, and with Elsa now also looking for somewhere..."

"Ben, listen," Dwight said, and I expected him to start launching into me, to try and talk me out of it, maybe even tell me how much of an idiot I was. But he didn't. "Every lawyer worth their salt reaches a point in their career where they feel it necessary to branch out on their own."

"Really?"

"Yes, of course. How do you think I opened this place? Sure as hell wouldn't have if I'd stayed at Jackson and Dwyer all those years ago. You're an incredible lawyer with an ambitious heart and an even bigger drive." He stood and held his hand out a second time. "I've never been more proud of seeing one of my own leave the nest to grow their own family."

His reaction caught me completely off guard, and I expected him to pull his hand back the second I went to shake with him, watching his face turn to scorn and for him to yell for me to leave the building. But that wasn't who Dwight was. He shook my hand a lot firmer than the first time and then watched as Grace gave me a hug.

When I walked out of the building carrying a small box an hour later, I did so a free man on so many levels. If anybody would have told me that in just seven days, I would find Naomi's killer, mend my relationship with Watson, solve the Libby Young murder, and quit my job in order to start a new business, I would have laughed in their face—and yet that was exactly what I was doing. Freedom had swept me up into its arms and welcomed me onto a new level of existence.

Elsa was already at Jeff's office when I arrived shortly after leaving Carol standing in the foyer of my former workplace, shaking her head in disbelief. I told her it still hadn't sunk in for me either, but during the drive to the real estate office, I did feel somewhat renewed.

"There he is," Jeff said when I walked in and shook hands with me. "I was just showing Elsa this place over on Fifth. It's got great views, close to the business district, courthouse, and plenty of eateries."

After a quick kiss, I handed Elsa the keys to her car and sat next to her.

"How did it go?" she asked.

"As well as can be expected," I said. "There weren't exactly tears, but they were pretty surprised."

"I bet they were," Elsa said. "They're such a wonderful couple. I wish I could have gotten a job there."

"Maybe you should apply for his," Jeff said from behind his desk with a smirk as Elsa laughed. "I hear there's an opening." He flashed a grin at me, and I picked up a stapler, pretended to throw it at him, then set it back down.

"Laugh it up, buddy," I said, flashing my own smirk at him. "But I happen to know you work on commission, so be careful who you offend."

"Jokes aside, I think the office on Fifth is perfect for you guys. Should we go over and take a look?"

One look at Elsa, and I knew she wanted to go for an inspection, and I guess I did too. The quitting part of my day still felt very fresh, and in a weird kind of way, I felt guilty for moving on so soon after walking out of my previous job.

"All right, let's go take a look," I said, and twenty minutes later, I found myself walking into an office most people could only dream about.

Elsa looked almost as stunned as I was when we first walked in. Most of the decor looked brand new, and each of the two offices was tucked into a corner of the building and provided world-class views. Elsa opted for the one on the east side of the building, and I on the west. I preferred mine, as it offered partial river views, with the occasional boat adding yet more character to the scene.

We did end up checking out three other places that Jeff insisted on showing us, but honestly, none of them compared to the first one. It's hard to beat a great first impression, and the building on Fifth just had it all. Elsa and I signed the application later that afternoon and received confirmation that the landlord had accepted us just before dinner. The meal we had intended to have to celebrate our new beginning turned out to be blessed with the signing of our lease, which Jeff brought down to us personally and then stayed for the entree.

It's funny how things turn out sometimes. One second, you're standing in a courtroom fighting a case and wondering why you're always drawn to the smile of the prosecutor, and the next, you're signing a lease with the same woman now sharing your meal, your bed, and your life. Imagine what the next second could bring.

THIRTY-ONE

I EXPECTED life to throw me the occasional curveball over the next weeks and months or so, but for once, it felt like life had finally turned a definitive corner. Elsa ended up setting herself up down at the courthouse and started taking on some of the overflow cases from the public defender's office. The smile she used to display while working as a prosecutor grew even more intense. I had never seen her so happy and at the same time so motivated.

What I expected was to also dive into work, but I found that I wasn't quite ready for that. It had been close to a decade since I'd taken any serious time off work, and after having spent countless months and years working cases, I wanted a break.

"You need to find yourself a hobby," Elsa told me one night just before we went to sleep, and I found myself staring at a laptop screen at two in the morning, going through gaming websites.

I had never been into video games before that night. Sure, I'd seen others playing games on their phones or laptops. Even Grace used to sit at her desk playing something called Candy

Crush. I tried it once and wondered whether I would get the ten minutes I spent on it back somehow. What I didn't know was that gaming wasn't just about simple apps on a cellphone.

By the end of the first week after Elsa told me to find a hobby, I'd rearranged one of the rooms in our new home, emptying it of everything except the desk. A day later, I went out and purchased a gaming computer, the tower looking more like a light show than an actual machine. The monitor the guy convinced me to buy looked bigger than the television in our living room, the thing curving across the length of the desk.

It wasn't long before I found myself disappearing for hours at a time into worlds filled with adventure, combat, and exploration. Some days, I would kiss Elsa goodbye in the morning, and then be all surprised when she reappeared, what felt like just an hour or two later, and find that I had wasted the entire day in some mythical world. Games like World of Warcraft, Call of Duty, and Diablo, names I'd only ever heard in passing, were now games I devoted entire days to.

But gaming wasn't the only change I made. If you've read any of my previous cases, you might remember me trying my hand at camping. Well, the good news is that Elsa has a bit of a history with that pastime. Her father used to take her and her brother out every other weekend, and she has some serious skills. We've spent multiple trips away already. One of them took us back to the same road where I first saw Max Dunning standing alone on the side of the road. I pulled over and shared the spot with Elsa. Camping at that location wasn't as bad as the previous time, and I actually managed to make it through an entire weekend.

There is one other thing I did want to share with you, though, one significant moment in time that I think might interest you. It has to do with a significant event that happened about two weeks after the arrest of Henry Altera and us managing to get Brian Watson exonerated.

Watson's recovery didn't go quite the way he had planned. Three days after the operation to realign his ribs, an infection set in, one that required extremely powerful medication to combat. There was a point in time when it appeared touch and go for him, with doctors giving him about a twenty percent chance of survival. I guess his good genes protected him that week because he ended up pulling through. It did, however, delay his discharge from the hospital by a few days.

That's not the part I wanted to share with you. The part I wanted to share has to do with what happened about a week later, the day I picked Watson up in my new Dodge Challenger. Yes, I know I swore that I would be a Mustang man for life, but man, this thing goes, and it sounds like a beast when the throttle opens up. Even Watson manages a goofy grin when sitting in the passenger seat during one of my occasional "engine throat clearings," as he likes to call it.

That day, we headed to a place where we hadn't been together since the day of Naomi's funeral, a day I know we both would much rather forget when it comes to our interaction. The cemetery had been somewhere where I normally went alone, not because I was afraid to share my grief with someone else but because I thought I needed to be alone.

It felt surreal to be walking in together. Watson still struggled to walk unaided, and he'd gotten used to using a cane, and so I walked slowly beside him as we made the short trek from the cemetery parking lot to Naomi and baby's final resting place. I could imagine the looks on their faces when they saw us approaching together. Naomi would have shed a tear or two; that much is certain.

Watson walked slightly ahead of me when we reached the row, and when he stopped before his daughter's grave and turned to face her, I saw the first tears begin to flow as he held a hand out to me. Feeling my own emotions rising, I reached out, and together, we stood before the grave of Naomi Watson, not just as a father and a husband, or a father-in-law and son-in-law, but most importantly as friends.

We showed her that we had finally let go of our past regrets and had chosen to move forward the way she would have wanted. Maybe it was time itself that we needed to heal, the years spent apart giving us the chance to experience the fragility of life itself. Whatever the reason may be, standing beside Brian that warm August morning proved to close the door on another chapter in my life, one I hoped I would never need to go back to. And the four of us finally had the chance to be together as a family.

Don't miss THE HOUR OF GUILT. The riveting sequel in the Ben Carter Legal Thriller series.

ONE MISTAKE COULD COST A YOUNG MAN HIS LIFE. ONE TRUTH COULD DESTROY THE MAN TRYING TO SAVE HIM. IN THIS COURT-ROOM, JUSTICE ISN'T THE ONLY THING ON TRIAL.

What began as a weekend away with friends turns into a brutal nightmare for Adam Rivera when he's accused of a killing he swears he didn't commit. Waking up in a tent with a dead girl and no knowledge of how he got there, his screams bring nearby campers running to investigate, including a lawyer who sees a kid needing help.

When Ben Carter is drawn to a mysterious murder scene, he watches on as authorities quickly take the young man into custody and eventually charge him with first-degree murder. But this is no ordinary defendant, and when Ben agrees to take on the case, he's unprepared for a revelation that will bring his own past into question.

Now with a personal interest in the matter, and a new client's life on the line, can he find the missing link before an innocent kid faces the executioner?

Purchase at: www.righthouse.com/the-hour-of-guilt
(Or scan the QR code below.)

NOTE: flip to the very end to read an exclusive sneak peek...

DON'T MISS ANYTHING!

If you want to stay up to date on all new releases in this series, with these authors, or with any of our new deals, you can do so by joining our newsletters below.

In addition, you will immediately gain access to our entire *Right House VIP Library,* which currently includes six original novels!

righthouse.com/email

(Easy to unsubscribe. No spam. Ever.)

ALSO BY DAVID ARCHER

Up to date books can be found at:
www.righthouse.com/david-archer

ROGUE THRILLERS
Gates of Hell (Book 1)
Hell's Fury (Book 2)
Ice Burn (Book 3)
Judgement by Fire

BEN CARTER LEGAL THRILLERS
Dead Man's Jury (Book 1)
Trial by Murder (Book 2)
The Hitman's Lawyer (Book 3)
Final Defense (Book 4)
The Hour of Guilt (Book 5)

JACOB HUNTER THRILLERS
The Kyiv File (Book 1)
The Bogota File (Book 2)
The Havana File (Book 3)
The Amsterdam File (Book 4)
The Saint Petersburg File (Book 5)

PETER BLACK THRILLERS
Burden of the Assassin (Book 1)
The Man Without A Face (Book 2)
Unpunished Deeds (Book 3)
Hunter Killer (Book 4)

Silent Shadows (Book 5)
The Last Run (Book 6)
Dark Corners (Book 7)
Ghost Operative (Book 8)
A Fire Burning (Book 9)
Dawnlight (Book 10)
Dead Ice (Book 11)
No Loose Ends (Book 12)

ALEX MASON THRILLERS
Odin (Book 1)
Ice Cold Spy (Book 2)
Mason's Law (Book 3)
Assets and Liabilities (Book 4)
Russian Roulette (Book 5)
Executive Order (Book 6)
Dead Man Talking (Book 7)
All The King's Men (Book 8)
Flashpoint (Book 9)
Brotherhood of the Goat (Book 10)
Dead Hot (Book 11)
Blood on Megiddo (Book 12)
Son of Hell (Book 13)
Merchant of Death (Book 14)
Extinction C-14 (Book 15)
A Vengeful God (Book 16)

NOAH WOLF THRILLERS
Code Name Camelot (Book 1)
Lone Wolf (Book 2)
In Sheep's Clothing (Book 3)
Hit for Hire (Book 4)
The Wolf's Bite (Book 5)

Black Sheep (Book 6)
Balance of Power (Book 7)
Time to Hunt (Book 8)
Red Square (Book 9)
Highest Order (Book 10)
Edge of Anarchy (Book 11)
Unknown Evil (Book 12)
Black Harvest (Book 13)
World Order (Book 14)
Caged Animal (Book 15)
Deep Allegiance (Book 16)
Pack Leader (Book 17)
High Treason (Book 18)
A Wolf Among Men (Book 19)
Rogue Intelligence (Book 20)
Alpha (Book 21)
Rogue Wolf (Book 22)
Shadows of Allegiance (Book 23)
In the Grip of Darkness (Book 24)
Wolves in the Dark (Book 25)
Olympus Must Fall (Book 26)
Children of the Empire (Book 27)

SAM PRICHARD MYSTERIES
The Grave Man (Book 1)
Death Sung Softly (Book 2)
Love and War (Book 3)
Framed (Book 4)
The Kill List (Book 5)
Drifter: Part One (Book 6)
Drifter: Part Two (Book 7)
Drifter: Part Three (Book 8)
The Last Song (Book 9)

Ghost (Book 10)
Hidden Agenda (Book 11)

SAM AND INDIE MYSTERIES
Aces and Eights (Book 1)
Fact or Fiction (Book 2)
Close to Home (Book 3)
Brave New World (Book 4)
Innocent Conspiracy (Book 5)
Unfinished Business (Book 6)
Live Bait (Book 7)
Alter Ego (Book 8)
More Than It Seems (Book 9)
Moving On (Book 10)
Worst Nightmare (Book 11)
Chasing Ghosts (Book 12)
Serial Superstition (Book 13)

CHANCE REDDICK THRILLERS
Innocent Injustice (Book 1)
Angel of Justice (Book 2)
High Stakes Hunting (Book 3)
Personal Asset (Book 4)

CASSIE MCGRAW MYSTERIES
What Lies Beneath (Book 1)
Can't Fight Fate (Book 2)
One Last Game (Book 3)
Never Really Gone (Book 4)

ABOUT US

Right House is an independent publisher created by authors for readers. We specialize in Action, Thriller, Mystery, and Crime novels.

If you enjoyed this novel, then there is a good chance you will like what else we have to offer! Please stay up to date by using any of the links below.

Join our mailing lists to stay up to date -->
righthouse.com/email
Visit our website --> righthouse.com
Contact us --> contact@righthouse.com

facebook.com/righthousebooks
x.com/righthousebooks
instagram.com/righthousebooks

EXCLUSIVE SNEAK PEEK OF...

THE HOUR OF GUILT

CHAPTER 1

AT EXACTLY 6:21, on the morning of April 24th, 2022, I woke up to the sound of bird song coming from somewhere high above me. It took me a few moments to remember where I was, given that camping hadn't exactly been at the forefront of my favored weekend activities, but after staring at the roof of Elsa's tent for a little too long, the previous night slowly returned to me.

I slowly turned my head to where Elsa continued sleeping, the soft snores rising and falling with repetitive frequency from somewhere underneath her long strands of golden hair. Despite my arm feeling devoid of any hint of feeling thanks to her using it as a kind of pillow, I didn't want to move, at least not at that very moment.

There was something tranquil about the moment, a brief period of quiet perfection appreciated by the only person conscious of it. I gazed at where her face lay hidden, an urge to stroke the cheek that I had held the previous night while caught in that moment of passion. At the time, feeling Elsa's lips on mine made the rest of the world disappear as we explored each other in ways we hadn't dared to previously. Maybe our decision to set up the tent away from the rest of those using the campground hadn't been a subconscious one after all; perhaps one of us was planning for that kind of intimacy all along.

Feeling the tender part of my shoulder begin to cramp, I was about to try and pull it out from under her neck, but a scream suddenly echoed through the air, the kind that brought the hairs on the back of one's neck to attention. I managed to slide my arm out and make it to my feet in one move. Elsa stirred almost immediately, pulled into the morning more violently than she probably planned, as I froze when the voice cried out again.

"HEEEELP," the young male voice called, the panic adding a shrillness to it that instantly made me move. "PLEEEASE, HELP MEEEEE."

"What is that?" Elsa muttered, her head rising enough for me to pull my arm out but her face remaining hidden behind the wall of hair.

"I don't know," I said and tried to grab my shorts while stumbling, bent over towards the front opening of the tent.

It took me several attempts to find the little zipper, mostly because of the thick clouds suppressing most of the morning's sunlight, but a third scream from the kid did the trick. I pushed through to the outside after winding the zipper most of the way around the arc of the opening, and when I saw a couple of people running through the campground, I visually followed their general direction to where a lone tent sat under a massive oak a couple of hundred yards from our own.

I heard Elsa call something out to me, but another scream got my legs moving, this one filled with the kind of guttural pain that hit a little too close to home. Others also emerged from nearby tents to see what the ruckus was about, but few actually ran to investigate the situation for themselves. It wasn't until I reached the side of the building holding the campground's facilities that I saw the half a dozen people running to where we all assumed the screaming to be coming from.

"Did someone die?" I heard a topless man with reading glasses on top of his head muttering to his wife. Another woman standing in front of a small camper called for her partner, Larry, to call the cops rather than just use the cell phone she was holding.

I watched more and more people emerge from various forms of shelter, some squinting their eyes against the morning sun, while others stood in complete bewilderment. The screams resumed, causing some to flinch, including one woman who physically pulled her husband before her to use him as a shield.

Rather than stand there watching the crowd, I continued running to the tent where a small crowd was gathering. By the time I finally reached the back of it, one older guy with a goatee beard stretching nearly all the way down to the top of his shorts had the presence of mind to try and open the zipper, the rest looking on. The screams had stopped by then, but I noticed one teen with a bemused grin holding his cellphone out, ready to capture whatever Insta-worthy footage he could.

Goatee man bent down, tried to pull the zipper handle, and barely got his fingers to it before a kid no older than maybe sixteen or seventeen rolled screaming out of the opening, giving everyone a jumpscare, including me. The terror I saw in those eyes is something I will never forget, the raw fear reaching all the way into his soul. The people watching had to jump out of the way as the kid half crab-crawled backwards from the tent as if trying to escape hell itself.

"P-please, help her," the kid stammered, the horror of his ordeal seemingly squeezing tears of fright from his eyes.

Another guy standing near the back of the crowd didn't jump out of the way fast enough and found his legs tangled around the kid's shoulder as he continued escaping from whatever nightmare remained inside the tent.

"Hey, watch it, boy," the middle-aged man cried out before he tumbled to the ground with a painful yelp.

"Please help Holly," the kid repeated. "She needs... she needs help."

"Somebody help him," the woman standing next to me called out, and that was when I took a couple of steps and knelt down. I grabbed one of the kid's arms and put a hand on his shoulder as he continued staring wide-eyed at the tent opening.

"It's OK," I whispered to him, trying to sound as empathetic as possible. "You're safe, just calm down, OK?"

He looked at me but only for a brief second before he turned his attention back to the tent. Tears mingled with snot as one arm slowly rose before the index finger pointed to the tent.

"S-she's... she's dead," he tried, his top lip barely able to form around the words trying to escape. Still hanging on to his other arm, I could feel every part of him trembling, the shock of his ordeal taking a complete hold over his self-control.

"Knock it off," someone suddenly said from above me, and I looked up to see a guy with a military crew cut lean in toward the teen with the cell phone that continued filming the kid. Something about the voice convinced the teen, who lowered the phone and took a couple of cautious steps back. The military guy watched him for a few extra seconds before looking down at me. "You got control of him?" I nodded, he returned the gesture with a single nod of his own, and I watched as he walked to where several of the crowd were staring into the tent. "All right, let's get back, folks," he called out, pushing his way through to the front.

"There's a girl in there," someone near the front called back. "Should we see if she's alive?"

"I'll check it," Military Guy said when he managed to get through the front part of the crowd. He paused near the tent opening, then leaned down enough to peer inside, no small thing considering I estimated him to stand somewhere near six foot eight. That's when two things happened in quick succession. First, the military guy straightened up again almost immediately and looked solemnly at the guy standing next to him before slowly shaking his head. I guess the gesture didn't need much translation, because the kid began squirming almost immediately, his one free hand pulling at the hair on his head as he resumed groaning.

"Oh, no...oh, shit, what have I done?" He tried to pull free so he could roll further away, but I held strong.

"You need to calm yourself," I said, getting a look inside as one of the men pulled the side flap of the tent aside. "Nobody knows anything yet, so just keep a grip, OK?"

Feeling the kid's trembling ease just a bit, I looked back at him and tried to calm the situation for him.

"Let them deal with that side of things," I whispered. "You just sit here with me until the police arrive, OK? They'll sort this out." He looked at me, the expression one of total confusion. His mouth continued trembling, but I could see him trying to talk. "It's OK, just save your strength," I said.

"She's my friend," he finally managed, the words barely loud enough to reach me.

"What happened?" I asked.

"I DON'T KNOW," the kid said, looking from me to the tent and back again. "Is...is she d-d-dead?"

"Adam?" someone suddenly called from somewhere in the

distance. I tried to look through the tangle of legs encircling us but didn't see anybody in particular until a couple of kids, appearing similar in age to the scared one sitting next to me, pushed through to the middle of the crowd. "Adam, what's going on?"

"You know him?" I asked when one of the boys knelt next to me, his fiercely red hair almost as bright as the morning itself.

"Yes, he's a friend of ours," he said while trying to get a sense of the kid's mental state. "Dude, what the hell happened to you last night?"

I saw Elsa approach the crowd, but I waved for her not to approach. The last thing I wanted was to get the kid all worked up again, and I felt like I was beginning to calm him enough with my presence alone. His hand also took hold of my wrist, as if he needed to keep me near.

A siren rose above the sound of the nearby crowd before Adam could answer, its wailing slowly building until it drowned out most of the other sounds. I felt the kid tense up even more as he nervously tried to place the source of it.

"You're fine," I said, giving his wrist a slight squeeze to get his attention. "The police will sort things out."

Things happened quite quickly from that moment on. Once the first police cruiser arrived, two officers climbed out and split up. The first immediately began to move the crowd back, while the military-looking guy got the second's attention. The pair spoke for less than a minute but still managed to look in our direction four separate times. When the second cop carefully stepped into the tent with one foot and reached in to do what I assumed to be checking for vital signs on whoever lay inside, another police vehicle began to approach.

I watched a sergeant climb out of the second cruiser and start conversing with one of his officers. The conversation almost mirrored the one he'd had with the military guy moments earlier, right down to the number of times they looked in my direction. Each time they did, Adam flinched, as if the eyes physically attacked him.

"Oh, geez, I'm done for," he whispered and looked at me for help that I knew I couldn't offer.

"Son, you got some explaining to do," the sergeant said when he eventually walked over to us. An ambulance had turned up, and I could see a couple of paramedics rushing to the tent.

"He's in shock," I said, turning back to the sergeant. "He might need a moment to get himself together."

"I'm sure he would be," the sergeant said, giving me a brief glance. "You know him?"

"No, Sergeant Baier, I don't," I said, noticing the man's nametag. "I just happened to be camping nearby when I heard the boy calling for help."

"I see," he said, turning his attention back to the kid. "What's your name, son?"

"His name is Adam Rivera," the redheaded friend said from behind me, and this time, the cop didn't take the answer too kindly.

"Any chance I could ask the suspect a question without someone else answering for him?" He sounded more annoyed than frustrated. "Deputy," he called over his shoulder and waved for one of his men to come over. "I want a statement from this gentleman," he said once the cop who'd arrived first on the scene approached. The redhead's cheeks began to match his hair.

"Right away, Sarge," the officer told his superior and waved for Adam's friend to follow him.

"All right, on your feet, son," the sergeant said as he turned his attention back to Adam. Another deputy walked over and stood beside his superior.

I didn't think the kid would respond, but he rose to his feet, looking around nervously. Several more phones appeared to be pointing in our general direction from the crowd. I don't know why, but I felt a sudden urge to stand between them and the kid, if only to save him the humiliation of finding himself plastered all over social media.

"How old are you?" Baier asked.

"I-I'm eighteen," Adam said, his tone weak from the nerves still gripping him.

The two cops walked Adam over to one of the cruisers once Baier gave the other cop a nod of approval. I followed close behind and stopped when we reached the vehicle, where the deputy asked him to put his hands on the hood of the SUV. He began patting the kid down, giving each of the pockets of his cargo shorts a squeeze. When he reached one of the lower pockets, he paused and looked up at Adam before turning his gaze to his superior.

When the cop pulled a small, clear satchel from the pocket, Baier stepped closer with an outstretched hand as Adam stared at it in confusion. I could see his puzzlement but wasn't sure whether the reaction was genuine or just an act. Baier inspected the contents a little closer before holding it up for Adam to see.

"What's this going to turn out to be?"

"I've never seen that before," Adam said as he looked nervously from me to the cop and back again. He shook his head side to side, looking more like someone trying to wake up from a nightmare than denying the bag's existence. "I swear, I don't know what it is."

"Just keep quiet, Adam," I said, suddenly feeling the overwhelming urge to speak for him. Baier completely ignored me as he turned to his deputy.

"Read him his rights and get him back to the station," he told the man before handing the evidence to another nearby deputy.

Adam gave me a final look after being cuffed before quietly taking a seat in the backseat of the police cruiser. I felt Elsa walk up and stand beside me as I watched the door slam shut on the kid. I kept wondering whether it hadn't been a simple decision on my behalf about camping there in the first place, or whether this was another one of those moments where fate intervened.

"That kid is going to need representation," Elsa whispered under her breath, and when I looked at her, I knew that the universe worked in mysterious ways. With us starting a new law firm only a few weeks earlier, this was exactly the kind of case we had been waiting for.

CHAPTER 2

ONCE THE POLICE cruiser pulled out of the camping ground, Elsa and I raced back to our tent and packed it as quickly as we could. We barely spoke, more focused on the task at hand. It took us less than ten minutes to not only throw our gear back into the bags but also to break the tent back down into its simplest form, with all the bits neatly tucked into a single bag.

"Do you think Adam will be OK?" I heard someone ask from behind us, and I turned to see the red-haired kid standing next to another kid who had been in the crowd watching the cops deal with their friend.

"Adam is going to need a good lawyer," I said as I tossed the tent into the back of the car, and then, figuring it was a good moment to gather some crucial information, I stepped toward them with an outstretched hand. "I'm Ben Carter. This is my... partner, Elsa."

"You a cop or something?" the red-haired kid said as he shook with me. "You sounded like one back there."

"No, actually, we're lawyers. What was your name?"

"Scott Baless." He swung a thumb at his friend. "This is Nathan, but everyone calls him Nate."

"Yeah, and he's Scotty," the other kid said.

"Scotty and Nate, cool," I said. "And you know the kid they took away?"

"Adam Rivera," Scotty said. "He came up here with us."

"What were you boys doing up here?"

"My eighteenth," the red-haired kid said, sounding more than a little proud.

"Oh, nice," I said. "So I'm guessing that smell I detected in Adam's tent was part of the celebration?" His cheeks immediately began to glow the same color as his hair. "It's OK," I said. "I won't say anything."

"We know we shouldn't have, but we just wanted to celebrate," Nate said meekly, and then, more to himself, he added, "My parents are going to kill me."

"He's only seventeen," Scotty said, adding context to the statement.

"Guys, we're going to do everything possible to help Adam, OK? Right now, we need to get packed up and head to the station. Can I grab your cell phone numbers in case I need more information from you?"

"Yes, of course," Scotty said, and once I pulled out my own phone and opened the screen, they both rattled off their numbers. They even gave me Adam's, but I had already seen his get taken by the deputy and knew calling it wasn't going to work.

"When are you guys heading home?" I asked once we had finished exchanging details.

"As soon as we're done here. I borrowed my sister's car," Nate said.

"OK, cool. All right, well, thanks for chatting with us, but we'd better get going," I said, and after waving to the two boys,

I continued helping Elsa pack the rest of the gear into the car. There were only a couple of backpacks and a few grocery items left, plus a bag I ran over to the nearby dumpster behind the toilet block.

"Pretty efficient there, Mr. Carter," Elsa said as we finished getting all our things into the car, and before I needed to ask her, she reached around into the back to make sure the one item I always insisted on carrying had escaped any sort of crumpling mess. "It's fine," Elsa said after examining the suit. "Want me to drive and you get changed?"

"Sounds like a plan," I said and ran around to the passenger side.

When I climbed into the car, just a few seconds later, still missing shoes and a tie, Elsa threw the Mustang into gear and headed for the park's exit while I focused on getting the rest of myself into a somewhat presentable shape. The tie I kept with my emergency suit had already been tied, so I just slipped it over my head, straightened it before pulling it tighter, and then spun around to find my shoes in the bottom of the suit bag.

"The kid seemed pretty out of it," Elsa said as she drove. "Did you smell the alcohol?"

"Yeah, it was pretty strong," I said, finally slipping into the shoes and tying the laces. "Just hope the kid doesn't take any drastic action before we get there."

"It was good that his friends came over to see you."

"And that we got their numbers," I said. "Hopefully, this won't turn out to be a wasted trip."

We continued on for about twenty minutes until we reached the town of Indiana, Pennsylvania, the closest major center to the Yellow Creek Campground. I had already pulled up the location of the police station on my cell phone and guided Elsa along the roads until we pulled up across the street, where I saw a number of cruisers in the parking lot located down the side of the building.

"I'm heading straight in." The second Elsa pulled the car into the curb, I opened the door and climbed out.

I barely felt the warmth of the sunny late April morning as I hurried to the police station's entrance, and once inside, I made my way to the front desk manned by a single officer who was talking to an older woman asking about fishing licenses.

"No, ma'am, you can do it all online these days," the cop said, trying his hardest to keep his frustrations at bay.

"Oh, so we don't have to come in here? It's just that my husband was so sure he needed to come in here to avoid a fine of some sort," the woman said, looking over at me with an embarrassed smile. "Better to be safe than sorry, I always say," she whispered in my direction.

"That's very good advice, ma'am," the cop said as he exchanged a look with me, one I didn't think he cared to share, regardless of how insincere it appeared.

"Well, thank you, Officer Grey. You've been very helpful."

"Anytime, ma'am. We are here to serve." The woman had barely turned away from the counter when the cop shifted his attention to me. "Can I help you?"

"Your officers brought a kid in from the Yellow Creek Campground just now. Adam Rivera?"

"You're his father?"

"No, I'm Ben Carter. I'm hoping to be his..."

"Ben?"

Surprised to hear my name, I turned to see a woman sitting in a kind of waiting area of the station. A dozen chairs stood around the outside of the area with a random box of toys in one corner. A noticeboard hung on the wall facing the reception desk with multiple flyers and announcements pinned to it.

The woman sitting underneath it appeared confused and bewildered all at the same time.

"Ben Carter?"

I wish I could tell you that I recognized her the way she did me, but the truth is, I had so many thoughts running through my mind that I barely recognized my own name when she spoke it. I looked back at the cop who remained standing behind the counter, appearing impatient, and held up a finger.

"Sorry, Officer, just give me a minute." The cop shrugged his shoulders and headed toward a nearby desk.

The woman pushed herself out of the chair and slowly walked toward me, her eyes still looking frightened and curious, as if unsure of which emotion to focus on.

"Is that really you?"

That was when it hit me, the visible features finally coming together to form a name in my head. The dimples, the deep green eyes, the long black hair, all the features I remembered falling for when I first saw them in that bar all those years earlier. But it was the necklace that finally brought those memories back, that distinctive gold leaf with the emerald set into the middle.

"Sydney? Sydney Becker?"

When she took a couple of steps towards me, she appeared close to collapse, and I gestured for her to retake her seat. When I got close enough, I held out a hand, and she took it before following me to the chairs closer to us.

"Oh, Ben, you're the last person I expected to be running into today." She looked around the room. "Especially here."

"What are you doing here?" I asked.

"They..." She spoke close to a whisper as she looked over at the reception desk, where just the top of the cop's head remained visible over the partition. "His friends called me to say that he's been brought here."

"*Who* has been brought here?" I asked.

"My son."

Something inside me tightened as the hairs on the back of my neck stood to attention.

"His name wouldn't be Adam, by any chance?"

"Yes, h-h-how did you know?"

"I was at the campground when they arrested him," I said and looked to the reception desk. "I actually came to see if he needed legal representation." I felt her hand tighten on my arm.

"You're a lawyer?"

"I am, yes. My partner and I started our own firm just recently, and when I saw your son get arrested…" Rather than react, Sydney looked toward the desk and shook her head.

"Nobody is telling me anything. Adam's friend phoned me this morning and said that the police brought him here, but he didn't say why." A tear slipped down the side of her face as her fingers curled around my wrist. "Ben, I'm so scared. Did he get hurt?"

"Sydney, Adam is going to need legal representation."

She looked at me, bewildered. "What?"

Breaking that type of news to a frightened parent isn't how I'd imagined gaining new clients, but not only did his mother need to know the truth, I needed to get in the room with my potential client while he was being questioned. The sergeant at the campground had followed every protocol required, and if he continued in that direction, my guess was that he had offered Adam a chat and now had him in an interview room without a lawyer present somewhere in the station.

"Sydney, there's no easy way of saying this, but Adam has been arrested. He was found in a tent with a dead girl, and it looks like there might have been drugs involved. I was there when they searched him and found a small bag of something in his pants pocket."

Sydney visibly flinched as she listened to my words, the emotional horror continuing to grow on her face as yet more tears began to fall.

"Dead girl? Who? But how?"

"I don't know the specific details yet, but if you hire me as Adam's attorney, then I can get in there and help him."

"Is it...will Adam be charged with murder?"

"It's too early to know that, but right now, you need to get the best legal counsel for your son." She looked at me wide-eyed.

"Will you?"

"Yes, of course," I said just as Elsa walked in and found us sitting in the waiting room. I beckoned her over. "Listen, Sydney, this is my partner, Elsa. She will take you through what happens next while I will go in and sit with Adam, OK?" She nodded, but I wasn't sure how much she actually understood. I could see her fighting both the tears and the emotions causing them, her eyes unable to focus on any one point as her brain lost control of the moment.

Once I was sure that Elsa had Sydney's focus, I walked back over to the reception desk and called out to the cop who was busy typing on the keyboard of the computer terminal.

"Oh, you're ready now?" he said impatiently.

"Yes, I'm here to see my client, Adam Rivera."

"Who? Oh, yes, the kid from the campground." He pushed himself out of the chair and disappeared down a nearby corridor. I heard his boots echo for a few seconds before pausing, and mumbled voices rolled back toward me.

"OK, come this way," he said once he returned, and I walked down the side of the reception desk to follow.

When I walked into the interview room, I found Adam looking almost as scared as his mother, sitting on one side of the table with two officers on the other, one of whom was the sergeant from the lake.

"Questioning my client without his lawyer present, gentlemen?" I said as my escort closed the door behind me.

"Your client waived his right to have an attorney present," Baier said smugly.

"Who? This eighteen-year-old kid who has never been in trouble with the law before and wouldn't understand coercion if it slapped him in the face?"

"There was no coercion," the other officer said, and given his lack of uniform, I suspected him to be the detective assigned to the case.

"Well, now that I'm here, we can restart the interview." I took my seat and set the wheels into motion on the first real case of the law firm Carter and Schwartz.

CHAPTER 3

ALMOST TWO HOURS had passed by the time I finally managed to get out of the interview, and despite my attempts to get him released, Adam remained in custody pending an investigation. While no definite limit of time existed for suspects allowed to be held in custody without charge, the police generally followed a forty-eight-hour rule, meaning they could hold Adam for at least two days while they went about investigating the circumstances surrounding the death of the victim.

Elsa and Sydney were still sitting in the waiting area when I walked out, but rather than talking inside the police station, I suggested we head out to the parking lot, where we could speak freely without others listening in. Plus, it gave Sydney a chance to get some fresh air into her lungs, something she looked like she needed after I saw her hands visibly shaking.

"They're going to hold Adam while they conduct their investigation," I told Sydney, and then to Elsa, I said, "We'll need a place to stay, maybe a hotel to begin with, or—"

"I have a rental you can stay in." Sydney swallowed hard to

try to control the shaking in her voice. "My husband and I own a couple of properties around town, and the one on Oak Street is currently empty." She tried to force a smile. "It's also furnished, which should help."

"You sure?" I asked. "We don't mind finding a hotel or something."

"No, don't be silly. There's no way I'm letting you stay in a hotel while you're fighting for my son."

"Sydney, listen," I said, turning the conversation serious again. "This isn't going to be easy, especially the next few days. There will probably be—" That was as far as I got before the sound of squealing tires cut me off. We all turned to see a Dodge Ram come speeding to the edge of the parking lot. It stopped, and a man and woman climbed out, the latter looking just as shocked as Sydney had been when I saw her. Elsa and I exchanged a look and immediately knew.

What I didn't expect was Baier to walk out through the station's side door and call out to the man, who turned and immediately headed for the cop. The woman held the man's arm and allowed herself to be dragged along. Given that we were standing just a couple of dozen yards away on the other side of the parking lot, it wasn't hard to hear the subsequent conversation.

"What's going on, Damien?" asked the man who I later learned was the victim's father. "Is it Holly? What's wrong with her?" When the sergeant didn't answer quickly enough, the woman joined in.

"Where's my baby? Is she OK?"

There is never going to be an easy way for a parent to find out about the death of their child, and I can only tell you that the heartbreak that followed hit hard. We watched a mother first find out the truth and then subsequently break down in a painful scene of screaming and crying before she fainted from the ordeal. The father tried to keep the anger from exploding, but he lost the fight when he took a few steps back toward his truck and began kicking the step beneath the door repeatedly while Baier tried to calm him.

An ambulance eventually showed up just after Elsa finally managed to get Sydney into her car and leave, and I watched them attend to Holly's mother. They eventually helped her onto a stretcher and loaded her into the back of the ambulance, where I was sure they sedated her. The father, a man named Bishop Mills, as I later found out, eventually managed to calm himself enough to listen to Baier, a conversation that included a couple of looks in my direction before I climbed into my own car and left the scene.

The house on Oak Street looked like just the kind of place I would have bought for myself had I had the money and the freedom to choose a new location to live. Charming is the word Elsa used when we met up again a short time later, and when Sydney opened the front door for us, the inside of the place proved every bit as beautiful. If only the circumstances had been different and we could have inspected the place for friendlier reasons.

"What will happen now?" Sydney asked when we eventually took our seats at the dining table.

"I will apply to the court for Adam's release, and if the police charge him, we will go for bail," I said. "The thing is, I don't think it will take them long to charge Adam. He was found inside the tent; they found drugs on him, plus the alcohol. There's just too many mitigating circumstances here."

"I can't believe that he would have done drugs," Sydney said adamantly. "He has always insisted that he hated the mere mention of them. He doesn't hang around friends who do them." She looked from me to Elsa and back again. "Why would he lie?"

"Maybe he isn't lying," Elsa said. "Until we know the whole story, we need to keep an open mind."

"Elsa is right," I said. "Let's just wait and see what the police come back with. There's no point getting ourselves all twisted up over something that may or may not happen."

It took Sydney a few minutes to get herself back under control after another moment of tears. Elsa remained by her side as I went and grabbed her a glass of water, and once she finished taking a couple of sips, she changed the topic completely to help her regain some composure.

"So a lawyer, huh? I remember you mentioning something about a summer gig with a law firm as an intern."

"*Unpaid* intern, if I recall," I said, a broad smile crawling across my face.

"And how long have you two been together?" she asked next, the question catching both Elsa and me off guard.

"Why do you think we're together?" I asked.

"Come off it, Ben. Have you seen the way you two look at each other?" She grinned. "I can tell you're more than just business partners, right?"

"A few months," Elsa said, and then added, "Long enough to know that we have a lot in common, which is why we decided to open a law firm together."

"You're a lawyer as well?"

"I used to be a prosecutor in Pittsburgh," Elsa said, smiling at the look of surprise on Sydney's face.

"Wow, a prosecutor. So did you two ever fight each other in the courtroom?" Another smile from Elsa as she looked at me.

"Once or twice." Sydney also looked at me, and I felt the heat in my cheeks reach all the way to the tips of my ears.

"OK, OK, quit it, you two," I said. Both women giggled, a welcome sound given the tension of the previous hour or so.

"All right, I need to make a call, so just hang out here for a bit."
I made my exit.

I headed out into the backyard before opening the cell phone and calling my investigator. Linda answered on the third ring, sounding out of breath.

"You had enough of camping already, boss?"

"Not quite," I said. "Can you talk?"

"Sure. I'm just running through the park. What's up?" I heard her slow down and take a couple of controlled breaths.

"We've had a bit of a case come up."

"On your camping trip?"

"Yeah, a possible murder case." I looked over toward the fence as a dog began to bark at me, and to try and escape the noise, I walked to the side of the building where a gate separated the back yard from the front.

"Did you say murder case?"

"I did," I said and went through the details of the morning, including as much as I could about the case specifics as I knew them.

The problem I had was that I had no clue whether I even had a case worth trying to fight. All of the evidence pointed to a couple of kids hooking up during the night after partying way too hard, and one of them ending up dead from a potential overdose the next morning. Adam denying even knowing the girl was dead didn't mean much, considering the smell of alcohol on him. The first impressions were probably the most likely, that he'd likely overindulged a little too much in whatever the alcohol had been, followed or led the girl back to the tent, and then tried some of whatever had been in the satchel, which the cops quickly identified as heroin.

"You guys coming back to Pittsburgh?" Linda asked.

"No, it turned out that the boy's mother is an old acquaintance of mine."

"Old acquaintance?"

"Yeah, from back in my college days," I said.

"What are the chances of that?"

I grinned. "The world isn't as large as it used to be," I said. "We have a house in Indiana. Nice place. I'll send you the address."

"OK, I'll get down there by mid-afternoon, if that's OK."

"Perfect," I said. "But before you do, I want you to check out a guy named Bishop Mills. He's the victim's father."

"Anything specific I'm looking for?"

"I'm not sure," I said. "Call it instinct. He just flipped out a little too over the top at the station when told of his daughter's death, instead of going to his wife. I get people react differently to such traumatic news, but I also know that people tend to gravitate towards loved ones, unlike this guy."

"Flipped out how?"

"Like kicking the crap out of his truck, kind of flipping out," I said. "His wife pretty much collapsed to the ground and he just left her there."

It wasn't Bishop Mills kicking his truck that got me thinking, but rather his lack of attention toward his wife when she fell to the ground. Unfortunately, I had seen parents receive such devastating news in the past, and I couldn't recall any husband or partner ever walking away when the mother collapsed from sheer grief. He was the first, and he did it in such a very public way.

"All right, I'll check it out," Linda said.

"I think he also has connections here in town. One of the police officers knew him on a first-name basis, and they seemed to know each other more than just in passing."

"I'll look for links."

"Thanks, Linda." I was about to end the call, but then remembered where I was. "Hey, wait, you still there?"

"I'm here."

"Can you swing past my place and grab the two laptops? We kind of wanted to unplug for the weekend and didn't bring anything work-related."

"Sure thing," she said. "Anything else?"

"No, that's it for now. Thanks," I said and ended the call.

I didn't head straight back inside. What I couldn't get out of my head was the sight of the girl's body inside the tent. There was just something about the whole thing that felt...off. To me, at least, anyway.

During my many years of defending cases, I had taken on numerous drug-related clients, a number of whom involved overdoses. This just didn't feel the same. The girl didn't seem to fit the profile. The way I heard Baier described the girl made her sound like the kind of girl who helped old ladies cross the street and washed the church windows for free whenever needed. If that was the case, and she had no history of using drugs, then that put the spotlight back on Adam, and if he didn't know anything about drugs either, then that meant someone else could have been involved.

I swiped the cell phone screen awake a second time, and after unlocking it, I made a second phone call. Scott Bales answered almost immediately.

"Hello?"

"Scott, it's Ben Carter, the guy from the campground."

"Oh, hey," the kid said. "Have you managed to help Adam?"

"I've met with him, yes, but there are a lot of details to go over," I said. "Hey, I'm wondering if you'd be up for a chat."

"A chat?"

"Yes, just a quick one to go over some details about the party you guys had."

"It wasn't really a party," he said, suddenly sounding defensive.

"I get it," I said. "But I'd still like to catch up, if that's OK."

"Sure, when?"

"How about right now?" I asked. "We could meet at a local café, if you know any."

"A café?" He didn't sound like someone who understood the meaning. "There's a Starbucks near my house. It's on 11th. You know it?" I recognized the number.

"That's not far from me either. Make it twenty minutes?"

"Sure," the kid said and ended the call.

I headed back inside and found Elsa and Sydney talking like a couple of old friends. It honestly felt good to see the mother regain her composure enough to hold a normal conversation.

"Listen, I have a meeting with one of the boys from this morning," I said, and before I could excuse myself, Sydney got up from the couch.

"You guys need supplies," she said. "Why don't you two go to this meeting, and I'll go grab some groceries for you. Just let me know what you need."

"No, hey, that's very kind," I began, but Sydney waved it away.

"It's the least I can do, given what you guys are doing for Adam."

"Why don't I come with you?" Elsa said. "Ben will most likely want to go to this meeting alone, anyway." She looked at me. "Right?"

"I actually would," I said, reminding myself that Elsa knew me better than most people in my life. She also had a lawyer's way of thinking, and so she understood certain things about specific types of meetings. "It's a young kid, and so it's probably better if I go alone."

"Which one of his friends?" Sydney asked.

"Scott Bales," I said, and her face turned stern.

"Scotty was there? I mean at the park with them?"

"Yeah, why?" I asked.

"Adam promised me he wouldn't be there. That kid is bad news. Comes from the kind of family most towns try to avoid." She looked up at me. "Scotty's older brother, Aidan, is currently serving time for car theft, and his other brother, Jack, is part of this biker gang. He doesn't come often, but when he does, trouble tends to follow, if you know what I mean."

"Do you know the family well?" I asked.

"I should," Sydney said. "They lived in one of our rentals for years before we finally managed to have them evicted. Trashed the place, and the renovations alone set us back six figures."

My mind ticked over as I considered the fallout from such a situation, particularly for the family who'd trashed the home. People like that rarely cared about what damage they caused and were more interested in avenging getting kicked out in the first place.

"How close are Adam and Scott?" I asked. "I mean, how close would you say their friendship is?"

"They're not," Sydney said. "Or at least I didn't think so. As far as I knew, the two boys didn't even speak after they had that fight a couple of years back."

"Fight?"

"Yes, a typical schoolyard fight between boys. Scotty brought two friends with him, and they beat Adam up enough for him to spend the night in the ER for a concussion."

"And yet they were apparently drinking together last night," I said, more questions forming in my mind.

"If they were, then that is one hell of a surprise to me," Sydney said.

We walked out of the house together, and after Elsa gave

me a quick peck on the lips, she followed Sydney back to her car. I waited until the two women had driven around the next corner before I climbed into my own car and headed in the opposite direction. 11th Street literally crossed Oak Street on the other side of the block, and after driving along the street for just over a mile, I found the Starbucks. What I didn't expect was three police cruisers to be sitting in the adjacent parking lot.

righthouse.com/the-hour-of-guilt

Printed in Dunstable, United Kingdom